ANOMPOLICHI
THE WORDMASTER

ANOMPOLICHI
THE WORDMASTER

PHILLIP CARROLL MORGAN

White Dog Press
• Ada, Oklahoma •

ISBN 978-1-935684-16-9

Design: Chickasaw Press
Symbols for chapter titles courtesy Chickasaw Nation Archives

White Dog Press
c/o Chickasaw Press
PO Box 1548
Ada, Oklahoma 74821
www.chickasawpress.com

This book is dedicated to our ancestors who built and inhabited great towns and colorful cities during a better era of life in North America.

HOLISSO CHAFFA

BOOK ONE

CHAPTER ONE

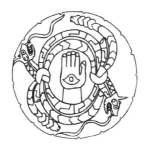

THE DREAM

T HE *MAHLISHTO*, THE DANGEROUS WIND, HAD PASSED DURING THE night, and Iskifa Ahalopa played some of the sweetest notes ever piped from his traveling flute while he ambled along the rocky path in view of the cool blue *okhata ishto*, the eastern ocean. The orderliness of his brightly colored costume contrasted with the panorama of storm-ravaged coastal vegetation and leaf-littered beaches.

He had seen sixty-five winters, but Iskifa felt the vigor of a much younger man. He had seen tropical gales and hurricanes before and once again felt an uncanny sense of joy at such powerful displays by *Aba Binnili*, creator of all. He marveled that his dream had drawn him toward the storm and again to this coastline, after many seasons of absence from it. He felt full of anticipation for his next discovery.

A whelm of scent from a *lowak pakanli*, a fire flower, stopped him, and as he stood to take in its fragrance, he spied a coastal black cap bird clinging upside down with tiny feet to a branch of the *lowak* bush, not two feet in front of his nose. *Lowak* petals lay scattered about. The diminutive bird inspected its one remaining flower.

Iskifa slowly, evenly, let his hand holding the flute return to his side. He gazed quietly at the bird, until it seemed to have enough of him and took flight. He chuckled like a child. He loved watching birds. He

1

had looked forward to seeing the coastal black cap ever since a word-master, one like himself, described it to him in Chunuli, many winters ago. The curious bird was smaller and more delicate than its cousin who lived farther west.

Iskifa did not venture to the coastline often, even though he loved the ocean. Coastal people could be uncouth. He dismissed their worthiness while inland, saying they were so numerous it was hard to walk a hundred flight—a flight being the length of an arrow shot—without running into one of their towns. "*Naniapa,*" fish eaters, he would call them, and he would laugh uproariously.

That often did not seem funny to others, he noticed. Apparently such name-calling was judged inappropriate for an *anompolichi*, a wordmaster. That made it all the more appealing to him. After all, he was not just an *anompolichi*; he was a Yukpan *anompolichi*, a Yukpan wordmaster. Most of the nineteen languages he spoke had separate words for "to bless" and "to laugh." Only Iskifa's people used one word, *yukpa*, for both, thus equating blessing with laughter. They called themselves Yukpans, so they were known everywhere in *yaakni moma*, the world, either as the Blessed or the Laughing People.

Iskifa identified personally as Chikasha, born in a Chikasha town to a Chikasha mother, but his father was Chahta, so he felt affection for both tribes, which in the past had been one. Both were members of the Yukpan Confederacy for many generations, and because his relatives scattered throughout their land, Iskifa felt loyalty and a great sense of security in the confederacy. It included tribes from the south coast all the way north to the Tanasi and Ohiyo rivers. Wordmasters like him were indispensible for keeping the confederacy together and responsible for communications between its tribes.

The salt-spray breeze brushed Iskifa while he stood on the seaside trail, once again drawing intoxicating vapors of *lowak* blossoms to his nostrils. He stepped forward, cupping the lovely crimson flower in his left hand, and pulled it close to his nose. The scent reminded him of the *okla*, the town, where he stayed the night before.

He felt more than reluctant to make himself known in any coastal town, but the afternoon gust front of the storm, coming in from the sea, told him it would be a bruiser when it made landfall. He reasoned the repugnance of vulgar people would be less uncomfortable than a howling summer fury. Transplanted *lowak* bushes stood in gardens in the town, and their cut blossoms adorned shell vessels in the humble home of the local wordmaster, Kaheto, and his wife, Nuktala, where Iskifa begrudgingly sought shelter.

It was bad enough to be quarantined all night with fish eaters, but to make matters worse, the couple's widowed daughter, Hosiini, also lived there. She possessed an uncommon beauty and a needfulness Iskifa found tempting. She performed a dance after their meal, a tasteful one that became suggestive only when she faced him.

If she had come to his bed during the night, he felt sure he probably could not have resisted her. Although Yukpans were sometimes polygamous, wordmasters agreed to only one wife at a time, so as not to distract them from their duties and studies. Wordmasters typically did little farming and had small immediate families, so they had little need or means of support for more than one wife.

Iskifa delighted in getting back to his journey. He found Kaheto tiresome and had to speak in his tongue because the fish eater only knew snippets of other languages. The wordmaster traditions had grown weak among the coastal peoples. They mostly lived in small, disconnected towns, intermarrying up and down the seemingly endless shores so often the customs and language of one tribe seemed barely distinguishable from the rest. Even while they spoke somewhat exotic languages, Iskifa noticed elements of at least two foreign tongues mixed with Kaheto's native Onnaha. Kaheto did not seem aware of that. The boat people who traded up and down the coast brought a mixture of influences to Onnaha culture. Iskifa and Kaheto discussed language, as wordmasters, but Kaheto's knowledge was quickly exhausted, and their talk degenerated into the same argument Iskifa heard all along his journey.

"How many of your people are going to the *Yamohmi*, the fashionable event, Iskifa?" Kaheto asked cheerfully, sounding eager to change the subject from language.

The question touched a nerve inside Iskifa. The *Yamohmi* was the traditional intertribal stickball contest held every ten summers, pitting the best players from the Yukpan Confederacy against players from tribes of the Allahashi domain whose capital, Tochina, lay north of the Ohiyo. The *Yamohmi* was planned for midsummer in Tochina and hosted by the Allahashi ruler, Yoshoba, whom Iskifa did not trust in the least.

"*Iksho*, none," Iskifa replied stoically.

"None?"

"None."

"Don't you know it is going to be the best stickball competition ever held?" Kaheto asked, astonished.

"I know it's going to be the biggest mistake ever made," Iskifa rebutted.

"How can it be a mistake? Don't you Yukpans like stickball?" Kaheto asked snidely.

"Everyone knows that we love *toli*, stickball. What we do not love are the Allahashi and Yoshoba," Iskifa explained, knowing Kaheto already understood his position.

"Well, this is our chance to show him for a fool on the field of honor, is it not?" Kaheto appealed nevertheless.

"It is a chance to be shown as fools ourselves," Iskifa retorted.

"The Allahashi are rich in trade goods," Kaheto persisted. "Their cities are large, and they produce a large surplus of food, I'm told. What they make is artistic and very high in quality. Most are saying that only a few old fools are against trade with the Allahashi and even fewer are against this great competition."

"That's what they said about the great teacher, Anoli, and previously about Komok, the prophet," Iskifa said, "and did they turn out to be old fools?"

"But things were different then," Kaheto argued, "those old hatreds died with our foremothers."

"I'm not so sure," Iskifa cautioned. "The Allahashi have always worshiped strange gods. They require blood sacrifice, and they think of

4

the sun as equal with *Aba Binnili*. They surely must have come from the great mountain range far to the south and west. Very strange and foreign in their ways."

Kaheto reacted indignantly. "I do not believe it. Human sacrifice has been against our laws for many generations, even in that part of *yaakni moma*. Their people would not tolerate such abomination."

"That's what their name means, you know—children of the sun," Iskifa said. "They've drawn several new and large tribes into their confederacy and have become more decadent than ever. I've also heard from reliable people, traveling builders, that Yoshoba has re-instituted human sacrifice into their temple worship."

Kaheto stared at him, stunned.

"But, of course, I hope you are right, honorable master, I hope you are right," Iskifa added, wishing not to upset his host. "All I counsel is to ask yourselves if the gains are worth the risks. Where is my bed, kind master?" he asked politely. "I have walked three hundred flight today, and I am spent."

"Hosiini," Kaheto called to his daughter, "show the wordmaster the bed you have made for him."

Smiling broadly, Hosiini showed Iskifa the smaller of two sleeping lofts at either end of the crude log house. He made no gesture toward her while she watched him climb the ladder to the loft.

The pallet was laid out neatly, its coarse mat woven from what Iskifa figured to be the fronds of the *tala* tree, the palm tree, found in that part of the coastline. The Onnaha traded such mats inland, along with dried fish and shell art, as part of their principal trade goods with the Allahashi. The sky had cleared. Moonlight filtered through the open smoke hole in the thatched roof, illuminating a *lowak* blossom lying on his pillow like a promise. Everyone will have to wait until morning, he thought, for the vigor of youth to show up in this tired old man.

Iskifa slept deeply and without dreams, awakened at dawn by a buzz in his ear. He was troubled by a ringing in his ears sometimes at night while he tried to fall asleep and occasionally when he woke up. It worried him because it did not sound musical. This morning's sound, however, seemed to have a bit of a tune to it. He identified it as the buzz of a bumblebee landing on the *lowak* blossom still on the pillow.

"*Kiyo!* Do not get any ideas, my friend, that I am competing for your nectar," Iskifa whispered to the bee. "If *Aba Binnili* sent you, assure him we are keeping our stingers to ourselves. If my wife, Nanitana, sent you, I know I am to be stung for even taking the thought."

He smiled and looked at the gray-blue dawn sky through the smoke hole. He thought of morning views at home and the sweetness of waking up with Nanitana. He missed her most acutely in the mornings and looked forward to his return home from what was becoming a very long walk.

He heard a light crack and looked down to see a small flame in the fire pit. Hosiini knelt in front of the new fire, raven-black hair flowing over her shoulders. He felt impressed that she could kindle the fire without noise.

Iskifa admired quiet people, like most Yukpans. He was particularly fond of women and loved how they could move about a house quietly and efficiently, the same way they hunted and snared game. Hosiini arranged a cooking pot, and he could not help but notice the nice roundness of her hip under her summer wrap. He rose for a better look.

The bumblebee took off from the *lowak* blossom to touch briefly on his head and flew up through the smoke hole. Iskifa composed himself and took his cap from his pillow to lay it in his lap, purposely distracting himself to admire its vibrant colors. His cap was made of soft, dyed leather, embellished with shell ornaments and feathers. Its purple-red color, made from raw *koshibba*, poke weed and berry juice, was his favorite to look at. Boiling the *koshibba* juice, mixed with some *takonlo lakna*, yellow plum, juice and a little water, changed it into black dye. The hardest color to come by was the yellow. He made it by boiling a particular type of *chomak*, tobacco leaf, which originally grew only on the banks of the *Hayi Bok*, Walnut Creek, near where he was born. He had to dip the leather in the hot *chomak* dye and let it dry five times. Looking at the colors this morning transported him for a moment to his beloved home.

He was not prone to sentimentality, so he could think fondly of home without getting too homesick. He carefully arranged the colorful cap on his head and tucked away the small stick and stone he picked up for luck on the path yesterday. The night had been cool and treacherous, so he kept his breechcloth on. He picked up his mantle and pulled it on over his head, gathered the rest of his gear and headed down the ladder before any more bees could fly through the smoke hole. Hosiini met him, looking radiant with a *lowak* blossom over her left ear, where single women wore flowers.

"Where are your mother and father?" Iskifa asked in her language.

"They usually fish in the surf before dawn," she answered, smiling. "They are probably seeing what kind of damage the storm has done. Would you like some…?"

"Yes, I would like some hot…*ashiila*…." He felt suddenly embarrassed—he couldn't remember the Onaffan word for boiled cracked corn, the regional choice for the first meal of the day. The wordmaster was at a loss for words. He gestured clumsily toward the meal urn, moving toward it, out of her reach, nodding, as if pleading for her to understand. She laughed understandingly and cocked her head, smiling at him again, as if to give him one last chance to change his mind. Regaining a bit of poise, he politely raised his eyebrows and nodded toward the corn meal urn. She chuckled again and went back to her cooking.

Iskifa walked outside to take in a deep breath of ocean air, refreshing and moist this early in the day. He glanced at the fish eaters' houses scattered along the coastline, all standing on high ground above the beach, like Kaheto's.

He liked the atmosphere of fishing villages. Everything was so practical and useful and obvious. The fish-drying racks and smoker sheds stood near the piers and wharves where fishers came in with their catches. This morning, of course, quite an array of boats lay on the higher reaches of the sandy beaches, their ropes running farther up the banks in case they needed to be pulled out of the path of a storm surge during the night.

The brunt of the storm had passed farther north. Though the winds were strong, they did not cause much destruction in the village. The fish eaters were out re-rigging and re-staging their boats and repairing minor damage to piers and drying huts. The only thing lost to the storm, as best he could tell, was the morning's catch.

Checking for new aches and pains, Iskifa bent gracefully to touch the ground with his palms, stretching and limbering. He reasoned he might be getting close to the goal of his journey, although he felt no strong intuition of imminent conclusion.

He only knew the strange, pale-skinned man in his dream came walking up out of an ocean much like this one. Of course, this was the only ocean coast he knew besides the *mahli okahta hochito*, the south ocean, and he saw no evidence that his dream pointed south. It was a fact about dreaming in his experience, as his mentor, Atanapoa, taught him, that you could not see any place in a dream you had not seen while awake. You could see people you had never seen before, they agreed—even people from your ancestors' lives—because people and their spirits move freely in the world.

Iskifa did not depart from Atanapoa's teachings. Since his time with him, he gathered little new knowledge other than from practical experience in trades and arts. He did believe *Aba Binnili* dealt with him more in dreams than with Atanapoa. Iskifa learned to trust and respond to his dreams. He did not question them.

They frightened him while he was younger, as did the unusual adventures they put him through. He learned through his life journey, however, to embrace them, because to do so was to embrace the *Hina Aalhpisa*, the forward path, and ultimately to embrace *Aba Binnili*. Wherever the infrequent but powerful dreams placed him or showed him, he went.

It became for him a simple and fundamental fact of life that any creature's central purpose was put in him by the Creator; that everything the Creator creates has a purpose within a potentially perfect design. The peculiarity that separated people from other creations, like rocks or animals, was that people could choose to abandon their purpose, their place in the design.

No other part of creation could do anything but what it was designed to do. But men and women could choose. People could choose evil or good. They could choose to love or choose to hate. They could choose to make peace or war. Iskifa believed that if you opened yourself to all creation, *Aba Binnili* would keep you on the *Hina Aalhpisa*. The reasons the Creator did this were unknown.

Although many who knew about the Creator regarded *Aba Binnili* as a father figure, Iskifa viewed him more as a whole spirit, with all potentials and qualities. He did believe *Aba Binnili* prescribed certain roles for men and women, young and old. The only thing sacred about how a person "chose" to pursue his or her *Hina Aalhpisa* were the rhythms the Creator set in motion for each person and for each family or larger group of people. One rule never changed: respect your elders.

With Kaheto and the fish eaters now several flight behind him, Iskifa felt happy to walk along a path overlooking the ocean and more certain his strange dream would prove true. Many along his journey, now twenty-four days' strong walk from Chunuli, ridiculed him. No one but a fool, they jeered, would go on such a walk.

They found it particularly asinine that he looked for a "white" man. Many did not accept the possibility such creatures lived anywhere in *yaakni moma*. Still, some traders said a northern group of people, the Delamac, once had a "white" man in their midst, and that he spoke an unknown tongue—but no one else believed them. Traders would tell whatever lies suited the promotion of their business. Iskifa, however, listened to their tales with great interest, because they seemed to be repeated more often the farther north and east he traveled. He had in fact sent his apprentice, Taloa Kinta, three winters earlier to study with Anli Basha, the wordmaster of Anoli, who had heard and believed stories about pale-skinned people who spoke a strange language.

The sun, now directly overhead, beat down on the beach, so he stayed on a fairly worn wooded path just above it, passing bushes he had never seen before and identifying a new variety of a familiar tree, all of which fascinated him. He kept a keen eye open for new birds or animals. He had not earned the reputation as one of the foremost experts on trees and things made from wood by owning a lazy eye. He felt proud of his understanding and knowledge and gathered more wherever he traveled.

The blue skies, the scents of coastal flora, the fresh sound of the rolling surf, and the occasional squawk of a shore bird provided high entertainment for the Yukpan wordmaster. Such sensations made him recall the brightest adventures of his lifetime. The sudden appearance of a fish crow changed his mood.

The bird lit on a turn of the path and held an odd-colored scrap of something in its beak. Iskifa recoiled with surprise, and it quickly took flight. He chided himself for being spooked, but he could not dismiss a sense he now felt. He had never been wrong about such a perception before—not when it felt so strong.

And it felt strong. It felt like death. Death was unmistakable. Death was near, not as an odor, but as another sense. It felt like human death.

It did not feel like his own death threatened him, but he drew an arrow from his quiver and readied it on the bowstring. A skillful hunter, Iskifa could shoot the eye out of a squirrel. He had never killed an enemy in battle, although he had been present at many. Wordmasters were protected because their skills were often essential to achieve peace after men had been killed. Hoping against killing, he crouched and tested the wind. He still sensed death ahead.

He stole away from the trail to find a higher vantage point straight up the hill and found a large *osak*, a hickory tree, with low, scaffolding branches. He crouched, balancing the bow and arrow between his teeth, and with silent hops made his way up the *osak* to see the beach over the under-story of brush. The scene he saw through the forking branches, toward the sea, turned his blood cold.

CHAPTER TWO

THE NAVIGATOR

CAPTAIN ROBERT WILLIAMS COMPENSATED AS BEST HE COULD for the rocking of the waves, sighting in the North Star through the eyelets of his brass navigating device. He held it still to see which number the plumb line intersected. Fifty-six degrees north latitude would take him straight west and far enough south to miss the Gulf of the Hebrides and the deadly riptides and coastal rocks of the Barra Isles.

Sailing this night instead of waiting till morning would save him nearly a day to the outpost and take him that much sooner back to Celia, his enchanting redhead, the angel who consented to marry him. What puzzled him, however, even while he became intoxicated with the blackness of the night and the white light of the constellations, was the northeasterly breeze across his cheek. The wind never blew out of the northeast this time of year. It started as a whisper, became a hum, began to declare itself, and turned into an agitation.

The year was 1399. Robert Williams the fourth was, in his opinion, at least, one of the better seamen in Scotland and one of its most progressive. For example, he believed the earth was round—or certainly not flat, anyway—and based his belief on his observations, like the way a ship's mast sinks steadily at the horizon while it moves away from you. Some of the better thinkers he met in Glasgow, even clergy among them, believed the earth was a sphere or perhaps egg-shaped, even if the official position of the Church said the earth was a disc around which the sun, moon, and stars spun.

And there was the matter of a new and unexplored world. Some men, descended from Norse refugees who married into Scots clans generations earlier, told of men from their tribes who sailed across the ocean centuries ago. A few returned, they claimed, all warning the journey was beyond treacherous—the sea was full of ice, and the strange lands across the ocean were inhabited by all manner of savage beasts and barbaric peoples. They spoke also, however, of unimaginable resources and treasure, a detail that always tantalized Robert.

Many of the better navigators he met around Europe and the Mediterranean agreed about the roundness of the earth, but none had sailed more than forty leagues from European shores. Robert had weathered thorny gales and incisive brushes with just about every kind of coast the known world offered. He was practically born on the ocean and imagined many times what might be required to cross it.

The son of one of Scotland's better-known shipbuilders, Robert preferred sailing to shipbuilding. His younger brother, Seth, inherited the responsibility of the boat-building business. Seth was a land lover. Robert's father let him know he felt grieved that his eldest refused to inherit the business, but he got over it. He was a wise enough man to know people do what they will. His wife, his beloved Ruth, regularly reminded him that things work out for the good, a sentiment which he held likewise and liked to be reminded of.

Robert's ship sailed for the remote village of Barabhas on the northwest coast of Lewis Island in the Hebrides. Once he landed there, he would deliver a shipload of provisions from Glasgow and pick up a load of Barabhan virgin wool, a robust component of Scotland's trade goods with the rest of Europe. The Lewis Islanders husbanded the largest flocks of short-tailed sheep in the kingdom, and their looms produced marketable quantities of the valuable fabric.

Still, he wanted to save time more than to make money. Every day he saved meant a day closer to the ravishing Celia. Her stormy red hair, apricot skin tones, and polar white smile dominated his mind. In her presence he always felt consumed by her radiance.

It would be faster, but more dangerous to sail north past Islay, then straight west into the open Atlantic. Most navigators feared that turn because it ventured too far from land, and they didn't like to lose sight of land. But Robert felt confident with his navigational instrument and with his skill and intuition.

Further, despite frequent conflicts with Seth, Robert credited his brother with a confidence-building genius for ship design. Seth bought the cog Robert sailed after the English navy retired it. It reputedly survived the great sea battle of Sluys with the French, the first battle of a war that had gone on without any permanent resolution for more than sixty years. Seth added a forward lateen sail, like cogs used in the Mediterranean, making it the first so equipped in all Scotland.

Robert always liked the stories of *Manannan*, the Gaelic god of the sea, so he retained the name she held after they bought her from the navy. The lateen sail made the *Manannan* the most precisely maneuverable ship he ever captained. He would simply time his course to the west, make a sharp turn north-northeastward, and slide up the west coast of the Hebrides to Barabhas.

The standard route to Barabhas was to sail the more protected and populous inside passage through the Gulf of the Hebrides, past the Isle of Skye through the strait called Little Minch, and then through the gulf called North Minch. There weren't many settlements on the west coast of northern Scotland and none on the west side of the Hebrides.

After that, the *Manannan* would pick up the woolens, sail north and then east around the Butt of Lewis, through Pentland Firth into the North Sea, then south along the east coast of Scotland to Aberdeen. In Aberdeen, trade goods would be loaded and the burgeoning shipment would terminate in Edinburgh, where the Lewis Island wool would begin its journey to London and points south.

Robert then would sail into the Firth of Forth to Dunfermline, home of the Scottish kings, and dock there. From there he could take the ferry to Falkirk and hire one of their fine horses, just like he did a month ago, when he asked Celia to marry him. From Falkirk it was only twenty miles overland to Hardgate, just downriver from Glasgow and the home of the celestial Celia.

He recalled how, upon his last visit to Dunfermline, he traded bolts of wool for an engagement ring for her. Stories about how the ancient Romans offered rings to their betrotheds interested him. The Romans believed the ring finger of a woman contained a vein, the *vena amoris*, that ran straight to her heart.

He remembered with immense delight and a little embarrassment how he found her at work in her cottage, how clumsily he proposed, and how she at first simply stared at the ring poised upon his out-stretched fingertips. Shards of her fiery red hair, loosely pinned up in the flurry of her labor, flew about her head like fairies trailing cobwebs as she at last accepted his proposal. His relief when she let him place the ring upon her finger was equaled only by his senses of success and happiness.

Robert recalled those memories dozens of times over the past month, and indeed savored them now while his ship gently rocked, deck boards giving slightly under his feet. A thin cloud appeared in the night sky.

The next time he saw her, after he sailed a two-hundred-league loop around the north end of Scotland and back to his home port of Glasgow, they could only just contain their urges for each other, so they set the date for the wedding six weeks hence, after his next two voyages and two returns, a regular trading cruise to Portsmouth, England, and a hit-every-port run around the north end of Scotland, down the east coastline and back.

Now he sailed the second of those voyages, and the glorious con-summation of their love appeared imminent. He would do the over-land jaunt from Dunfermline once more for the final preview, and to this end he made the swing to the west side of the Hebrides to save a day's journey, to put him closer to Celia.

But the night launch and the brisk breeze from the northeast began to worry him. Robert Williams could tack across almost any wind with the best of helmsmen. He could maneuver a large, square-sail cog as well as an average sailor could a smaller craft. Still, the unexpected northeaster at that time of year distressed him.

By late spring, winds coming off the Mediterranean and Spanish rock-heated air masses commonly overtook the northers to flood northwestern Europe with welcome south breezes. The currents ran gently up that western coastline, although with Robert. He felt confident of his time-saving course, particularly if he could reference off Castle Bay, the fortress built in the eleventh century to intercept Viking invaders on the south end of the Barra Isles.

If he got blown off course, however, he would be less familiar with the smaller Barra Isles, and the inherent hazards of sailing in unknown coastal waters shook his usual confidence a bit—but he did not care. Celia's smile and sunset hair brandished through his mind's eye while he watched the buffeting main sail. He thought of her freckled hands and delicate feet. A vague shadow appeared on the deck, made by quarter moonlight blocked out by the ladder netting. He stared transfixed at the delicate shadow for a moment until it vanished.

A dark cloud obscured the spring tide moon. He smelled smoke from the men's cook fire. A queer mood settled over him—sudden cold and loneliness. The gust front hit him forcefully and jarred him off balance. The smoke scent left, replaced by the familiar, foreboding smell of ice in the wind, a wind of force.

He flashed for a moment on Vikings in their long boats and horned hats they no longer wore, but for which they will always be remembered. He thought of them with the toothy arctic wind at their backs, sailing toward Scotland to rape, steal, and kill. The weight of his predicament sunk into his shoulders like a whaler's poon.

He shouted to his crew to put out their fire and make ready for a storm. He made the decision, in anxious recognition of its tardiness, to turn south and try to tack east. He frantically calculated in his head the force and navigational effect of the sudden northeaster and could not escape a chilling deduction that with this much wind at eight degrees west, only a miracle could deliver him to the northwest coast of Ireland, never mind Scotland.

Unless it abated at once, the white boreal wind could blow them out to a sea unknown to him and his crew. He barked orders as quickly as his eleven men could accomplish them. They made a skeleton crew for the usually uneventful cruise around the north end of Scotland by the inside passage.

"Stow those barrels," he cried. They were caught unawares with loose cargo on deck. "Secure those lanyards and tie those bales," he yelled. "Denny, haul in that goat before she bloody drowns," he commanded, almost seeing humor in the irony of the king's goat washing overboard. The king's physician had ordered the milk of this particular species of goat for the monarch's heartburn. They picked her up on the island of Islay and were to deliver her to the winter palace in Dunfermline.

The northern sky turned completely dark. Waves slapped the side of the ship, sending up great wisps of spray, like a giant stomping in a mud puddle.

"What have we got, Robert?" asked Denny, his old friend and first mate, returning from the hold, having saved the goat.

"Looks like a damned cold easterly, mate. Not good," replied Robert somberly. "I'm geared south and as much east as I kin. We'll hit Ireland if we're lucky. If not, we might be roasting that goat in Barcelona."

"You act like we've never been lost before, Robby. What's this compared that bruiser in the Irish two winters yon? And that turned out all right, didn't it? Got to spend two weeks in Cork with the prettiest Irish lassies a brigand might fancy. And the Irish grog wasn't bad, neither." Denny was always optimistic.

"That's fine for the wishin'," Robert continued in a contrary tone, "but this is a crumb more of a pickle than that was, laddie. We had wind blowing us toward land, that day."

Denny looked up at the lateen sail. It vibrated like a violent cricket's song. He pulled his cap tight to his eyebrows and clasped his top button. Robert nodded toward the sail, and Denny called Willam Wainwright, the eldest crewman aboard the *Manannan*, to help haul down the lateen. Nothing more was said. Robert stayed at the helm while the crew scurried to secure their cargo. The seas mounted quickly, and his hopes vanished that the gust front would be the worst of it. He knew it was only the beginning.

Within an hour, Robert gave up any idea of tacking east. The waves and troughs were so immense his highest hope now was to hold line with the wind and pray the old cog would hold together. Never in his sailing life had he seen wood so stressed to its sinuous limit. The wind and waves twisted and stretched the vessel like a strong-handed wash-woman wrings a towel.

The wind gained momentum so fast the main sail rent down the middle before they could gather and secure all the cargo and loose gear. The crew hauled it down before it blew away. Robert and Denny took turns at the helm, taking twenty-minute shifts to prevent succumbing to the wet chill and simple exhaustion from titanic wrestling with the rudder wheel. The storm at first pelted them with eyeball-size hail and two hours into it, stung them with horizontal sleet. Crewmen worked below deck to make space for shelter in the cramped hold. They tried to supply dry blankets for the spelled helmsmen who slipped below to thaw out. A pass of the whiskey jug was made.

"I'm hoping this thing will pass," Robert said to Wainwright. "Have ya ever seen one like this at this time of year, Willam?"

"Noo, I haven't, lad," he answered, "but ask ole Russell over there." Russell Tain sat on a stool, staring into the floorboards in the rolling room, within earshot of Wainwright's comment. Tain did not respond. Robert fixed his eyes on the rugged seaman. The cracked skin on Tain's hands seemed the only dry feature of the man in prayerful posture, as if that skin lay so open it could no longer possess moisture.

Robert asked, "Russell, have you?"

"No sir," he answered, "but I've heared of it."

"Well, tell, man," Robert insisted.

"When I was a wee lad, me da didn't come home," Russell said in a monotone, hesitating.

"Yes," Robert added intently.

"Me da was a sailor, like us. He sailed regular in the navy and then on a freighter all around Anglund and Eire. In June of sixty-four, when I was five, we had one of the coldest storms I remember. In June, mind ya. It came out of the nor'east, jest like this'un. They were deliv'rin' a load of feed 'round to Galway. They never seen 'em in Galway. That nor'easter blowed 'em clean away. No one ever seed 'em again." Tain never looked up.

"Well, that's a fine report," Robert said, reacting strongly. "Well, let it be known, mates, the *Manannan's* not goin' down, and we're not dying. Is that clear?" He quickly jerked his eyes around the group, making eye contact. "Clear?" he asked again forcefully. The crew grumbled half-hearted affirmation.

Robert's optimism was naïve. The storm lasted for six nights and five days. Every crewman took a turn at the rudder wheel and none, he observed, slept much. All sooner or later hurled their stomach contents, as much from fear as from seasickness. It horrified them to believe they were blown over a great abyss of ocean. Some feared being driven to the edge and into an even more frightening, perilous, and evil unknown. They were all so wet and cold, the thought of death felt inconsequential to Robert.

When the storm-ravaged ship finally came to rest in sunny doldrums at unknown latitude and longitude, Robert and the others lay incapable of understanding or interpreting any of it. A few nibbled on dried fish, beetroot, and garlic from the stores and sipped from a water barrel before falling into deep, exhausted sleep. The *Manannan* drifted for eighteen hours before Robert regained enough presence and energy to wake.

"Celia," he moaned unconsciously. A knifing pain in his spine jolted him at sunrise. The next sensations his brain acknowledged were the saltiness of the blanket over him and the sensation of his cracked lips, like crumpled parchment. He felt battered, beleaguered, and speechless, like one returned from hell without a memory, a newborn orphan adult in a blank landscape with no guide. He battled for command of the moment, but nothing he learned or experienced prepared him for it. He considered and meditated as all seamen of all eras do, upon what lies "beyond." His mind staggered while he waded through an inventory of pain in his body. His left wrist looked purple and swollen, and he couldn't tell whether it was broken or badly sprained by one of the uncounted howling gusts that threatened to capsize his vessel during the recent infinite past. A tender, stinging gash over his left eye felt raw.

The other eleven littered the deck like nautical rag dolls, some covered by blankets, some sprawled where they fell, all blistered, scabbed, and oozing blood. If he was not fairly certain of his own painful state of being alive, he surely would have judged the spectacle as a collection of corpses. Apart from an occasional slither and groan, they looked inert.

At mid-afternoon, useful navigation readings were impossible. He could look at the sun and determine directions, but he couldn't judge his latitude without the North Star. All notion of longitude was gone. So he stared at the water, azure and swelling gently. "Flotsam," he thought finally, feeling the rocking-chair lullaby of the swells under his pathetically insignificant vessel.

He began to walk the deck, quickening somewhat from his painful torpor. The scrambled impulses in his brain began to collect, like fat in a broth, to resemble thoughts, then patterns of thought. "What are we going to do?" was the first to take shape in his mind. The arithmetic was easily calculable, but he found himself avoiding acceptance of the results. Six nights and five days of travel at top de-sailed speed put them not only in unknown waters, but in a virtually unimagined place, too.

None thought of coping with such experimental reality. They once laughed about possibilities like this over pints of ale, but none seriously contemplated or feared them—except Robert. He had pondered the "beyond." He was inquisitive and independent in thought, always the outsider, which explained why he couldn't take over the family business. He could not portray himself in a locked-in place. He never felt interested in the status quo, but always in the *mutatis mutandis*. Now, on a watery plane of all but certain death, he recalled one of his brother's recent remarks.

"Robert," Seth said while they inspected the *Manannan* during her last docking in Newark, after Robert told him of his engagement to Celia, "What makes you think you can settle down to one woman?" The rhetorical tone of the question bothered him then and now. Seth sounded as if the answer was obvious to anyone who knew him.

"Of course I can," Robert blurted, startling himself with the sounds of his first words in many hours. Sharply, his mind returned to the deck of the *Manannan*. He clutched the skin on his chest and needle-like pains bolted up his spine, jerking his head backward. He winced, closed his eyes, and Celia's opalescent smile appeared. "I must find a way," he whispered with his first hint of strength.

He began to behave instinctively, like a ship's captain, going to his charts, even if they were mostly portolan and better for navigating coastlines. He stared at the blank western region of the ocean on his map and thought of the blue swells outside his cabin. He reasoned they drifted about two hundred leagues west of Ireland, but it was harder to calculate how far south they were.

The farthest he sailed before without landing was four days and even then he rarely lost sight of land. He recalled sailors bragging of sailing four days straight west into the Atlantic and returning, but such claims always came from blowhards, not serious seamen. The prevailing breeze, he noted, pushed them southwest, so it would take a fairly large loop for them to tack back east—and again, he had no idea how far south they sailed.

Known enemies to Scots lived and sailed ships to the south and east, all feared worse than unknown threats. The more he calculated and festered with the variables, the greater an inspiration rose within him that his safest bet might be to sail west and try to find the land he imagined might be there. Robert enjoyed every primitive land he visited, and the imagination of discovering new territories began to take hold on him.

He was not greedy, but discoveries and exotic treasures haunt the dreams of all voyagers. If land lay west, then there should be people, and if people, then provisions and knowledge of winds and currents, the least they would need to get back home. No expanse of sea where he captained before lay more than a day's sail from land. Already they were six nights and five days south and a considerable, if uncertain, distance west.

"How much farther could it be toward land?" he mumbled over his charts. "We won't sail over the edge. Somehow, there is no edge. There's got to be land." His words seethed slowly.

"We've got the provisions," Denny announced optimistically, walking through the open door of the cabin and overhearing the captain's utterance.

Robert reflexed painfully. "Lord, ya scared me, man. How are ye?" he asked, scanning his bruised and tattered friend.

"Keel-hauled," Denny replied. "Where's the whiskey?" Robert pointed to the jug in a chair nearby, and Denny swiped it up for a quick swallow. Denny not only was an optimist, he also held tremendous confidence in Robert Williams. Robert had sailed them out of so many scrapes, Denny never questioned him.

"We've talked about it plenty, Denny. It just doesn't stand to reason that there's not land out there. And anyone who thinks the world is flat with a brink is too stupid to recognize the color of shyte, wouldn't ye agree?" Robert asked rhetorically.

"I'd say so," Denny replied collegially. "You convinced me a long time ago, Rob. It just don't make sense to the eye to say the earth is flat. Anybody who's been to the top of a mountain or sailed the sea much kin see the world's got a curve to her, like a woman's arse at eye level." He paused to give Robert a chance to react, pleased with his comparison. He raised a foot to the chair, leaned on his knee, and let the whiskey jug dangle from his finger. "Only those damned book gnats and clergy who never go outdoors could hold to a silly notion that the world is flat," he concluded.

"So you think we might have a chance to find land to the west?" Robert asked.

"Don't make me repeat me-self, Bobby. I said we had the provisions. It seems possible, if not likely. And like ye say, our chances are worse than bad, trying to go south and east," he replied, showing some anxiety about that idea. "We're prob'ly dead men anyway we spit. But we've got food and water for thirty days, and if we get lucky and find a route to Chiny or India, and can find our wee back, we'll be the kin of kings," he reasoned more cheerfully. "Hell, man, we even have milk and a decent supply of whiskey."

"And what do you think the others will think of the notion, Denny?" he asked. "They didn't sign up for China or India."

"Well, they didn't sign up for a six-day gale, neither, Robby, but that's what they got," he answered, resignedly. "I 'spect they'll see it the same way we do."

"So be it, Denny," Robert said, more formally. "Organize the rations. Get the men up, tend to their wounds, and mend the sails. Let's put the *Man* back into shape."

The next few days saw the crewmen of the *Manannan* bring themselves back together with food, water, sunshine, and the sweet song of survival—for the present and the less certain future. No one's wounds were too severe; mainly cuts and bruises except for Tain. Sleet blew into his eyes during one of his midnight turns at the wheel, and he lost his sight for two days and two nights. A week later he still saw only blurs and suffered eyeball ache.

The crewmen reluctantly accepted the captain's rationale for proceeding west, reckoning one fear to be no better than another. They were obedient by training, a necessary quality of good seafarers. All knew democracy had no place on a ship and in fact, hardly any place in the human world of the fourteenth century. The king's law was absolute, the captain gave the orders, and common people did what they were told.

The men regained strength and enjoyed fair June weather, the blue skies and spectacular starry nights. A giddy excitement even took them once in a while, especially after Robert ordered a once-daily whiskey ration during the first week after the gale. They gained the full fledge of adventure.

Robert calculated their latitude on the second night after the storm at forty-seven degrees, three degrees farther south than he had estimated with the charts. The westerly winds caused his earlier misread. Apparently the wind blew more northerly during the storm, which accounted for the ice in it, but prevailing winds from the southwest yesterday had greatly diminished and began to turn. They set the sails, and Robert gave instructions to continue tacking south until they could pick up currents and winds off Africa. Although incomplete for that part of the Atlantic, his charts suggested they would push the *Manannan* westward. Under no circumstance would he consider letting the westerlies carry them to Spain or Africa.

The *Manannan* successfully tacked southward for three more days until, to Robert's delight, her sails began to pick up the warm winds off Africa that daily felt more tropical. In another two days they blew almost straight west and so they sailed, blistering in the sun at twenty-six degrees north latitude, in hopes of finding a new world. Infatuation with the open sea was a new experience for the band of Scotsmen.

Although none of the *Manannan* crewmen had experienced such hot weather, each day seemed more intoxicating to Robert. Surely they would have gone over the brink in the first days, if there had been one. The winds blew brisk and steady, an encouragement to sailing men anywhere encountered. Each new day built confidence they would find land. The changes in their surroundings were subtle and only eerie when considered together. June was a big month for bugs, but not an insect had been seen for days. Also, significant time had passed since they saw waterfowl of any kind, meaning they sailed far enough away from land, in any direction, to be out of range of flying insects and birds.

Robert, at least, understood his best estimate of the completed part of the voyage was at most half. On his first reckoning of that, which came at the end of the third week, he recalled Denny's optimistic declaration of thirty days' provision.

He became grave and prayerful. He had never registered such a sharp perception of his own triviality amid matters fully outside his control. No swagger fit the situation, no bracing of the wits or will. This was a new realm, a spectacular, off-the-chart voyage, defying his attempts to rationalize it. The wind varied day to day, but had not completely subsided even for an hour in two weeks. It was a hell wind of destiny. It was a burning-bush wind. It was handwriting on the wall, and no Daniel present to interpret. His imagination failed him. His preconceptions, his psychological reserves, his old sayings, his father's advice, and the sage counsels of the old, white-bearded seamen at whose feet he learned held no wisdom, no comfort. The sense they were even on the same earth began to leave him, like an opium dream.

They only sailed, at twenty-six degrees, into an abyss of ocean. Maybe this land he hoped for was like the stars that seemed close enough to touch, although somehow he knew they were very far away.

Even stranger, he sensed something in that abyss more liberating than the first sense of facing its unknowns had produced. To realize his fate lay beyond his control, out of his hands, had a puzzling, calming effect on him. In fact, none of the men seemed frightened. Most grew quiet and went about their chores without conversation. Some talk arose at the rationed meals they took together, but even then a strange calm overtook them.

By the end of the fourth week, a couple of men began to spook—not toward the captain or the voyage, but internally. The new language of open sea was not fitting with the old pictures of coastal voyages, familiar landmarks, and ports. Seamen are not, by nature or choice, sentimental family men, but none had known removal from customary surroundings for so long. Most of the *Manannan's* crew were single. Robert, like other ship captains, was careful to hire bachelors, but Tain and Willam had married since signing on. Men without wives and children, however, still connected to strings of associations that might include the butcher, the baker, a minister, a pub proprietor, a constable, a neighbor's family, aging parents, a mistress, brothers and sisters, pets, and even rivals and enemies. Robert understood how long ocean voyages could make any man feel small, alone, and insufficient.

He noted slow and steady erosion of their conditions. What had been exhilaration, then calm, now looked like the climate of weakening. The men were true to their tasks, but running out of capacity, and he feared their communal conditioning was not enough for the rigors of this journey. It was painfully easy to extend the signs of weakness toward insanity. The younger men showed signs of emotional fatigue. They were more volatile in the first place, without the backlog of suffering to fall against, like older men. Robert remembered the scripture that said tribulation works patience.

His darkest reveries centered on how he would handle demented behavior if it arose. "How do you think the lads are holdin' up, Willam?" he asked old Wainwright one day while they stood on the bow stage, staring into the open sea.

"Young Braemar's gettin' shaky Cap'n. I've heared him whimperin' at night lately and mumblin' about his mother," Wainwright replied. "And in the daytime he don't say a word; nay, not one, sir."

"What are we gonna do if he snaps, Willam?"

"I dunno Cap'n. I 'spose it depends on what he does when he cracks," Wainwright replied thoughtfully.

It settled Robert down just to broach the subject, especially with a man as solid as Wainwright. He was the tallest man Robert knew and the most substantial physically, six-foot-four and built like an ox. He had the red hair of a Gael, but Robert was convinced his cheekbones were Norse. In no other variety of human had he noticed such mountain-ridge cheekbones like Wainwright's, except among Norsemen. None of the soft roundness of Scot facial structure was evident in Willam. His coarse carmine hair was always braided, more like knotted, dangling around a working man's head. He had the skull of a lion on the torso of a wrestler. The bass tones in his voice, with their Gaelic intonations and halting melody, felt like soothing syrup to Robert's ears; fatherly, brotherly, remarkably sage.

"Let us keep an eye out for any dangerous madness, my friend," Robert continued. "Better to bind with ropes for a while and let 'em come off it. Catch 'em 'fore they get lethal. Right?"

They faced the deep blue ocean at the oak rail beneath a bright blue sky holding one cottony cloud, high and thin.

"Aye, Cap'n," Wainwright replied. Robert loved the way such a vastly superior physical human being like him could convey a sincere attitude of equality, or even superiority, to a captain.

Denny walked up to complete a triumvirate, noticing the others' political postures. "Another beautiful day, gentlemen," he quipped.

"Aye, Denny," Robert responded. "How long can it last?"

"I hope it doesn't last too much longer, Robby," Denny said, "'cause our water barrels are good for another seven days, outside."

"Have you noticed any men going flaky or talking crazy, laddie?" Robert asked Denny.

"Tain's got that eye twitch he gets before he goes off, and Braemar looks like the living dead," he replied quickly, as though he already knew the topic of conversation at hand.

"Let's keep close watch, Denny," Robert ordered. "Wainwright here is on alert, too. We'll bind 'em with rope if need be, to keep 'em from hurtin' themselves or others. I've got some terebinth with opium if we need to dose anyone." Robert was happy to have two salty seamen like these for friends and allies, no matter how peculiar the circumstances. They could be trusted to hold together as well as himself, he hoped.

"Aye," Denny replied calmly, like it was routine to be a month into a voyage into an outer realm, believed by most people on earth to be the very definition of doom.

CHAPTER THREE

THE LANDING

THE HYPNOTIC BREEZE AND BALMY OCEAN TRANSFIXED Robert, Denny, and Willam at the *Manannan*'s forecastle rail until sharp bleating shattered the spell. They knew the sound as the call of Lizbeth, the king's goat. The crew named her, tongue-in-cheek, after Elizabeth Mure, the famously well-endowed and somewhat scandalous mother of Robert III, king of the Scots since 1390.

Lizbeth's large udders originally were a curiosity of amusement for the sailors, but had become a primary source of comfort and nutrition. They roasted one of her kids on the first weekend after the storm and the other a week later because her milk supply became a staple of the crewmen's diet. Several took turns milking Lizbeth, and everyone on board zealously monitored her grain and hay supply.

Robert recognized the healing benefit of the milking chore since it was, besides this ship, their only connection to their previous earthly life that now existed only as a remembered acquaintance, like a dead relative, the ghost of a life drowned at sea three limitless weeks ago. After suspension in purgatory for days, each man was resurrected into this nether region, neither heaven nor hell.

Beyond a source of nutrition and comfort, Lizbeth also was something of a mascot and a one-character comedy. As anyone who knows goats would suspect, the intelligent and cantankerous creature constantly sought opportunities for chicanery. The wellspring of curiosity never runs dry in the brain of a goat. The storage of the ship's galley grains required re-fortification on many occasions, especially after Lizbeth chewed through an inch-thick pine storage door latch to get to them. That episode nearly resulted in her death sentence, but her value as a renewable milk supply outweighed the loss of a pound or two of millet. The game was always to keep Lizbeth outwitted and observed.

Robert came up with a solution. He ordered the round timbers that took up so much deck space to be lashed more tightly together so they couldn't roll much on rough seas. That killed two birds with one stone, because it also supplied a platform for a cage of sawn timbers, fastened with good English nails and ropes, so the stubborn goat couldn't kick her way out if she disagreed with her accommodations. "The Barabhans won't be needin' the lumber," Robert told the crew when he gave the order. The space around the logs let air circulate under her cage. He ordered hay strewn inside it and that its floor be scoured with salt water every day. The sailors usually put her in her cage at night, when no one could watch her. Especially during daytime, Lizbeth seemed to have a knack, a goat's intuition, for times when no one was looking at or thinking about her.

Her somewhat long fur was mostly white with a few large brown patches. Her face was slender, even for a goat, and put a decidedly feminine cast to her features. She was almost attractive and might even have seemed cuddly, had she not fully retained the characteristic fragrance of her species. Everyone's favorite pose of Lizbeth's was her preferred daytime position, standing on the farthest forward and highest part of the bow stage, statuesque, front legs on a little step at the bow point to get the most breeze on her face. She could remain thus for unexpectedly long periods of time, peering forward as if eager and confident to sight land. If that was actually a concept or impulse in her goat's mind, she was all but alone in it. The crewmen of the *Manannan*, in Robert's estimation, had forgotten the possibility.

Two more weeks passed, and the men, to Robert's surprise, did not go crazy. They just got weaker. The drama intensified steadily after Robert, Willam, and Denny talked about the dwindling water stores. Water rations were cut and work schedules trimmed to a minimum to minimize thirst, but a blessed twenty-four-hour rain shower, beginning with a frighteningly strong gust front, replenished the rain barrels about four days before the supply's expected extinction.

Not only was it relief from the threat of thirst, but also from the monotonous weather pattern that became as oppressive to Robert and his crew as the fear of death. A more subtle and equally serious problem, although not as consciously anticipated, was sickness the men began to suffer for lack of fresh fruits and vegetables. Tain and Donnchadh McLaren—two of Robert's eldest and most capable seamen—suffered scurvy, a rare and little-known problem. Robert knew deprivation of certain foods caused disease, but had never seen a case. The illness developed slowly and still did not seem as dramatic in his mind as the gnawing fears he once suffered of watching his men die one by one of thirst. For that matter, he imagined a half-dozen other perils as distinct possibilities, all greater than malnutrition.

The refilling of the water barrels and the break in the drone of weather restored some hope among the voyagers of the *Manannan* except Robert. From the captain's perspective, he remained unsure. The others apparently felt they no longer sailed into an endless abyss but perhaps, just perhaps, on a normal, but much larger, sea in the realm of earth, with weather patterns similar to those they knew.

He acknowledged the fresh aroma of rain as a welcome revival. And with the reflexes necessary for a functional captain, he felt some relief that he had not, so far, cracked under the pressure of venturing into the unknown. He found himself comparing his feelings of the past four-odd weeks since the big gale ended to ones he remembered clearly from when he was a lad exploring the narrow, deep highland caves above Glasgow with Seth. The sense of familiarity colliding uncomfortably with the mysterious and exalted unknown was strangely similar. The strains of trying to maintain his composure and of marshaling the impulse to panic were not completely new. The channeling of the impulse into devising strategies or into mapping out escape contingencies, existed now for both struggles in his memory, side by side—images of terror, images of exhilaration, images of survival.

○ ○ ○ ○

Robert leaned over his charts in his cabin, toiling with information about currents and winds, trying to set a course based on reason. The crew teamed up a few seasons earlier to build the small cabin under the sterncastle of the *Manannan* as a place for him to study his charts and bills of lading, and even sleep, in privacy.

"We're gonna make it, Robert," Denny proclaimed with aplomb as he entered. "I've a real strong feelin' that we're gonna find that new world that you've been dreamin' of, and it's gonna be a land filled with gold, silver, whiskey and beautiful women. I know it, Bobber, I kin jest feel it," he added with a display of optimism.

In his four years of association with Denny, his cheerful talk had become the thing Robert liked most and least about him. "Your feelin's mean nothin', Denny," he said bluntly.

Denny stood half in and half out of the doorway, hands on his waist, inhaling deeply the storm-rarefied air, flowing sweetly now from the south and east. He looked at Robert quizzically. "My feelings are right, you arse," he said.

"We might drown or starve, but we won't be expirin' thick-tongued, Denny McClendon," Robert replied curtly, "that's all you can say."

"Who put the stickers in your braies, Robert?"

Robert's fists clenched and his forearms stiffened where they rested on the chart table. He turned his head mechanically and glared at his friend and first mate. "I just get sick of hearin' your drivel. We're in the worst fix of our lives and all you can talk about is your feelin's," he snapped.

Denny flushed, stepping all the way into the cabin. "What would ye have me talk about, shyte-face, the price of pork?" he retorted angrily.

"How about some figurin' on the wind or the current, or better, the riggin'? You're a seaman, aren't ya?" Robert growled.

Denny's face contorted around the mouth and eyes. He hooked his thumbs under the waistband of his breeches and leaned threateningly, chest out, toward his captain. "Oh, yeh, Bobby, I'm comin' around to your way of thinkin', now. I'm seein' what ya mean. Right now, I'm figgerin' a way to fit the jib riggin' up your arse," Denny snarled.

Robert's fists came off the chart table in one fluid motion with the rest of his body, into a vicious swing at Denny's jaw.

Denny reflexed backward a little, only enough to deflect the force of Robert's punch, which caught him on the chin and knocked him back into the doorpost of the tiny cabin. He winced at the impact of his backbone against the doorframe. Robert lunged again, and Denny dropped to the floor, rolled, and came up beside him, punching him in his ribs, knocking some of his wind out. Denny threw another overhand punch to his ear and knocked him flat to the floor.

"I'm feelin' better than ever now, Bobby," Denny said, heaving breath and glaring down at him.

Robert felt dazed. "You reckless little bastard," he grumbled, rising slowly to all fours. Without looking up, he swiped Denny's legs from under him with his strong helmsman's forearm, and the mate hit the wooden floor like a sack of turnips.

Denny flexed quickly, but Robert was atop him before he could roll free, spreading a hand to press hard on his face while he delivered a couple of hard blows to his abdomen.

Denny shook his head violently from side to side, managed to pull one of Robert's fingers into his mouth, and bit down.

Robert yelped with pain, jerking his hand away. Denny shot the heels of both hands up to Robert's chin with enough force to bowl him over backward and off him.

By then Wainwright and McLaren had arrived. Each grabbed a combatant. The two struggled briefly against the older men's grips, shouting the last of their insults at each other before they surrendered limply into silence. The elder sailors released them to let them stand, minding to stay close enough to grab them if their tempers flared again.

Robert's and Denny's eyes finally met for one of those short moments men share from time to time when they feel the intimacy of brotherhood, its love and its hate. Robert focused on the cracked, sun- and exposure-grooved skin around Denny's face, bearing evidence of their agonizing strivings with this and other mighty seas. The weath- ered skin poignantly framed tender blue eyes that had sounded many waters alongside his.

○ ○ ○ ○

The winds kept fairly steady, still blowing them west, and the water warmed notably over the following week. A steady current propelled them even while the winds laid still in the warmest clime any aboard had known.

It had been many days since Robert last thought of Celia—not since the night of the revival rains, when he remembered getting caught with her in a sudden chilly squall in Hardgate. In a flash, again, he could smell her wet auburn hair, and the thought of raindrops on her lips strummed his heartstrings like a knife. He had to dismiss it. It was too painful, like touching bare skin to a hot coal, and he had to get away from the thought.

"Cap'n, have ya noticed how warm the water's got the past few days?" Wainwright asked in the evening while Robert manned the wheel.

"Aye," Robert replied. "What does it mean?" he asked the elder sail- or, noting his pensive and uncertain eyes.

"Well, with the bit o' northerly current we crossed just yesterday, I'd say water's a-comin' against land, which is turnin' it. Further yet, I'd say as warm as the water's gittin', we might be in for some weather."

Wainwright made his report with such analytical wisdom that Rob- ert felt moved to accept it. "How far do you figure we might be from land, mate?" Robert asked.

"A guess would be about a hunnerd leagues, me Cap'n friend," Wainwright estimated, squinting a deep-set hawk eye towards Robert. "Don't bet your life on it, though. I might be right. I might be wrong," he added, gesturing with a half jerk of his head to his left and back again. "I might be right. I might be wrong," he repeated as if it was the refrain of an old song.

As the portent of Wainwright's lyric percolated through Robert's mind like a monk's chant, he felt a soft and completely puzzling thump atop his hatless head. He looked up to catch a high, quick, departing smudge of flying color in the dimming sky. His eyes widened as though awakened, and he reached up slowly to touch his crown. He moved methodically with a quizzical frown, drawing his hand down before his eyes, turning toward the light of the oil lamp. He stared upon the thick, white, paint-like material on his fingers.

"Shyte, Willam," he muttered incredulously. "Bird shyte."

"Holy Mither of God, Cap'n," Wainwright exclaimed. "I was right. We're closin' in on land." He smiled broadly, burying his eyes yet more deeply into their sockets. He turned to gaze confidently, with apparent vision, across the blue ocean.

Robert approached each member of the crew, simply presenting his hand with the white substance smeared on its fingers. He gave each time for the information to soak in. Before long the entire assemblage jumped for joy. Lizbeth darted playfully, nipping at their hands while they danced arm-in-arm, fiddle blaring. She seemed to understand.

"Shyte, shyte, the bird has shyte. Our hearts are filled with pure delight," they sang, quickly composing a lyric to go with the fiddle jig. Robert broke out a cask of spicy mead from his cabin he once intended to save for trade. The occasion was too grand—their first real hope of survival since the norther called for immediate celebration. "Poor, weary devils," Robert said to himself, watching the men dancing a jig hand-in-hand like maidens around a maypole.

"I want to propose a toast," Robert proclaimed above the din of music, adding, "to the Blessed Laird Jesus." He held his sloshing cup of mead high, the foamy overflow sliding down his muscular forearm. The men quieted solemnly upon hearing the name of the Lord, as if Robert had waved a magic wand. They held their cups more outward than upward. "And also I want to drink to good friends … to good winds … to Scotland … to the greater world … and … to bird shyte," he squealed, breaking the spell. The men hooted, guzzled, and resumed their revelry, continuing well into the night.

Robert noticed Lizbeth had not been present amidships for more than an hour. The men were settled into slightly drunken, highly philosophical, but a great deal quieter conversation, so he slipped away to check on her. As soon as he left the circle of his fellows, he was struck by the beauty of a clear summer night. The moon, orders of magnitude brighter than any ever seen in the Scottish North, hung fat in a deep black sky. The tip of the rocking mainmast, from where he stood, bobbed back and forth over it like an upside-down pendulum. He stared a moment at the odd motion and image. The inky blackness rendered the stars almost blindingly bright, even in the bath of moonlight. Robert expected each man aboard must feel the same strong sense of worth as he did. He looked down to observe his dense shadow on the deck of the *Manannan*.

A sharp bleat from Lizbeth jerked his attention back to the deck. She stood in her favorite position at the bow stage, the breeze slightly fluttering her floppy ears. He smiled. The familiar sight comforted him. His heart swelled a little while he considered she might again graze on living grass. He lingered in that imaginary green pasture for a moment, until he caught a whiff of fish coming from the water, and suddenly, a superstition arose in him. He had learned to trust his intuitions. His blurry glimpse of the shorebird, less than the blink of an eye, returned to his mind's sight, strangely colorful—so colorful he suspected at the moment he might be hallucinating.

A queasy fear in his bowels suggested perhaps the omen was bad instead of good. He thought of the colorful serpent that deceived the first woman in Eden and of the simple conventional wisdom that things are not always what they seem. He focused on the smell of the air, a different air than his nose ever registered, unusually warm and moist; a bit like the air in the deeper highland caves. His mind ran from there to the memory of the first black man he ever saw, on a moldy ship stopped for repairs in the Williams Shipyard in Newark. Robert had boarded with the yard foreman and immediately noticed strange, barefoot, and poorly clothed black men doing the work of seamen at the foredeck. Another black man, dressed and shod relatively well, greeted the foreman.

"Welcome aboard the *VanWort*, mate," he said in decent English,

"I'll show you our problem." The two went below and Robert remained on deck, looking as long and often as he dared at the ragged black men. Shortly, the headman returned alone. "Your uncle will return soon, little mate. What be your name?" he asked in a thick, robust accent unfamiliar to Robert.

He replied politely to the strange-looking chap and in the conversation that followed, learned the man called himself a "trustee" and that he came from somewhere far to the south, a place the man called "Afriker." Robert remembered something from their conversation, because he had memorized it.

Robert asked about the weather in "Afriker" and the strange man said, "Remember this: June, real soon. July, stand by. August, it must. September, remember. October, it's over." The man did not explain. Robert assumed he talked about bad weather.

It was hard to fully imagine anything horrible on so pleasant a night. He chided himself to dismiss such old-womanly fears, declaring it sacrilegious not to be thankful for what God gave. And certainly, he concluded, God delivered to them the thing they needed most—hope. He rejoined the resting crew, got out his latest whittling project, a carving of Scylla, and relaxed into the wood, a favorite pastime.

He considered over the next few days Willam's estimate about possible landfall. Birds appeared more frequently. The fish life grew more abundant, and the men were regularly entertained, amused, and nourished by catching new species on their troll lines. Finding land seemed inevitable, and Robert shared a ballooning sense of ecstasy with his lost brothers that they might actually survive their incredible adventure. The apprehension of what they might find in the unknown world also was present. He found only ironic comfort and minor relief in his relative certainty they would not confront people they were already at war with.

Talk about what they might encounter ashore ranged from madmen to monsters and paradise to parched desert. Every siren, every Cyclops was considered, but Robert had long since judged such pagan myths to be the fancies of childhood. As captain, he had one dominant concern, and that was to land his ship, his men, and his cargo safely on a stable shore.

The weather turned warmer, uncomfortably so. He questioned his decision weeks earlier to keep the west-southwest heading, having reasoned at the time that they were more likely to encounter rains and therefore drinking water in a more southerly clime. Of course, he had been rewarded for that, but with welcome rains sometimes come unwelcome winds, like the ill-spirited one that blew them into the unknown. He held back a sudden rush of anxiety at the thought.

Robert reviewed that decision from time to time, but kept their heading, lining up with the prevailing ocean current, which, of course, meant swifter travel. His whole thorny thought process brought them, according to his previous night's calculations, to about thirty-three degrees north latitude. He had to use more wind for the past day or so, and rudder more steadily into a strong south-to-north current, but still they progressed almost due west. He had sailed as a cabin boy one voyage to the Mediterranean, during a lull in the war with the Franks, but now he was four hundred leagues farther south than ever as an adult seaman.

Even if their outlook improved with fresh fish on their plates, the *Manannan*'s crewmembers' health had not. Several were seriously weakened and suffered sores in different places. Some food had spoiled and molded, and their diet deteriorated despite Robert's effort to manage and ration. Only Willam and Denny seemed to hold their own, health-wise.

Robert kept well dressed in the evening, when the air cooled off, proud of the fact that he was noted for that. He thought it helped maintain morale and discipline if he dressed like a gentleman. He washed his clothes regularly, like his mother taught him, and his ships always carried a good supply of soap. "Cleanliness is next to godliness," she said so often to him when he was a boy. He could still hear the tone of her voice.

On the afternoon of the thirty-ninth day of the *Manannan*'s voyage, Robert spotted a buildup of blue-black clouds due south. He felt certain they neared land because of the increasing numbers and variety of gulls and other land-based birds—in fact, they might already have landed, if he hadn't taken Denny's advice two days earlier to turn more due south. Denny had a "very strong feelin'" that they were going to miss a land mass and insisted on the turn. Robert didn't trust Denny's "feelin's" any more than anyone else's, but did not want another fistfight, either.

The foreboding sky filled him at once with the most morbid fear he ever knew. What tragic irony it would be to be blown back out to sea with land so near. Or perhaps, God forbid, to sink into the unknown ocean, transforming a heroic voyage of discovery into a long journey into unheralded death. His boldest dreams of discovery were no match at the moment for the sirens of despair howling in his ears.

"Reduce to the main sail," Robert shouted, ordering the men to take down the lateen. The men scurried—only a blind man could fail to see what lay at stake. Robert knew some thought he was spoiled and privileged by birth. He once overheard one say he thought he betrayed his father by leaving the running of the business to his "incompetent" brother. Robert valued loyalty, and such remarks hurt deeply, but he knew when the inevitable crises arose, he could count on his men to obey orders. And they knew from experience that Robert could be relied upon for heady decision-making under the most desperate conditions. If the pecking order were natural, instead of based on class privilege, Robert felt he still would be every crewman's first choice for captain. It was not a popular idea of the day, but Robert strongly believed at least in the practicality of a principle that those who were governing needed the consent of the governed.

When he felt the powerful gust front of the storm, he immediately knew his best tactic was to turn into it. He couldn't outrun it and, like a fistfight with an Irishman, the best bet was to stand toe-to-toe and give it his best shot.

"Land ho!" Tain blared from the crow's nest. "Land ho!" he exclaimed again, pointing due west.

Robert quickly climbed to the platform, delighted to confirm Tain's sighting: low clouds hanging over a green coastal forest about three leagues due west. His delight at the sighting was blunted only a little when the first blast of squall line rain hit him in the face.

"Land ho! Land ho!" Robert called down enthusiastically.

All the men, and Lizbeth, stood staring up at the crow's nest in anticipation. The men cheered, and he shouted down again, repeating his order to turn into the wind. Three leagues might as well be a thousand, he thought as he climbed down. He admonished himself for doubting.

He rehearsed his training as a young sailor: "Tack directly into a storm wind until you can judge its force. Then, and only then, try tangent maneuvers," his sailing masters said. Robert had the best tutors in Glasgow and could have studied at Cambridge but, despising the life of a cleric, begged his father to apprentice him to one of his captains, because that's what he wanted to be. Being from a wealthy family never impressed young Robert. For as long as he could remember, he always preferred seamen to business and society men.

Still, he felt gripped by the terror of this new storm, and at the same time by the sublime rapture of glimpsing a new world. All his science, his religion, his worst terrors, and his wildest dreams collided, and yet his face broke into the bright, instant smile he was well known for. Survive one more leg of the race and the prize of a new world was his. For the first time since he left Scotland, he felt near to the sense the world was at his command.

"Let's tame the wench!" he cried. The men took their duty stations, some scurrying to remove loose items to below deck. "Bind your cargo, lads!" he ordered, well aware that every man knew his duty amid such winds. Robert bitterly loved the melody of crisis and to tune his voice to the harmony of danger, the perfect pitch of challenge. He knew the voice of decisiveness reassured frightened men fighting to rise above the noisy chaos of disaster. He saw the resolved sense of determination in the countenances of the men, but also noticed how debilitated they looked. "Lord, have mercy on us, poor sinners," Robert whispered as the wind began not to bite, but simply to paw and push. It was warm and moist, almost caressing his face, like the gloved hand of a lady, unlike any he knew from the north seas.

The sea seemed to swell into huge walls of water with inordinate speed. He figured they would be into the rain shortly, and as he gazed into the blue-black void of the storm a strange apparition appeared—a broad whitish column, like one of smoke, rising from the sea to the clouds, proceeding in front of the storm, toward the *Manannan*. He heard crewmen call out to each other, astonished.

It couldn't be smoke, he puzzled, yet at a loss to understand what his eyes told him. It looked like a long, white rope, twisting from the surface of the water up into the ceiling of the clouds. He wondered if it perhaps was the devil goddess Scylla, come to enchant and enslave them. The narrower the *Manannan* closed the gap, the more amazed and confused he felt. The wind intensified, and as the *Manannan* got close enough for him to focus on the monster, he forced his unwilling brain to accept as fact what his eyes attended to—a giant whirlwind on the face of the sea.

By his own reckoning, the best young seaman in Scotland was about to meet his match, if not his Maker. "Holy Mither of God!" he heard Wainwright exclaim, coming around from starboard, chasing Lizbeth to put her in her pen and spying the waterspout.

"Christ's-sake, Willam, what is it?" Robert yelled, raising his voice over the howling wind.

Wainwright looked at Robert, his sunken eyes wide with apprehension. "I never thought I'd see one, Cap'n," he said, glancing back and forth between Robert and the cyclone. "I've heared they have 'em in the Mediterranean," he added, "but I've never seen one."

"What do we do?" Robert yelled, wrestling harder to hold the rudder wheel.

"Try to steer awee from it if'n ya can," Wainwright puzzled remarkably calmly. "And if'n ya can't, Robert, jest pray," he said. Then to Robert's amazement, Wainwright smiled a wide, exaggerated grin, a wide gap between his two front teeth.

Robert hesitated and ordered, "Secure the goat, Willam." Wainwright caught Lizbeth, led her to the aft deck to put her in her cage atop the timbers once meant for the lumber-poor Barabhans, and tied its door tightly shut.

By the time Wainwright returned, Robert was resigned to take the cyclone head-on. It once began to withdraw into the clouds, but to his renewed horror, stretched down again. He managed to rudder-tack closer to shore because the squall line was intermittent and realized what he first took as a mainland shore was instead a long island or slender peninsula, with other shoreline beyond, farther west. The rains blew solid now, and the island or peninsula was the last thing he saw before the watery curtain closed. He steered blindly that way with what little westward travel he could make and stay safe while bearing into enormous troughs. He knew the worst thing that could happen was for the *Manannan* to turn sideways to the waves.

Now, he felt, the main event of his life was at hand. He killed the wild boar in the deep woods of Ben Nevis and whipped a lion of an Irishman in Cork, but was not sure if the Lord himself could deliver him from this Philistine devil wind. Within a few hundred yards of the spout now, he could hear its roar above the din of straight wind and slapping rain. He saw lightning flare inside its fiendish funnel and smelled its rarefied air. There was enough light left in the late afternoon that he thought he could see through the spout to the other side, into a picture of man's insignificance, he thought. In the foreground the crewmen stood transfixed, clutching the bow rails like tiny, two-legged insects, the whirlwind dominating the horizon. "It's the fingertip of God," he said out loud, even if none could hear him. It comforted him to hear himself speak the name of God.

"Get them below and hang on!" he screamed to Denny, who had struggled back to the helm.

"But what about you?" he yelled back.

"All hands below, mate; that's an order," Robert commanded.

"But—"

Robert cut him off. "Go!" he barked.

Denny hesitated but obeyed, rounding up and herding the crew down the hatch. Wainwright went last, stopping at the helm to look sternly into Robert's eyes.

"Go," Robert said respectfully, wagging his head toward the hold. Wainwright ducked inside.

The *Manannan* slipped closer to the spout, which dissolved into a solid, gray-black wall of water. The circling wind was entirely new to Robert—it came from all directions at once. He heard the lateen sail rigging snap and saw it disappear. Other rigging broke loose and left into the wind. The mainmast groaned once, crunched, and fell to the deck like a tree onto virgin forest floor.

The storm now seemed to suck things up and into itself. Barrels tossed, rolled, and lifted from the deck. The *Manannan* moaned and cracked with a chilly song. Pieces of the rails, floorboards, and splinters flew up into its black abyss, a hungry, roaring hole in the sky. The devil wind lifted Robert up, steadily, until topsy-turvy, yet clinging to the rudder wheel, feet over head, straight up toward the heavens. His shirt ripped away. His loose-fitting deck boots sprang off into oblivion. He thought the sinews in his arms and shoulders might snap like the rigging. Finally, amid a grotesque crescendo of stretching and buffeting, he made the split-second and conscious decision to let go.

The certainty of death was beyond his doubt, but he felt strangely awake. In fact, the stinging sensations everywhere in his skin proved he was much alive, either suspended or rising inside the devil draught. He saw some of what might have been debris from the ship swirling above and below him, and bits of things were flung against him, driven by the wind. He felt a quick and intense pain in his left calf, as if someone plunged a dagger in it but, mixed with the incredibly confusing avalanche in all his senses, it passed as only another painful sensation. He understood he was spinning and spread his arms and legs out, more or less by instinct, which slowed him down. He felt the sensation of falling.

It was hard to judge directions, but he figured he dropped because the density of the water inside the funnel seemed to increase. With only enough realization to catch his breath in a bare moment, he found himself under water.

Robert had always been an active and skilled swimmer and knew how to behave even if disoriented. He knew sometimes people drowned even in shallow water because they lost their sense of direction, panicked, and swam down instead of up. He kicked his feet to regain uprightness in the water and broke the surface.

He gasped for air, bobbed back under an enormous swell, and felt the quiet peace of the mother ocean envelop him. In the next few eternal seconds he skimmed what thoughts he could, including the realization of daylight in one direction.

He kicked to the surface again, confirmed the glimmers of light, and took that as a bearing west, toward land. He could see he was some distance yet from the possibility of shore and as near to extinction as when he was inside the whirlwind. His only chance of survival was to stay near enough to the surface to catch a breath of air now and then.

He managed with a combination of swimming and floating. His body felt like a swollen bundle of numbness and pain, mixed like bitters and water. With each submersion in a swell, he knew his life was over. Each time he came back to the surface, he thought he might live another breath or two. On one trip to the surface, he caught a glimpse of twilight.

The rain eased somewhat and the wind laid, too. He thought he made out a dark silhouette of land. Too dumb with pain to register hope, he intuitively locked in a bearing toward the shape of an unknown earth once far from his reality.

At some length of time unmeasured and unconscious to him, a great tongue of sea swell spat him onto the shore of a strange world. He laid there until, by instinct alone, he crawled inch by inch out of reach of the surf and fell limp. Darkness enveloped him.

CHAPTER FOUR

DEAD MAN

FROM HIS PERCH IN THE *OSAK*, ISKIFA COULD SEE A MAN'S FORM lying face down at the edge of the surf. Each wave lapped over the feet. A fish crow bounced onto the body and picked at it. Another waddled nearby, fanning its oily black wings.

Death was confirmed. Iskifa panned the horizon for living enemies who might have killed the man, although he judged the body probably washed up there. He climbed down to make his way to the beach.

The corpse's pale, pinkish-white skin and orange hair shocked him. Along with blunt amazement at this human's odd pigments, Iskifa registered a rush of anxiety about his dream. He turned the limp man over and looked into his pale, sad, hairy face.

He fell to his knees in the wet sand, crushed. "This is not right, *Aba Binnili*," he mourned aloud, staring north, with the fingertips of his left hand resting lightly on the dead man's hairy chest. "He was alive in my dream."

Iskifa wrung his hands, sinking into despair. He had walked twenty-four days to meet a white man, and his white man was dead. He turned away from the body, dazed, and walked back toward the treeline. Crows tried to sneak back to the corpse, and he turned again to chase them, waving his arms and yelling. He sat, took out his pipe, filled its bowl and smoked. The sand felt good against his legs.

For a moment he felt pangs of homesickness and soothed his despair with warm thoughts of Nanitana. He soon dismissed them, though, because they made him want to cry. He tried to focus instead on what happened. He knew he must gather himself. He took his traveling flute out of his bag and played a sad tune for the dead man. As the mournful sounds poured like teardrops out of his flute, he regained his composure.

His dream vision still seemed at least part true. He had walked to the eastern ocean and found a man almost white in skin color—but unlike his dream, the man was dead. What could that mean?

Again the crows tried to return, and he ran them off. He felt an urge to protect the body from the scavenging birds, so he went to the treeline for armloads of *tala* limbs and fronds. He found rocks to weigh them down, and added to them wooden planks washed up on the beach, along with a big, empty, strange-looking box with a hinged lid. He carried them to the body and piled them atop it, weighting down the fronds until he felt satisfied the protection was enough to keep the birds from desecrating the body, at least for a while.

The strange objects also made Iskifa believe the pale-skinned man drowned after his boat crashed on the rocks off shore. It confused him, however, to imagine where he might have come from. Perhaps he was one of the white men he heard rumors about from up north. He had asked Taloa either to verify the accounts or find them to be rumor and vapor while she studied in Anoli, fifteen days' walk east and south of Chunuli.

If the corpse was one of those white men rumored to live north, but still west of the long mountains, why was he so far south and on the coast? Iskifa puzzled while he walked the beach, finding other exotic objects that washed up in the surf. One was a necklace with pretty, hard, lightweight beads the color of darkened rose petals, at the bottom of which hung a neatly carved wooden stake with a cross bar, similar to the symbol for a star in the paintings and symbols of the ancients. Iskifa studied the string of beads and put it around his neck. He had never seen anything like them anywhere in his travels.

Though none of the answers he considered to his many questions satisfied him, it occurred to him that the white man's boat may have been big enough to hold many others like him, and another one or more might still be alive. The sand dunes and woods on the barrier island less than twenty flight from the beach, as well as any of the coves and marshy inlets, could harbor a living white man like the one in his dream. Still, except for the color of his hair, the dead man was very much like the one in his dream.

He picked up his flute to resume the sweet melody in honor of the dead man. If his spirit hovered about, heartfelt music would cause it to feel more comfortable while crossing over into the next world. The music soothed his own soul while he relaxed and played, trying to push back the sad thoughts accumulating at the end of his difficult journey. At almost the very instant his mind returned again to consider the possibility of survivors, he heard an agonized cry to the north. He stopped and stood, alert.

He felt sure the cry sounded human.

CHAPTER FIVE

NEW WORLD

THE SOUND OF A HUMAN CRY OF DESPAIR PENETRATED THE FOG around Robert's mind. He felt numb. He could not organize a thought. He tried to move his legs. He felt more pain, so he knew he must be alive. He remembered crawling into bushes and out of a hot morning sun. "I can't move," he thought, fearfully. "I might be paralyzed." He squinted a moment, upward through strange, fanlike leaves waving above him, at a blue sky dotted with wispy white clouds, before drifting back into the fog.

When he awoke again, he thought he heard music. It sounded almost like the clay whistles the Irish play. It stopped a little while and started again, a strange and sweet melody he could not quite make sense of—it seemed so out of place. The wind is playing tricks on me, he decided.

The ache in his left leg seemed loudest among his angry mob of distresses, making it hard to focus on much else. He tried to look at it, but his eye that was not stuck shut could not see that far.

With excruciating effort, he cupped his hands under his head and pulled up to look down his torso. His loud cry at the sudden and sharp pain in his neck surprised him. He fell back to his sandy bed. The whistling music stopped. He took another quick breath and slowly exhaled. "I'm Robert Williams," he whispered, affirming the world.

"You're alive," he answered himself.

This numb puzzle. The voice. The voice. He flexed again, straining, up to one elbow. "Denny!" he called out.

Now he felt a flash of fear. His voice sounded too loud. He rolled with a jerk, a little more up onto his side, hardly able to summon thought against his body's universal anguish. Nothing looked or felt familiar. The trees looked strange—and the plants, the sand, the heat. Nothing made sense. His memory swam, too loaded with bizarre stories to trust it. He struggled to recall what happened and to understand what was happening.

He tilted his head toward the direction the voice and faint music came from. More suffering. I must have dreamed it, he reasoned. He raised a hand to the eye that was swollen shut and pried it open with stiff fingers. It joined the other to reveal blurry, blue-white surf lapping on blond sand. A brief sensation of relief touched him. He was not in the water. He welcomed the smell of the beach. He tried to rub one of his eyes, felt sand grains, and stopped. The irritant watering blinded him. When tears hit his parched, cracked lips, they stung. He tried to add sorrow to his weeping, but couldn't gather enough of the idea. The surf's rhythm urged him to relax and think about moving again.

He brushed sand off his fingers and rubbed his eye again. His vision began to clear and the beach came into focus. The necessity to find drinking water crystallized as a thought. The necessity of trying to stand up followed it, along with merely sitting up. He tried to wrench his body upward, but his elbow left the sand only far enough that he crashed again onto his back, grimacing in pain.

His temporary relief disintegrated into an astonishing torrent of agony. He tried to repress his impulse with conscious effort, but could not keep from crying out again. He rolled and contracted into a fetal position to muffle himself. Moaning and whimpering, he closed his eyes and mumbled a prayer.

The hallucination of music gave way to a terrible sense of defenselessness, and he fell into despair. He allowed himself to recall the desperation of the whirlwind and the thresholds of underwater death. The fearsome mystery of his comrades' fates beset him, but he could not line up his mental soldiers long enough to decode such riddles. He blinked.

Buckskin shoes. Feet. An adrenaline rush thrust him up to sit, with success. He gasped for breath and shrunk away reflexively in the sand, still unable to stand. He bent his neck away by instinct, awaiting the blow to his head, any second, now.

The figure in buckskin shoes hung back warily, as if to forestall any more torturous retreat by the injured man.

Robert blinked and flinched, trying to bring the figure into focus. The sunlight behind the man to whom the shoes belonged made it hard to see his face. At least the stranger did not kill him right away, a fact that let his fear slip into amazement. He shaded his eyes for a better look.

Before him stood a creature unlike anyone he had seen. The man's skin was an unusual tone of dark brown, and Robert felt struck by the colors of his clothing—his richly hued and ornately embellished cap and a vivid green sash at his waist. His legs were bare but for a breech-cloth. He noted another sash the strange man wore from shoulder to waist, a big bag and two smaller ones slung from his shoulders with leather thongs. The man laid a bow and a sling of arrows gently on the sand, suggesting, Robert hoped, he meant no harm.

No threads of identity were familiar to Robert except for what looked like rosary beads with a small wooden cross hanging around the man's neck. He lowered his hand. "Are you going to kill me?" he asked, his voice dry and thin.

"*Kiyo*," Iskifa replied, shaking his head once, in a tone suggesting both understanding and "no" to Robert. He unslung a bladder from his shoulder, pulled out a cork-like stopper, and extended it.

Robert stared at the bladder, at the brown man's stunning dark eyes, and again at the bladder.

Iskifa hefted the bladder again, with an urgent nod.

Robert took it, held it over his mouth, and let a few drops of water dribble onto his lips. Their slight stings gave him welcome, life-restoring sensations. His arms went limp a moment and fell to his lap, clutching the water skin with both hands as if in prayer. He lifted the vessel again and took a swig, deeper. "Thank you," he said, coughing a little.

"*Chokmashki*," Iskifa replied, with a little smile and a curious, rhythmic gesture, leveling his hand and forearm with his chest.

Robert realized his leg lay tucked awkwardly beneath him. He held the water skin for balance to switch gingerly to a cross-legged seat and drank again, deeply.

Iskifa smiled broadly and dropped to sit, cross-legged also, facing him. He looked as if he had run into an old friend.

Robert found his attention shifting between the strange brown man and the multiple complaints of his body. The pain in his leg begged loudest. His left pants leg was ripped at the calf, a dark red stain extending to its tattered cuff. The stranger looked at it also, he noticed—as if studying it, really.

Iskifa bent to pull on Robert's trouser leg gently, indicating concern about the injury. He rose to his knees, the cross dangling from his neck, and bent for a closer examination of the wound.

The sight of the cross was strangely comforting to Robert, although he couldn't think why. He repressed panic with the thought, "new world, new people," although the sight of this man generated a new experience of amazement. He came to believe he was something of an old man. He extended his wounded leg toward him, tacitly.

The antiquated fellow worked Robert's pant leg up skillfully and gently to expose the wound in his left calf. Every twitch and movement hurt immensely. Iskifa took a pouch from his sash and sprinkled powder into the palm of his hand. He added a few drops of water to make a paste and rubbed it gently around the wound, dripping water on it until the gash looked clean. Robert could see the end of the shard of wood the whirlwind had daggered into his leg.

The old man nodded at it, as if conclusively.

"Can you get it out?" Robert asked.

"*Ii*," Iskifa answered, with a nod as if he understood. He reached into one of his bags to produce an extraordinary-looking knife—small, with a sharp, flaked-stone blade, its bone handle inlaid with bands of bright copper.

Robert checked his anxiety with an inward concession that some sort of instrument needed to be used. He shifted his weight onto his hip. "Be careful, please," Robert requested, almost childishly.

"*Ahaa*," Iskifa responded.

He can barely speak, Robert thought.

Iskifa stood, looked about, and fetched a stalk from a nearby plant similar to the Haver cane found at the foot of Ben Nevis. The old man broke off a piece between two joints and made a long split in it with his knife, carefully opening the jaws of the split reed to clamp the end of the finger-size sliver of wood in Robert's leg.

He made more paste and massaged it into the gash. Last, he took the sash off his waist, twisted it with a stick, and tied off a tourniquet around Robert's calf above the cut. Reaching into one of his bags, he retrieved another, smaller bladder. He popped its cork and extended it. "*Chibanna?*"

Poison, Robert's thoughts squealed. "No," he replied, fear in his eyes.

Iskifa raised his eyebrows, shrugged, and took a drink. Carefully lifting at the knee, Iskifa pulled Robert's calf farther off the sand and laid resting on his elbows, allowing him to grip the split-cane device. Much to Robert's welcome surprise, the old man steadily withdrew the tapered piece of wood without much more pain than he already felt. The wooden missile looked about four inches long.

Robert exhaled, realizing he had held his breath all the while. A gush of blood issued from the wound, and the old man tightened the tourniquet. The bleeding slowed after Iskifa opened another little pouch from his bag and staunched the wound with a poultice made from a fresh green herb that looked to Robert like Scots yarrow.

Returning to the small medicine pouch, Iskifa withdrew a strip of leather to wrap neatly around the calf at the wound and tied it off. He examined Robert's lesser cuts and bruises, cleaned them all, and applied poultice to the worst. "*Taha*," he declared as he finished.

So far, everything the old man said sounded like the same grunt to

Robert. He felt surprised someone so primitive could doctor so well.

Iskifa coaxed him to back up against a tree and laid a rolled-up bag behind his head. Robert relaxed, beginning to feel some trust toward the gentle savage. Iskifa unwrapped another package from his bag to bring out three small dried fish and offered one to Robert.

The thought of taking food, a normal activity, overwhelmed Robert at first. He started to cry. The old man set the fish on its wrapper beside Robert and walked into the bush. In a short while he returned with a handful of pleasant-looking plump fruit, pale red and yellow in color. He ate one, apparently to head off any doubt, and handed another to Robert.

Robert took the fruit and ate. It was juicy and sweet, its powerful flavor momentarily overwhelming his pains. He composed himself enough to take a bite of the fish before Iskifa came back, and his appetite returned. He realized while he ate and drank more that one of his worst aches was the hunger in his belly. He had not eaten since noon the previous day on board the *Manannan*.

The ship. It seemed like a dream, a past nightmare. A thousand years had gone by and everything had changed.

He focused on the strange beach, the beautiful blue ocean, and the clear sky, where a few frail, snow-white clouds contrasted against the azure firmament. He took in the trees, the incredibly warm air, and this new creature, an apparently primitive human being, a strange, brown, colorfully capped jester who saved his life. He had sailed into oblivion, gone to sleep, and awakened in another world, as if he became a different person.

Robert dozed and Iskifa did not attempt to awaken him. "Denny?" Robert awoke a short while later with the question on his lips. He felt delirious for a moment, but with some strain and effort, lifted himself onto his better leg, to stand. "Where's my crew?" he asked in no particular direction. "Where's the old man?"

Iskifa came up from the beach into the shade and handed Robert his staff fashioned from a dark, oily wood, with an intricately carved face at its knob. "*Minti*," he said, gesturing that Robert should follow.

Robert invested yet more trust in his new savior. What little hope he could muster centered on this mysterious inhabitant of this new world. The man could have killed him. He could have ignored him and Robert likely would have died. So he followed.

Iskifa led north on the coast trail, Robert hobbling close behind on the staff. They had not walked a hundred paces when Iskifa turned back toward the beach. Robert saw in the distance the odd-looking pile Iskifa left over the dead man's body. The first thing he recognized as he approached was the familiar trunk, the one where he kept his navigational instruments and charts.

And he saw a hand, a glimpse of flesh, flushing him with terror and anguish. His worst fears fell upon him. He staggered another step, let the staff fall, and dropped to his knees beside the pile, emptied by sadness. He carefully uncovered the dead man's face, quickly recognizing his old friend and crewman, Donnchadh McLaren. He winced at his gruesome wounds and broken bones. Men and women in his life had died before, but never his crew, never his men, never in an unknown world.

"Oh, Donnchadh," he cried, laying his head on his mate's lifeless chest, upon the man who sailed on every *Manannan* voyage Robert captained. "You poor man, you poor man," he sobbed. All the stored-up sorrow of a thirty-nine-day voyage into hell, of nightmares of calculation, of love lost, of pain suffered, of mental torture broke loose in a torrent from Captain Williams. He cried until all tears were exhausted.

The old man disappeared. Robert fell quiet, taking time to organize his thinking, remember his ordeal, and to consider the overwhelming probability that all aboard the *Manannan* had perished, save one soul, himself. Of all the others besides Denny, McLaren was the only one nearly as strong a swimmer as Robert, and here he lay fully dead. God had left him only, he knew, to suffer the guilt, shame, and punishment of losing his crew, ship, and cargo. He alone was cursed to travail in an utterly foreign wilderness. He felt sure the woe of Robert Williams had only begun.

The old man returned carrying a pole-and-mat contraption which he laid on the sand beside McLaren—a litter to carry his body. He politely pointed both index fingers at Robert, touched his own temples with them, and pointed at McLaren's body.

Robert felt comforted by his gesture, knowing the old man asked what he wanted to do with the body. Robert pantomimed shoveling and the sign of prayer with his hands.

Iskifa pointed at Robert, then to his own eyes and waved his hand northward in line of sight of the beach. "*Hollopi ish-pisah*," he said and repeated the signed message.

Robert could tell he meant for him to find a decent burial place for his dead friend before the body bloated any more.

Iskifa bent over McLaren's shoulders, waited for Robert to get his feet, and they hefted the body onto the litter. Robert registered amazement that the old man had been able to put it together in such a short period of time. It was made of a couple of parallel poles with heavy vines tied between them. Over that basic frame were laid boughs of a tree that began to look familiar to him.

They left McLaren on the litter and walked up the beach until Robert noticed a peaceful clearing circled by tall trees. "That's it," Robert said, pointing to it and looking at Iskifa.

Iskifa nodded with a thoughtful expression on his ruddy brown face, which Robert took to mean his strangely attired friend approved. They walked back, faced each other, and prepared to lift the litter. "By the way. Do you have a name?" Robert asked.

Iskifa looked puzzled. Robert realized he needed to sign and tapped on his chest, pronouncing his name, "Robert." He pointed at himself, his face, his torso, his legs, and repeated, "Rob-ert."

"Wa-ba," Iskifa responded gamely, his first try to imitate the sound.

"Rob-ert, Rob-ert, Rob-ert," he said again, pointing at his chest each time.

"Ra-bat, Ra-bat" Iskifa said, seeming eager to hear more of it. "Iski-fa, Iskifa," he said, pointing at himself. "Is-ki-fa."

"Iss-kuh-fuh," Robert said.

"Iss-*kih*-fuh," Iskifa corrected, methodically.

Robert heard kindness in his voice. "Is-ki-fa," he repeated, slowly. "Rob-ert," he added.

The old man nodded. "Rob-art."

"Iskifa," Robert said, more confidently.

Iskifa nodded. His bright eyes and white smile pleased Robert.

They bent to pick up the litter. "Iskifa," Robert said one more time. "Robart," Iskifa replied. They both smiled, and Robert forgot momentarily about the dreariness of the task. He felt somehow he had made important progress, if only a little.

Every step under the burden of the litter caused pain, but Robert intended to honor his friend with a reasonably dignified Christian burial. He would not leave him to scavengers. The sandy earth was covered with thin green plants and small bush saplings. Robert didn't know how they might dig the grave, but started nevertheless, pulling up weeds. Iskifa wandered away again and returned shortly with two planks—ones Robert recognized as deck boards from the *Manannan*.

Despite his sadness, Robert settled to the task, reasoning he should not grieve too deeply or he could not survive. He had never considered grieving a luxury before. He dug with a plank, removing much of the sand by hand. Iskifa watched—likely, Robert thought, to make sure he understood how he wanted it done. He joined in the digging, which went tediously, but took Robert's mind off his aches. He considered while he labored that the brown man and his people might not bury their dead. They might cremate them. They might eat them. He dismissed such thoughts.

The pains in his muscles and joints, in his cuts, bruises, scratches, and the puncture wound hurt, but Robert and Iskifa took turns working and resting until they hollowed a sandy vault about chest deep. They used makeshift baskets Iskifa wove from the long, slender leaves of the tree he called "*tala*" to carry dirt out of the hole.

They took McLaren's body from the litter and laid it feet first in the grave. Robert hated burying his man in the cold ground with hardly any clothing.

Iskifa handed Robert boughs from the litter to arrange them around and under his friend's body. The old man also found some flower blossoms he called something like "low walk" and some delicate clusters of blue flowers he called by a name Robert couldn't understand, and offered them to decorate McLaren's grave.

"Thank you," Robert said gratefully as Iskifa gave him a hand up out of the hole.

Robert rested briefly, stood, and began to speak. "We are gathered here," he said, not like a parson, but like a ship's captain, "to honor a fallen comrade." He glanced at Iskifa and then away, catching his breath. "Fairer friend, nor braver heart, nor truer faith, hath ever been found on God's earth than in Donnchadh McLaren. The gates of Heaven opened wide to receive his spirit. We who are left behind are better off for knowin' him and worse off for his leavin'. God grant us grace and mercy in this wilderness. By the Laird Jesus, Amen."

Robert began to dump the sandy dirt back into the grave, one basketful at a time. Iskifa observed quietly, suggesting it might not be his practice and perhaps he didn't understand it. After the pause, Iskifa helped fill the hole. After it was about half filled, they sat to rest on a few leftover *tala* boughs.

"A good friend, Donnchadh McLaren," Robert started, gazing into the ether, "but the damned evil wind …" He stopped because Iskifa stood and craned his neck to hear something, his expression reading like danger. "What is it?" Robert asked, not hearing anything.

"*Nashoba. Haklo,*" the old man said sharply.

"What?" Robert whispered, straining to hear. Finally, while Iskifa stood motionless, as if taking bearings, Robert heard it, faint, but familiar—squealing and barking, perhaps. "Dogs?" he asked, incredulously. It had been so long since he had seen or heard one. He couldn't believe his ears. A louder yip provoked fear in him. "Wolves?" he asked solemnly.

Iskifa stood still, tilting his head. "*Naninla,*" he muttered, which meant, "and something else."

CHAPTER SIX

ANOTHER SURVIVOR

ROBERT NOW HEARD THEM WELL—SEVERAL, AND SURELY wolves. No towns here, he was certain—they would have seen people if there were. He picked out another sound above the barks—a squealing, a bawling. Certainly, it was their prey, louder, clearer, bawling—bleating.

"Lizbeth!" he shouted. "That's Lizbeth!"

He jumped up, stumbled, and fell, grabbing his left leg at the bandage and writhing on the sand. Iskifa handed him the staff and he picked himself up, grimacing, hobble-hopping toward the beach.

Iskifa picked up his bow and bundles and ran in front of him. "*Il-ilohmi,*" he said, gesturing for him to stay near the brush. The farther they went, the louder came the bleating, and the more certain Robert was that he heard Lizbeth. He had been cooped up in close quarters too long with that goat not to recognize her voice.

"We've got to save her," he exclaimed.

"*Ma!*" Iskifa whispered, holding his fingers over his lips, crouching. They rounded a point of beach to creep behind a bush that looked like a Scottish blaeberry to Robert and saw the source of the dramatic noise—Lizbeth in her goat pen still nailed atop the Hebrideans' lashed

56

timbers, balanced precariously on a cluster of coastal rocks at the water line. Her well-built cage stood intact but for a broken bottom rail. Robert counted three wolves circling the rocks, the most aggressive of them trying to open the cage at the broken rail, jerking at it with teeth and claws.

All three snarled and barked. Lizbeth made butting feints, bleating her head off, and tried to keep her balance on the uphill end of the tilted raft. Robert felt weak and wounded, but knew his heart would break if he lost any more of his precious past. He felt compelled to save her. While his brain raced about to find a plan, he noticed Iskifa examining the contents of one of his pouches.

Iskifa took out what appeared to be a slender piece of bone—bird bone, probably. One end appeared hollow, the other tapered and shaped, with a string tied to it. The only thing Robert could guess it might be was a whistle. Iskifa hung it around his neck, checked his bow by touching it, took the staff from Robert's hand, and stepped out into the open beach, moving toward the wolves at a steady pace. Robert felt frustrated and scared. He wanted to help, but the old man behaved like he wasn't there.

Iskifa got within twenty paces of the wolves before one, of almost pure black fur, noticed and turned to face him, crouching and growling. The others, each gray and brown, turned about, showing long, white teeth at the old man. Lizbeth's bawls diminished into whimpering bleats. Iskifa raised the staff, holding it at its center, above his head. Their eyes followed it upward and they stopped snarling. Robert couldn't believe what he saw and speculated the primitive man must be some sort of magician. Iskifa raised the little bone hanging around his neck to his lips and held it there, blowing through it. Robert heard nothing. The wolves as if stung, yipped and scampered away. Iskifa followed a few steps, holding his staff aloft.

Robert could not interpret what he had seen. He hobbled toward Iskifa, his hand to his forehead. "Moses or the devil," he mumbled, and made his way as fast as he could toward Lizbeth's cage, past Iskifa, who kept an eye on the fleeing wolves.

Robert stopped short, seeing how the lashed-timber raft teetered perilously on the shoreline rocks. The front end looked stuck tight on the rough jumble, and the waves at low tide splashed over its aft, rocking it. The whole mess tilted up toward Lizbeth's cage, which might have been a good disposition if not for a tide pool of some depth just outside her gate.

It looked like Robert would need to wade or swim the tide pool, or he could try to work his way around on the rocks, like the wolf, although the footing looked treacherous. The more he studied, the more he concluded the wolf's approach seemed best. The broken cage rail was on the narrow end, aground on the rocks. If he could get a strong pole between those rails, he could pry enough off to get her out.

The poor goat looked so frazzled Robert didn't think she recognized him—who knew how long she had tossed on the waves before she came aground? The ship either broke up against rocks around a barrier island less than a mile offshore, or the whirlwind somehow released the raft to its rough voyage and probably, he reasoned, she washed in and grounded with the high tide last night. One of her legs looked bloody, either from the crash or a wolf's bite, and her udders looked painfully engorged.

He went to Iskifa, who seemed to elect himself out of the situation, asked by gesture for the staff, and started to pick his way along the rocks to Lizbeth's cage. He slipped painfully, and the rocks hurt his feet, but he maneuvered his way to Lizbeth. The closer he came, however, the worse she set up her bawling again.

He lurched for an end rail of the cage, gripping it, but she butted his fingers. He jerked his hand away, lost his footing, fell bouncing on his rump, and almost slid into the tide pool. "Fool goat, Lizbeth," he yelled. "I'm tryin' to help you."

She withdrew a few steps, wild-eyed, bawling obnoxiously. The throbbing in his leg came back. He pulled himself up to balance on the tilted raft and decided to wedge the staff between the top and second rails of the cage. "Now, mind your manners, Lizbeth," he coaxed, "I'm here to rescue your hide."

Lizbeth still bawled in fine voice, alert to his next move. He stuck the staff inside the top rail to pry against the next one. She darted toward him, biting at the staff. Robert respected her teeth, so he kept his hands and fingers out of reach. The good English nails held tight in wood swollen by water. "Come on, come on," he urged, rocking the staff against the rail, noticing the sun dipping toward the horizon. At last, the rail popped loose.

That caused more psychotic bleating from Lizbeth. She poised herself on her back heels. He tried to stick the staff under the second rail, and she would have none of it, charging to thrust her head and shoulder through, scoring a toothy nip on Robert's forearm. He dropped the staff inside her cage.

"Ow!" he cried, "Idiot goat! I should've let the wolves have ya."

Iskifa folded his arms, apparently taking it all in, but not laughing, at least.

Robert tried for the staff, but Lizbeth snapped at him. He felt pressure from the threat of sundown, after which the tide would lift her off, and she would be lost forever, like the rest of his life. Maybe he could distract her. He splashed water from the tide pool into her face and she cringed, letting him snatch the staff. He slid it up under the second rail and levered it against the corner post of the cage. She attacked the staff, but couldn't reach Robert, who pried the rail loose.

Lizbeth now came head and shoulders through the larger opening, bawling and snarling, berserk with fear. He took the lower route again, seeing one more rail would make an opening big enough for him to crawl through, and pried it off.

She saw he could get in now and retreated to the other end of the cage, her tail wedged into the uphill corner, bawling desperately.

Robert remembered how Tain used to call her in a falsetto voice while bringing food for her. "Lizbeth, Lizbeth," he called in his highest tone, imitating Tain. Lizbeth fell quiet. Somehow the high voice touched recognition in her fear-crazed brain.

"Lizbeth, Li-iz-zzz-beth," Robert repeated in the same falsetto while he pried off two more rails, giving him enough room to lead her out. The rope still hung from her neck, the one Wainwright left on her a little more than twenty-four hours earlier. She stood quiet, but didn't take her eyes off Robert while he climbed inside, moving slowly so she would not get upset again. He turned away to pry off the bottom three rails. "Everything's gonna be all right, girl," he cooed in his most tender tone. "Everything's... gonna... be... all right..." he crooned in time with each pry against the heavy nailed planks.

As soon as he pried the last one loose, with his back to her, Lizbeth burst out of her corner to butt him squarely in the backside, sending him flying out to bounce on his hands and knees on the rocks, landing with a splash in the tide pool. The shock of the cool water after his sweaty labor was intense. All sympathy vanished, and now he wanted to kill her. He scrambled up on the rocks, not watching his footing, and stepped on a nail in one of the planks he had pried off. He grimaced and cursed, scrambled over the logs and back into Lizbeth's pen. She held resolutely inside, the cage evidently the only thing familiar to her in this strange scape of sea and beach.

He squared off with her, balanced on his feet, slightly stooped in the pen. She inched backward into the corner and lunged again. He snatched her rope with one hand, head-locked her with his other arm, and wrestled her to the log floor. She kicked and struggled a moment and went limp. "Settle down, Lizbeth," he murmured, holding her firmly, "now, settle down."

All the fight left the king's goat. Her terror subsided into out-of-character submissiveness. Robert sensed it and stroked her little beard, talking gently and firmly to her, hoping she would remember him and their peaceful life on the ship.

It was almost dark when he stood, holding on to her rope. She rose to follow him like a pet out of the cage, off the raft and over the rocks, where the going was much easier for her than him. He suffered searing pain with each step from the wound in his leg and the new puncture in his foot.

The sand of the beach felt better under Robert's feet. Iskifa walked around the goat, viewing her from each side and angle, looking fascinated, appearing to tear himself away to negotiate over the rocks to the raft to get his staff. He also picked up one of the planks with nails sticking out and carried it with him back to the beach. He followed while Robert led Lizbeth to drink some rainwater from the hollow of a flat rock nearby, and to a grassy spot to tie her to a small tree so she could graze as he tenderly milked her to relieve her engorgement. At first he let the milk fall to the ground.

Iskifa watched with interest, produced a pottery cup, and offered it to Robert. "Thank you," Robert said. He filled the cup with milk and drank it. He filled it again and offered it to Iskifa.

"*Kiyo*," Iskifa declined, shaking his head with an appreciative smile.

While Robert worked to relieve Lizbeth's udders, Iskifa quickly gathered and cut some *tala* boughs and spread them on the ground and brought tinder and wood for a fire.

Robert finished milking her and lay, grunting with pain, on the boughs, exhausted. His heart weighed heavy with grief for his lost comrades, if lightened somewhat by Lizbeth's rescue. The pains in his body amazed him with their severity. His leg throbbed like a drum, and now his foot sizzled, too. Prying Lizbeth's cage apart aggravated his wrist that never got a chance to heal from the sprain he suffered during his titanic struggle with wind and waves at the helm of the *Manannan* during that terrible, icy storm in the Atlantic almost a month and a half ago. He felt a tug at his leg.

Iskifa had raised his pants leg again. The old man untied the bandage by the light of the campfire to clean the wound. He made a yarrow poultice for it from a vial in his pouch and a few drops of water and re-wrapped it. He cleaned Robert's right foot, left a daub of poultice on the new wound, and used the rest on Lizbeth's leg. She seemed to welcome it. Robert submitted to the old man's generous doctoring, marveling again not only at the remarkable color of his rescuer's skin, but also at the bone structure of his face, unlike any he'd seen. The distinctive colors in Iskifa's cap and mantle stood out dramatically in the firelight. He studied the buckskin shoes the old man wore. They appeared to be made of one piece of thick leather, with no separate sole, coming up to and just covering his ankle, tied with leather laces in a straight line along the top of the foot.

Stars appeared in the clear night sky. Robert remembered this night would see a full moon. He took small comfort in knowing he would not have to deal with total darkness during his first conscious night in a strange new world. Iskifa finished the new setting of the bandage. "Thank you," Robert told him. "I'd sure be dead if not for you, mate."

"*Chokmashki*," Iskifa replied, seeming to understand. He moved to the other side of the campfire to sit on the boughs he cut and laid for himself, pulled out another parcel and unfolded it, revealing more of the dried fish Hosiini sent him off with that morning. He offered some and a piece of bread to Robert, who gladly accepted. The bread was of a new sort to him, reddish in color, crumbly and grainy and delicious. He ate eagerly after the day's fantastic work. The fish had a nice smoked flavor and a bit of salt, reminding him of fish the Norse traded across the North Sea to Scotland. Next Iskifa produced two more pieces of the fresh yellow fruit he picked earlier, a nice finish for a welcomed meal.

Iskifa took the pottery cup he loaned Robert and heated some water in it. He dropped crushed dried leaves inside to make a tea and offered it. "*Chaloklowa*," he called it.

"Thank you," Robert said. The warm drink was soothing. Its flavor was not familiar and produced a cool sensation in his mouth, and he found it quite agreeable. For an obviously primitive fellow, the old man seemed to know a lot of tricks. Robert was intrigued and grateful, but sure this simple man with no horses or gunpowder would soon be fully known. He could tell by the way the old man studied him that he was not used to seeing white men. He seemed polite and did not stare, but his curiosity was clear. Robert felt sure he himself did not disguise very well his astonishment when he looked upon this resident of the unknown realm.

"*Fo-chik*," Iskifa said to Robert, pointing to the sky, wiggling his fingers.

"*Fo-chik*," Robert repeated.

Iskifa nodded enthusiastically.

"*Fochik*," Robert said, knowing by the way he wiggled his fingers that he referred to the twinkling of the stars. "Stars," Robert said. "Stars."

"Stahs," Iskifa responded.

"Star-r-r-s," Robert repeated.

"Stars," the old man said.

"Yes, good," Robert said appreciatively. "Stars, *fochik*."

"Yes, *gude*," Iskifa repeated, putting an odd accent on the vowel. He smiled broadly again, revealing almost perfect white teeth that picked up little orange glints from the firelight.

A sudden snort interrupted them from Lizbeth's direction. She lay comfortably with her legs folded under her, sound asleep, perhaps snorting a last dreamed warning at those wolves. Iskifa and Robert smiled at her and at each other.

"*Oklhili hashi*," Iskifa pronounced slowly, nodding toward the full, golden moon lighting the surface of the ocean, rising from the east horizon. It looked to Robert like a radiant egg yolk.

"Moon," Robert said. "Moon."

Iskifa smiled and cocked his head. "Moon," he said. "Moon. *Oklhili hashi*."

"Ok-lee-hash-ee," Robert recited, trying to remember all the syllables.

"*Oklhili hashi*," Iskifa repeated, patiently. "Moon," he said plainly.

"Ok-lily ha-shee," Robert said.

Iskifa nodded, encouraging him. "*Oklhili hashi*," he said once more.

"*Ok-lhi-li ha-shi*," Robert repeated proudly, catching on to the airy consonant cluster in the first word. "*Oklhili hashi*. Moon."

The old man nodded slowly and approvingly, his eyes closing, giving in to the fatigue of such a day. He took a thin, light cloak from his bag and handed it to Robert for a cover. "*Nosi*," he said, "*Nosi*." He lay down on his *tala* fronds and appeared to fall asleep immediately.

Again, Robert felt moved by the generosity of the primitive man. No ceremony. Just handed over his cloak. "It's hard to thank you enough," Robert said to Iskifa's back, now turned to him.

Iskifa only grunted.

Robert pulled the cover around his bare shoulders, glad to have it because the heat of the day was lifting. He lay on his side, facing the moon, now a milky ball a few degrees out of the water. The thought of how strange all this was could not develop beyond that. He tried to pray, but God seemed like a lost memory, as if He may not have arrived here yet.

He felt the torment of the necessity to finish McLaren's grave first thing tomorrow, but sleep weighed heavy in all his members and began to cover up the aches in his body, like molasses covers a griddlecake. He tried to focus on scripture, but could not. The only thing to stay afloat in his mind was a nursery rhyme, a Gaelic lullaby he repeated after his mother at dozens of boyhood bedtimes in the uppermost loft in the two-story family home in Glasgow.

He could see the single candle burning and smell the wax in the little finger-choil candle dish beside his bed. He felt the stroke of his mother's fingers on his forehead. He whispered it now with his mother's accent, while the stones settled against his eyelids: "Here I lie me doon to sleep, preein' the Laird me sool ta keep. If I should die before I wake, I pree the Laird me sool to take ..."

CHAPTER SEVEN

MOONLIGHT

SKIFA AWOKE WITH SURF SINGING IN ONE EAR AND A MOSQUITO buzzing in the other. "*Ishtokat chimmayyali*, I'm bigger than you," he told the insect. He waved it away, opening his eyes to a full moon in a black sky. He had fallen asleep almost instantly after he made medicine for the white man's leg. "Rob-art," he whispered to himself while his eyes adjusted to the nearly full moon. "Rob-art." He liked the way the sound felt on his lips.

His bed elevated his head with two short, heavy poles at his head and foot, and long *tala* fronds under the foot log and over the head log, giving his head and shoulders just the right amount of support. It was too late to teach the white man about that. Robart made a quick, flat pile of fronds and laid down right away.

The moon looked stunning, and brilliant arrays of stars shone in the darker quarters of the sky. Nanitana will be so proud, he thought, filled with a sense of accomplishment at finding his white man. The memories of his glorious day flowed through his mind—the crow, the dead man whose name was difficult, the outcry, the medicine, the rescue of the little beast Lishbit, the burial, and finally, the white man's glorious language.

His reflections turned perplexing. He could not fall back to sleep.

Doubts crept in. He had followed the *Hina Aalhpisa* and the dream *Aba Binnili* gave him. But now what? He had not dreamed again since he set out on his journey, and nothing in his first dream suggested what might come next.

Am I just supposed to take him and his strange animal home with me? he wondered. Maybe I should introduce him and his new animal to men of knowledge. Certainly I should learn his language as quickly as possible and hear his stories and about the world he comes from. If I can talk to him, Iskifa thought, it will be easier to keep him safe.

Robart's animal surely was domesticated for food, given the unusual practice of keeping the goat wet with milk and consuming it every day. Perhaps males of her type were used for meat. He remembered stories his mentor Atanapoa told him about the northern tribes who often had bigger towns than the southern Yukpans and tried many schemes for herding and confining animals. No tribe could predict the journey of the *yanash*, the bison, so they could not always depend on them for winter meat. He had seen a small herd of *issi*, deer, inside a strong fence when he visited the great city of Tochina as a young man. Chilantak, whom they would probably meet on their journey inland from here, was said to confine and manage a small herd of *yanash* so they would have the animals nearby for meat if hunts were thin.

Atanapoa also told stories of people of the past who used up all their food and had to abandon their towns. It happened, he said, especially during periods of long drought. Perhaps that happened to the white man's country. Possibly they ran out of food and had to search for a better country. The Yukpans generally built smaller towns, more spread out, for that very reason—to make sure there was plenty of food to go around.

Iskifa soon dropped out of such nocturnal musings, being old enough to know a good night should not be wasted on worry or ambition. The breeze brushed him while he stood and wandered off to urinate. The air felt comfortable and moist. Wisps of white clouds occasionally intersected the bright moon in the blue-black sky.

Shore birds fished in the silhouetting moonlight, swooping and billowing across the surface of the sloshing ocean. He placed his hands behind him, pressing against the bench of his buttocks, feeling the fatigue of a momentous day. The stretch helped him fill his lungs with moist coastal air. It never failed to amaze him how wonderful moist air made him feel and how it made his hair and skin feel right.

The white man groaned painfully in his sleep. Iskifa turned from the moonlit surf to gaze at him. A strong young man, he thought, remembering his athletic struggle to rescue his animal. He had never imagined a human being like him. His skin was very pale where it had been covered by clothing, but his face, neck, forearms, and lower parts of his legs were tanned ruddy by wind and sun.

Iskifa encountered a lot of people he thought were ugly. The fish eaters were small in stature, with flat, uninteresting faces. Some of the northern tribes people had big, fat, round faces with no visible bone structure. Robart's long, angular jaw and square chin were actually quite handsome, Iskifa thought. His hair was dark brown and thick and appeared cut fairly short not so long ago. His beard and moustache were thick and almost black, but his face had probably been shaven clean, he reckoned, within the last moon or two. His beard was only about a finger joint long and even. The dead man on the beach seemed much uglier to Iskifa, with hair on his head the color of a red fox kit and a long, curly, matted beard in various shades of the same color. His face, especially his nose, looked puffy and distorted to Iskifa's eye, even allowing for his being bruised and dead.

His white man was handsome, in contrast, with pleasant facial features—a ridged brow and straight nose of attractive prominence set in a ruddy face under a shock of dark hair, which generally made him more acceptable-looking. Maybe because of his almost decent looks, people wouldn't be so inclined, he hoped bravely, to fear and want to kill his white man.

CHAPTER EIGHT

INLAND

Lizbeth's bawl interrupted entombing sleep. Robert opened his eyes and jerked up to sit. The old native wasn't there. He instinctively whirled to scan for wolves, enemies, cannibals, demons. Only two living things came into view—Lizbeth, standing and staring at him, and a large mosquito buzzing curiously around his head.

Relieved to see no apparent immediate threat to his life, he slapped at the mosquito, breathed again, and let his eyes settle on Lizbeth.

She bleated in a way Robert understood to mean she had no great need other than for attention. He felt glad to have rescued her from the wolves and the waves. The sadness of losing his comrades prodded at his heart, but couldn't penetrate the thick hide of physical pain around it. His right foot throbbed from the nail hole, as did his left leg with its wound, and his left wrist still felt sore and weak. Besides those focal points, an overall ache seemed to have settled in his joints and muscles, making every movement harrowing.

As one inured to hard work, Robert knew he had to get up and move around to limber his muscles, no matter how torturous the prospect. With agonized grunts, groans, and jerks, he came to his feet and hobbled toward Lizbeth.

She bleated, approving of the idea, straining nervously but gently at her rope and arching her head, which Robert greeted with his hand, and petted her. He noticed her udders were full, so he hobbled back to the campsite, wishing to find the man's cup, and grumbling nervously about the old fellow's absence, hoping he had not been deserted. He spied the cup sitting on a rock that resembled a round loaf of bread, as if left there for him.

He returned to milk Lizbeth, which she seemed to appreciate. The warm milk tasted good to Robert, and he drank his fill. He saved a full cup to offer to the man.

Soon the old native brought a double handful of bright green leaves for Lizbeth, which she immediately preferred to the grass. He and Robert shared more fresh fruit and a good-tasting jerked meat of some kind, although the old man again refused the milk.

As if he recalled something, the old native interrupted breakfast to take the rosary from around his neck and, with a gesture both graceful and humble, extended it to Robert who examined it closely for the first time, a wave of unspeakable heartache washing through him. He could see now, it had belonged to Donnchadh McLaren. The strange little man must have determined to return it to one who knew the poor seaman, perhaps as a remembrance. "I'm too rattled even to remember his name," Robert whispered to himself, still having a hard time gathering his thoughts into an order that made sense. It came back to him, however, in recollection of their recovery of McLaren's remains. "Iskifa," he muttered, soundlessly. "Iss-kih-fuh."

While they shared cool water, Iskifa scratched pictures in the sand and spoke in his own language, communicating, Robert thought, that they should finish burying McLaren and head for a settlement. As near as Robert could make out, the old man indicated he could talk to the people represented in his sketch. That of course seemed preposterous to Robert since he understood only the two words Iskifa taught him and couldn't imagine understanding anyone else here.

Iskifa again dressed Robert's foot and leg wounds with the same poultice as before and wound an extra leather wrap around his injured foot. Robert's grief returned while they finished filling Mc-

Laren's grave, even while his thoughts turned toward survival. Iskifa had laid some flowers nearby and gestured for Robert to use them. Robert arranged the yellow, blue, and fire-orange blossoms at the head of the grave, bowed his head, and prayerfully said goodbye to his fallen friend.

The native, even if a savage, seemed to understand his need for privacy and walked to the edge of the clearing with his back turned until Robert finished his quiet eulogy and left to follow, leading Lizbeth.

Iskifa handed Robert his staff and led the way back to the coastal footpath. The walking was painful, but the earth lay soft on the shaded path, and a bit of athletic resilience began to return to Robert while they walked and rested. The old man did not rush the pace, seeming to know just when Robert's fatigue called for a respite.

Anytime they stopped, Robert studied the strange plants and trees around him. The taste of the fresh water from the two coastal streams they crossed was sweet, reminding Robert of the mineral-rich groundwater of the highlands. There were an annoying number of insects in this warm clime, especially small swarms of biting flies that assaulted from time to time. Robert noted the old man didn't seem bothered by them. Occasionally he spoke sharply to them, but he never swatted at them, like Robert.

After they walked northeastward about an hour, they came to a wide, shallow river mouth. Their well-traveled path turned almost straight north along a low ridge overlooking the west side of the river, leading inland. From there Robert could see several forks split off the main channel upriver and spread across a large, marshy delta crisscrossed by narrow tributaries.

Iskifa headed straight up the inland path. Robert felt an apprehension, a vague anticipation of an unwelcomed commitment, but followed, understanding he had little choice. He felt the urge to ask the old man where they were going, yet refrained. He was beginning to trust him, strange as he was. Fewer panics over cannibalism and other prepossessions hit him than at first.

The path narrowed to cut through a dense grove of tall trees choking the light down to a few shafts, and the air cooled. Robert let his attention drift from his hobbling, unbalanced gait to marvel at the almost whimsical flora of the grove's understory, full of plants of magical quality. They reminded him of dragons and strange flying things of childhood tales.

The forest opened to a round meadow, maybe fifty paces wide. In its center sank a round, shallow fire pit, not very wide across, its perimeter lined by set stones. The remains of past fires blackened its floor. Shaved logs, flattened on one side and set on short, carved log pedestals, served as benches in the sparse grass around the pit. Trees towered overhead. The path continued into the forest on the other side.

Iskifa sat on a bench, reached into one of his bags, withdrew something like a scroll, and beckoned Robert to sit beside him. Robert tied Lizbeth's rope to a limb so she could graze and took a place beside Iskifa while he unrolled the piece of light-colored buckskin and spread it between them.

Robert marveled at the drawings he saw on it, his experienced eye soon concluding it looked most like a map. Iskifa used his bone whistle for a pointer, indicating first what looked like an image of ocean and coastline.

"Coastline?" Robert asked.

"*Oka taakchaka,*" Iskifa confirmed. Robert followed his pointer while it traced up to small pictures that looked like houses. Beside each was a tiny symbol, like a fish.

Iskifa's whistle traced the coastline to a little squiggle that, to Robert, looked like ones that usually indicated rivers on his charts. A line parallel to it suggested a road or trail, and watching the old man's pointer as it followed that a short length, he saw a circle with the sign of a fire inside—the very place where they sat.

With a proud look, Iskifa pointed to the ground beside them. Robert chuckled and nodded, amused and gratified by the old man's ability to communicate. A shriek from the woods shattered his smile, sending a cold chill of fear ripping up his backbone. Iskifa nudged him and made a bird-winging sign with his hands. "*Foshi,*" he said, flapping his finger wings.

Robert chided himself for his childish reaction. "*Fo-shi*, bird," he repeated, both relieved and embarrassed. Everything was too foreign. "Keep a level head," he whispered to himself, reinforcing his intent to control his tendency to panic or lose temper.

Iskifa drew Robert's attention back to the map to show they would continue on the trail to what looked like other houses beyond. As he had done in camp that morning, Iskifa picked up a piece of wood and scratched some stick figures in the dirt and pointed to them, to his own lips, to Robert, and at last to the house figures on the map. Robert still could make no interpretation of the old man's signs other than that they would meet people he could talk to. He reconsidered the possibility, but the thought of someone in this place speaking his language still was more than he could imagine.

Iskifa rose to continue. Robert untied Lizbeth, allowed her to drag him over to the stream so she could drink, and fell in behind Iskifa, still limping.

He was exhausted by late afternoon and prayed the old man would find a stopping place. Iskifa chose a site on a grass-covered knoll over-looking the mouth of a small stream at its confluence with the river. Robert tied Lizbeth, who looked tired also, to a low-hanging limb after she took her fill of water from the stream. She lay down in the grass and folded her legs under her. He spotted Iskifa tossing a fishing line into the river at the mouth of the creek.

The foliage was lush and green and the air smelled fresh. Robert relaxed, reclining on his back, looking up into the forest canopy from the slope of the bank. An incredibly sweet smell, apparently from some yellow flowering vines climbing the trees nearby, enter-tained his nose. He focused on a couple of colorful birds flitting past and jolted at a new, startling image that arrived to suspend abruptly a few feet above him. He froze and focused on it. The image moved. Robert realized it was a very tiny, shiny, and colorful bird, hovering, beating its miniature wings so fast he could hardly see them.

Just as quickly, the wee bird darted away. He found it again a few feet to his left, suspended with others of its kind, all busy as if tending the tapestry of aromatic flowering vines. He allowed himself to marvel at the wonders of this new world.

The old man hooted. Robert looked back to see him pull a small fish out of the water. The catch pitched itself about on the bank. Iskifa laid his hand over it and removed the bone-white hook from its mouth, drew the sharp stone knife from his pouch, and made a quick cut in the top of its head. He released his hand; the fish lay still. He cut out a piece of the fish's flesh and baited his hook with it.

Robert felt a pang of hunger joining his appreciation of the old man's efficiency at harvesting food wherever they went. He rolled over and started to offer a compliment, but elected silence instead, content to watch. He noticed, through the semi-clear stream, how Iskifa's bait came to rest on a shallow shelf. Iskifa carefully pulled the line until the bait fell off the shelf into deeper water and waited, relaxing until he returned to an alert crouch. The string tightened, and Iskifa set the hook. After a short battle, the old man landed a relatively large, smooth-skinned, gray-blue fish.

Robert cheered, "Hi-ho!"

Iskifa pinned the large bounty to the bank, looked up at Robert, and smiled. He picked up his sharp stone knife from where it lay atop his carefully folded mantle and pierced the fish at the top of its head; it ceased its struggle. He slit the fish's belly, pulled out its guts, and tossed them into the river. "*Loksi*," the old man said.

"Very lucky, indeed," Robert responded, rather sure the old man meant something else. He took another reading on the hollow feeling in his stomach and figured he should do his part. Iskifa must have sensed his desire to help, because he looked around the creek bank where he had begun to clean the fish to find a dry, dead limb. He picked it up and showed it to Robert.

"Of course," Robert agreed. He rose to limp among nearby trees in search of firewood. He found many small limbs lying about and carried them back to the camp so Iskifa could kindle a fire. He ventured farther on his second trip, for larger pieces, and quickly became aware of vine-like briars growing along the ground that scratched his ankles and arms if he didn't pay close attention. He heard leaves rustle behind him.

"I can handle this chore by myself, old man," Robert said, turning to greet Iskifa. But the man who stared back at him was not Iskifa.

A fresh bolt of terror straightened him. He stared back at the dark brown-skinned man wearing only a breechcloth, with a dreadful-looking, purple-painted face, a white stripe shaped like a lightning bolt across his forehead. A bow and a quiver of arrows were slung over his shoulder, and he balanced in his hands a staff with the carving of a face on its knob. The man stood transfixed, probably surprised himself, Robert reckoned, because he could not have expected to see a man with a white face turn to meet him. The brown man's head bore no hair except for a tuft from the very top of his scalp. He made an offensive gesture with the staff, but did not advance or speak.

Robert stood wary and still. The man laid down his bow and quiver and repeated his two-handed thrust.

Robert's heart pounded audibly. He felt relieved the man did not immediately attack but, understanding he was being challenged, he carefully leaned over to pick up a stout-looking deadfall limb at his feet.

The man thrust again with his staff, this time holding it out in front of himself for a moment.

Robert locked his eyes on the wild-looking man, cautiously snapping small limbs off his stave. Another man appeared from behind a tree to Robert's right. He looked at a glance to be identical to the first savage, without the purple face.

Thoughts of escape raced through Robert's mind. Instinctively, he wheeled to face behind him, the only direction left. Standing there was yet another man, much older, clothed differently from Iskifa—in a breechcloth and a type of skirt, shirtless, with weapons and pouches slung over his shoulders and a similar, if plainer cap on his head. He smiled, nodding slowly toward the first man with the staff, who took a step toward Robert, repeating his feint.

Robert knew he was being challenged to fight. He turned and took a step forward, convinced he once again came face to face with death.

His opponent rushed forward several paces. Robert braced. The man stopped, looked him in the eyes, and faked a blow to his head with the staff, which Robert raised his rod to block. As he did, the purple-faced dastard swooped low with a round swing, sweeping Robert's legs out from under him. Robert hit the ground hard on his left shoulder. A stabbing pain ran up his left leg like a lightning bolt, and he expected to be pummeled on the ground. Rather, his opponent's companions cheered while he stood by, giving Robert a chance to get up.

As soon as Robert reached his feet, a rhythmic blow from the right side took out his legs again, and he crashed to his right shoulder, striking his head a glancing blow on a rock. Another cheer went up. The noise and the pain ignited his rage. He rolled away and up again, ignoring the ripping fire in his leg and foot, in time to spot another roundhouse swing toward his ankles. He jumped; it whiffed under his feet, and he brought a sharp blow with his rod to the side of his crouching enemy's head, sending him sprawling.

The others lifted their voices to cheer again, which surprised Robert. He stood, panting, returning the courtesy of allowing the wild man to regain his feet.

An issue of blood appeared over the other man's purple eyebrow while he got up to circle, shuffling his feet sideways. Robert moved in step with the primitive athlete, never looking away from his eyes.

The wild man smiled confidently, but the blood was getting into his left eye. He quickly swiped some out, and as soon as he raised his hand Robert attacked, punching the left end of his staff toward the wild man's right knee.

Surprised, the sylvan warrior blocked the blow by reflexing down with a one-handed defensive thrust. The move effectively broke the force of the blow toward his knee, but since he just had one hand on the rod, the strong strike by Robert knocked it out of his grip. Robert delivered the other half of the two-handed forward slap of his weapon to his chin. The other men laughed and hooted while the blow sent the native sprawling onto his back, but he used the momentum to tumble backward, landing like a cat on his feet again. With breathtaking agility, he dashed to his staff, swiped it up, and charged. Robert swung another strong blow with the left end of the staff toward the native's legs, which he blocked. Again, he delivered the logical right hand thrust, which his enemy ducked.

As if he had known Robert would try the same move, he whirled in a crouch on one foot, ducking the swinging rod, ending up slightly behind Robert. Completing the athletic spin, he delivered a powerful slapping stroke to the middle of Robert's back, deflating his lungs, flinging him off his feet, and knocking him face down.

Robert cried out. He rolled to his back quickly and sat up, although he could not breathe. The yips and hollers of the bystanders barely penetrated the veil of pain enveloping him. He saw the purple-faced wild man glaring at him, an attempt at a smile on his bleeding face, although it looked more like he was gritting his teeth. Still, he did not attack while Robert was down.

Robert's ribs racked with pain and his breath came as wheezes. But his fear was fully replaced by athletic anger. He had never shied away from a fight and always, even in a difficult row, could identify his adversary's weakness. He focused on the bloody eye sockets of the purple-faced wild man. He noticed his pupils were big and black as those of any man who took a heavy thump to the head. He might be woozy, Robert thought, and summoned his strength for his only chance. He jumped up quickly, still gasping, re-fixing the staff in a two-handed grasp. The purple-faced fighter charged as soon as Robert reached his feet. He anticipated that, swinging his rod for the native's ankles.

The native, matching the move, jumped to avoid the strike easily. Again, from behind Robert where he landed, the man wheeled and swung at the back of Robert's head.

Robert ducked, causing the native to miss, and twisted again, delivering a solid strike to the belly, hearing a *whoof* as the man doubled over. He came up with another stroke under the wild man's chin and sent him with a thud onto his back. He heard cheers and whistles. The man rolled again and came to his feet, although not with his previous agility. His chin was cut, his eyes were wide, and the smile was gone.

Still gasping, Robert could not stand erect. He faltered, remembering his limp while he and the native slowly circled each other, blinking through blood and sweat and dirt in locked gazes.

As if from nowhere, Iskifa stepped between them and held both his arms out straight, palms up, as if to say the fight was over. The native man came to attention when Iskifa looked at him. He turned to Robert, who, without knowing why, also straightened. The other men yipped and applauded.

Robert felt emotionally numb, if hardly so otherwise. He had been in quite a few fights before—even contests with the staff, at clan festivals—but never with such an unknown and mysterious foe in an unknown and mysterious world. He peered at his erstwhile opponent, who wiped blood from his chin and eyebrow with his forearm. The old man and Iskifa engaged in what seemed to be genial conversation, each glancing at Robert.

The third man cautiously approached Robert, staring while he wiped the dirt and sweat from his eyes and gingerly dabbed at a stubborn issue of blood behind his left ear. The man reached tentatively toward Robert, who slapped his hand away impulsively, distracted by a siren's chorus of aches.

The native chuckled and turned to follow his friends and Iskifa to the camp on the knoll by the creek. Robert trailed at a distance, trying to interpret what just happened. Iskifa stopped to look at Robert, who stared back, puzzled.

Iskifa bent to pick up a stick from the forest floor and raised his eyebrows at him.

"Oh," Robert muttered densely, "the firewood."

CHAPTER NINE

SECOND NIGHT

ROBERT THOUGHT IT ODD THAT ISKIFA HAD NOT FORGOTTEN his firewood chore, as if to disregard the fact he had just experienced another new and most extraordinary event in his life in a new, strange world. Still, he conceded that the old man always seemed in tune with what was going on.

After they shared a welcome meal of campfire fish, dried meat, and some tasty, if oddly tuberous, vegetables offered by their visitors, the eldest of the three men began to speak as if to give a speech. Iskifa had repeated to Robert the eldest man's name, Shonta, until Robert could say it. Iskifa seemed less interested in teaching him the others' names, although he made clear by signs that the two were brothers, and Shonta's sons.

Shonta reached into a bag and pulled out a long wooden tube. Robert figured it to be a kind of flute at first, because of the way the old man held it to his lips. Shonta stuck the tip of a small branch into the fire, raised it, set the burning end to an opening in the tube, and began to suck smoke from it into his mouth.

Robert could not believe his eyes. He leaned closer to make sure the flickering campfire light did not play tricks on him. After Shonta finished, he handed the tube to his son, seated next to him, and he sucked smoke into his mouth also. When he exhaled, Robert noticed, smoke came out of his nose. Works of the devil, Robert thought. He squinted so as not to miss a detail of the bizarre ritual.

A breeze made the fire flare and give off more light—indeed, they all sucked smoke from the tube. The light also revealed imprints or drawings of small fish in red and black on the men's shoulders. Robert felt a foreboding, recalling from scripture the warning against defilement by "the counsel of the ungodly."

Still, when they passed the smoking tube to him, he found he wanted to try it, tempted to take communion with these men of war. He held the tube at arm's length first, studying both ends. It was beautifully carved, with tiny seashells somehow embedded in it. He impulsively pulled the bowl and its smoldering contents under his nose for a sniff. The acrid smoke burned his nostrils. He coughed and snorted and thrust it toward the nearest native.

The rest laughed, as if amused at his unfamiliarity with their ritual. Still, they all seemed pleased to have Robert in their company, not at all like what he expected from fearful dreams and imaginations of unknown lands. The fight with the staffs was their idea of an athletic event, not a battle, or he would have been dead by force of odds. It was not so different, he reasoned, from the rough martial games he, Seth, and their young friends played growing up.

He recalled how enthralled they looked a little earlier, crouching and studying Lizbeth while he relieved her swollen udders, and how surprised they seemed while they watched him drink her milk. Like Iskifa, they refused, chuckling, when he offered the cup. He assumed they did not have goats in this new world—or perhaps cows, either. Lizbeth bleated kindly, and they petted her, if tentatively. She always seemed to get her way.

Iskifa, Robert observed, conversed freely with the men, although their speech sounded different from the language the old man used the day and night before. Also, these men had sharp, angular features, different from Iskifa's long, slender face punctuated by a narrow chin. Their shoes were different from Iskifa's, too. The clothes of the older man, Shonta, were not as colorful, and his ornaments stranger and more numerous. He wore round spools set in holes in his enlarged ear-lobes, glimmering like copper, and a striking necklace of shark's teeth. The stories and souvenirs of fishermen of long ago caused Robert to recognize and fear the tooth of the shark.

It did not escape him, though, that if these men used shark's teeth for ornaments, they might be men of the sea and might have ships and knowledge of the currents—the things Robert needed to return to Scotland. He felt encouraged and frustrated, because even if they did, Robert had nothing to trade for their help. He was stripped of all wealth.

The men rose to walk to the river for some reason, leaving Robert to wait. To pass the time, he inclined his ears to the noisy din of wildlife voices. They rang with ratcheting sounds of riverbank insects and frogs, interrupted only by an occasional cat screech or wolf howl. The trees sounded full of raspy bugs, buzzing, vibrating, louder than the teeming river bottoms of the Scottish lowlands.

The others returned, bearing flat, hand-size stones, and retook their places around the fire. Shonta straightened with an air of ceremony, holding his hands palm down, straight out from his shoulders, and the rest fell quiet. He looked up, raising his hands above his head, as if to search among the treetops, first one way, then another. He turned his palms upward, cupping them in rhythm with the turns of his head. Then he began to sing, displaying surprising range in his voice. The others, including Iskifa, began to clap the river rocks in time.

At length, their rock-clapping stopped, and to Robert's wonder, Shonta began to whistle, then chirp just like the birds Robert heard in the woods, and then to make sounds like the insects and frogs. He went back to singing and the rock clappers resumed, except for Iskifa, who took his flute from his pouch to play.

The young man who did battle with Robert earlier gazed directly at him, playing a steady beat with his river rocks. Robert returned his even gaze, feeling strangely at ease in the presence of his death-grip opponent of just a few hours ago.

The other young man skipped into a much faster beat, still in rhythm, continuing until Shonta stopped singing, leaving the notes of Iskifa's flute wafting over the rhythm of the rocks. Robert felt drawn pleasurably into the intertwining sounds, as he had toward the smoke-sucking but, fearing some evil spell might be spun, checked his impulse. On the other hand, the spirited singing and percussion was not so unlike the clan gatherings of his childhood and youth before he became so devoted to the sea. The clan gatherings always included dancing, however, he recalled.

Iskifa stopped, and the two brothers continued their rock-clapping until the fighter stopped, leaving only the faster one. Without breaking rhythm, the fast clapper came to his feet to dance, still keeping time. His gyrations amazed Robert. He danced on one foot, then the other, jumped and spun, keeping the feverish beat. He circled the fire, danced down the riverbank and back again. Shonta held his arms up straight, hands cupped, repeating the gestures that began the song. The young man danced to his place, stopped, and dropped into his seat. After a short pause, Shonta dropped his hands, and the four natives shouted, "*Shol shol shol aachi!*"—the crickets say, "*Shol shol shol!*"

Robert's amazement at the unearthly spectacle competed with sad reminiscences of merrymaking with lost friends on the *Manannan*. This was perhaps the first moment such feelings surfaced since Iskifa brought him to Donnchadh McLaren lying dead on the beach. The images swept upon him like a flood made strong by the surety he would never again see any of them and probably never see Celia, his mother and father, or Scotland, either. He rose, unable to control his tears and tried to distract himself by gathering boughs and canes for a bed. The others turned away to do the same, talking quietly. Robert lay on his mat and rolled to face away from the fire. Without speaking, Iskifa again laid his light cover on Robert's bare upper body. Robert floated through the river of pain in his joints and limbs, to find harbor in deep, dreamless sleep.

Lizbeth's bleating at daybreak awakened him to an annoying and fresh array of aches. Now accustomed to managing pain, he knew he must break through it, like thick brush. He stood in one excruciating jerk, hobbled and balanced with his weight on his good foot, picked up Iskifa's cup from a flat rock, and made his way to her. She shifted on her hooves with anticipation. Robert picked some leaves from a bush Iskifa once pointed out to him and gave them to her to nibble while he milked her. He spotted Iskifa dangling a line into the river at the mouth of the creek. A limp, smooth-skinned fish lay on the bank near the old native.

Shonta was nowhere to be seen, and the younger men lay asleep. Robert drank the warm goat's milk and relaxed into a sense of well-being in what seemed quite a beautiful forest, the more he studied it. He recalled the agility of his opponent of the past afternoon's contest and admired his own final maneuver of the match, the one-two punch to the belly and chin. If they owned no other credit, he reasoned, at least they fought honorably.

The fighter was last to get up, and his slow moving, an obvious distress from their contest, paid Robert a little comfort. Shonta returned bearing wild fruit. Iskifa handed the three fish he caught to the fast dancer brother, who roasted them over the fire. Robert's mouth watered with sweet aromas wafting in the smoke. "Thank you," he said genuinely, after the fast dancer offered him a nice piece of fish and two of the sweet fruits—his share, it seemed.

Soon they moved west on the trail together. The younger natives displayed a great deal of curiosity about Lizbeth. They took turns leading her, and she seemed to enjoy the attention, Robert noticed, jumping and nipping at them from time to time, as she once did with the *Manannan's* crewmen. Robert's punctured foot had improved remarkably, and the wound in his leg scabbed over nicely, to the point he walked almost normally after a bit of limbering up. Except for new scrapes and bruises from the fight, he supposed the rest and fresh food restored some vigor to him.

After about an hour's walk the trail came parallel to the river, overlooking it from a tall bluff. A disturbing rumor of voices bothered Robert's ears. He thought he heard laughter and singing similar to the campfire ritual from the night before.

To his astonishment, from around the next bend in the river came a long boat—maybe thirty feet, he reckoned, with slightly upswept bow and stern. His heart leaped, and he felt a surge of hope and unexpected joy. It bore a canopy as a sterncastle and was propelled only by the slow river current, although he could see several oar placements. An older man sat in a comfortable-looking chair under the canopy. His dark brown and hairless chest was bare but for a brief red vest. He wore a long, soft-looking loincloth of orange color, hanging past his knees.

A native woman on board looked much younger than him. She wore a straw-colored, one-piece dress and a red sash about her waist. An array of colorful flowers lay atop her raven-black hair. She sat in front of the man in another chair under the shade and appeared to be fishing, as did three young children clustered toward the bow. An older boy stood near the stern, manning a rudder stick.

Shonta and his sons waved and called out to the family, all of whom waved back with familiar smiles and shouts. Shonta pointed to Robert and Lizbeth and said something, a gesture that concerned Robert. The people in the boat became excited and rose to gape at him, although their view was not good through trees on the riverbank. The children pulled a stringer of fish from the water to show off.

Robert had never seen a boat like it. He studied it carefully, trying not to be too distracted by the people, especially the woman, the first he had seen in many weeks—too many to count. Her skin was more copper-toned than the man's darker brown. When she stood to peer at him from under the canopy, Robert noticed she was shapely and possessed unusual loveliness.

As for the boat, it appeared to have been made from one very large tree, hollowed out and shaped on the sides and ends. Its bow, which bore a striking carved image of a fish, stood taller than its stern. While it hove by, he noted its almost wakeless knifing through the water. He wondered, though, since he saw no mast for a sail, how this large craft could be moved back upstream with so weak a crew.

Alas, the boat slipped out of sight and his navigational reverie ended. Nonetheless, his faith was renewed somewhat. The drummings of woodpeckers and the occasional flicker of a squirrel's tail in the canopy reminded him that the temperate glens of this new world were full of life. At times he could almost release himself from his worries enough to enjoy the flora and fauna and the odd troupe he walked among.

Iskifa played his flute often, adding peaceful music while they walked, with a cadence that seemed to match the rhythm of their steps. Robert noted with bemusement the lineup they kept on the trail—a young man each at the front and rear, the older men in the center, always in charge, a submissive order toward which the younger men showed no hint of resentment.

More boats, smaller and narrower ones carrying one or two people, floated by, and Robert felt curiosity mix with anxiety at the prospect that they drew near a population center. Perhaps he could find sailors or boatmen to help find a way home. If they had knowledge and resources to build small boats, they might at least put him in touch with materials to build a larger one. Still, such thoughts made him nervous, too. He had nothing to trade and he could not communicate.

The river widened and the trail ran down to the water. They came upon many children swinging and dropping into the water from ropes hanging from high branches, paddling about on logs, splashing and swimming across the river. Many played cheerfully in the rocky mouth of a spring-fed stream whose clear water flowed into the murkier river on the near side. Robert noted, impressed, how well they swam for such young ones. They sprang out of the water to flock around him and Lizbeth, chattering, chuckling, and reaching out to touch him and the goat. The children made a big joke out of smelling Lizbeth, grimacing and pinching their noses. "*Issi kosoma, issi kosoma*," they repeated in a singsong chant. It made Robert happy to see so many young children, and he felt less like he was lost in an uncharted wilderness.

Past the swimming hole the valley turned treeless, widening into broad, green fields, and their trail became a road. Robert could see a few men and women working at distant points in the fields among well-ordered, healthy-looking crops. Again, he was dumbfounded. Anytime he formed a judgment of these people as primitive, some unexpected scene popped up to suggest they were perhaps civilized.

An orderly field of tall, leafy, stalk-like plants, unlike any he had seen, stretched before them. He assumed they were food plants because they were so neatly cultivated. In another field, vines tangled over the ground around large, melon-like fruit. The scale of the fields struck him. The first they encountered probably measured a furlong each in width and length, laid out in squares. As the valley widened, some—especially with the tall stalk plants—looked at least a mile long.

Shonta and Iskifa knelt often to examine the plants, talking. Their caps glistened colorfully in the afternoon sun. Lizbeth wanted to sample the cultivars, but Robert, hoping to keep good relations with the local farmers, led her instead to patches of grass between fields. One of the younger men gestured his desire to look after her while she grazed, so Robert handed him the rope and took the opportunity to examine the plants himself. He noted he had not seen, except for a few in the distance, many workers in these fields, although they looked steadily cultivated. Each large field had a small house in its center—a hut, really—built of logs, with a thatched roof.

"This might be their Sabbath," he whispered to himself. Robert reached for Donnchadh McLaren's crucifix hanging from the rosary beads around his neck, remembering how McLaren carried it on Sundays for shipboard services, and how Iskifa handed it to him over breakfast the morning they buried him. The people here are certainly not Christian, he reasoned, scanning the fields mostly empty of laborers, but they may have a day of rest, since so many are at their leisure on the river.

They continued through several miles of various crops and passed a side road branching west, headed between two steep hills at a distance. A small stream ran beside it, and a couple of furlongs down it Robert could see a stockade wall built of small trees stripped of their bark, set upright and lashed together.

"What is that?" he asked Iskifa, pointing at the fence.

Iskifa seemed to understand his question and conferred with Shonta before he answered. "*Yanash,*" Iskifa replied, holding his index fingers up to his head, suggesting a horned animal.

Robert thought he meant cattle, another thing he wished to make sure about after seeing the natives' unfamiliarity with Lizbeth. "I want to see," he said, signing with forked fingers from his eyes down the side road.

Iskifa looked at Shonta, who had listened to Robert and watched his signs, and made an affirmative gesture, saying, "*Ah.*"

Iskifa and Robert went down the side road. Robert noticed the fence spanned the end of a small canyon with walls of shaley-looking rock, much of it concealed by brushy vegetation. The cliffs rose to about forty feet on each side, like the bluffs above the river. The fence stood about ten feet tall with a set of double gates about the height of a man in its center. The stream ran out from under the east side.

The old man put his ear up to the gate for a quick listen, unlashed its rope lock, and swung it open. Robert followed inside to a small enclosure maybe ten paces square, with another gate in the opposite wall. Iskifa carefully closed and lashed the gate behind them, put his ear against the next one before unlashing it and poking his head inside to look around, then passed through.

Robert fought off uneasy apprehension, reminded himself that all this was his idea, and followed. Iskifa closed that gate, too, but did not lash it.

They had come to a boxed canyon. Just inside the fence, parallel with the stream, stood a simple, heavy post-and-beam frame built above a floor of logs, all flattened on top. Sturdy ropes hung from the beam and were lashed to the posts. Another broad log-beam floor lay behind the frame and floor. Iskifa led him beside the structures, making a quartering sign near the open floor to indicate that was where they gutted and quartered animals, pointing to the frame. He directed Robert's eyes to a large, round fire pit full of ashes and remnants of wood behind the open floor, apparently where they burned what they did not eat or use. Tools and large clay pots sat stacked in a corner of the open floor.

Robert tensed at the bloodstains on the ropes and floors. His apprehension wanted to turn into panic. Combined with a strange, prevalent odor, the sensation of seeing blood induced a whelm of alarm to his bowels. He scanned the canyon walls—he could easily climb out, he reasoned. But where would he be then? Lost, with no guide, no guardian angel. He forced himself to calm down. His best bet was still to trust Iskifa. I'm not a captive, he thought. I'd probably be dead if not for this generous old man who seems determined to protect me.

The canyon widened into a broader space with short grass and a conspicuous absence of trees. A commons where people gather to watch torture and execution, Robert feared, though trying to dismiss such thoughts. His agitated memory nonetheless flung forth a vivid and terrible recollection of a brutal public execution he witnessed in London when he was eighteen. A sound behind him caused him to whirl quickly—an innocent, bright green insect hopping in the grass. He felt the hair stand up on the back of his neck and goose bumps big as apple seeds standing on his skin. "Get hold, man," he whispered to himself, feeling urgency in his steps.

He focused on Iskifa's brightly colored cap bobbing ahead of him, trying to shake off the chills. They went about a hundred paces farther to another fence, through a similar arrangement of gates and an enclosure, and emerged into a wider part of the canyon, full of tall grass. Iskifa stopped to point. Robert followed the line of his finger to see a large beast drinking from the stream. Beyond it stood others of the same type, grazing in the tall grass. Iskifa looked wary and he could see why. Beasts from hell, Robert thought—large, dark brown, hairy horned beasts, resembling cattle with monstrous heads.

Iskifa squatted with his forearms on his knees, so Robert did, too. The old man seemed to enjoy his study for a while and turned to look at Robert, raising his eyebrows.

Robert relaxed with reassurance, regaining interest in the new world, and imitated the level forearm and hand sign he saw Iskifa use on several occasions, to signal gratitude for indulging his curiosity.

"*Yanash*," Iskifa said and made a sign with his hand to his mouth, suggesting eating. They left to retrace their steps back through the gates, lashing each closed. Robert then realized the first area was a grazed-down pasture, which the strange beasts had been moved off so the grass could grow back. He felt relieved and educated.

They rejoined the others, who rested and smoked their pipe in one of the huts at the center of a large field. Shonta had removed his cap, revealing long black hair, strikingly streaked with white. "*Minti*," Iskifa said.

All rose to leave, and the stick fighter untied Lizbeth's rope from the doorpost. Robert reached for the rope, but the young native gestured insistently that he wanted to lead the goat. He held up some leaves in his hand, which Lizbeth jumped and nipped at, like a trained pet, and they headed together down the road.

CHAPTER TEN

THIS WHITE MAN

I SKIFA WALKED A COMFORTABLE DISTANCE BEHIND ROBART, LISH-bit, and Shonta's eldest son toward the town responsible for these fine crops, once again feeling a sense of great confidence in his faithful journey and its accomplishments. After two nights and two days with this white man, however, Iskifa was no more certain about what he should do with him than on the first night.

The encounter with Shonta and his boys made a good test of how people might react to this white man and his strange beast. Shonta and he had never met, but they recognized each other as members of the Yukpan Confederacy. Shonta's tribe was from about as far to the east as allies of the confederacy lived. The fish-eaters had their own associations up and down the coast, but kept a neutral footing with most inland tribes, although they were usually willing to trade.

"What brings you so far east, Wordmaster?" Shonta asked after Iskifa stepped in to stop the stick fight late the day before. He had recognized the beaded image many wordmasters sewed on their shoulder bags, always of a campfire flame surrounded by four logs in a diamond shape. Besides the four directions, it symbolized the wordmasters' role of bringing people of disparate languages together in peace around council fires.

"I came to fetch this white man," Iskifa told Shonta. "*Aba Binnili* showed him to me in a dream, and I recognized your country and ocean in that dream. I've been here before. Atanapoa sent me over here at the end of my apprenticeship, when I was becoming a man, to collect your languages. I met some of your people. I recognized your colors, and that's why I speak your tongue."

"And I recognized your colors, my friend. You are Iskifa Ahalopa of Chunuli, aren't you?"

"You are correct, my friend, and you are Shonta the Trader. Am I also correct?"

"Yes, you are. I came as far west as Tashkalusa four winters or so ago, trading for black pearls. The wordmaster there, Hushihoma, told me all about you."

"And he later told me about you, Shonta. He spoke well of you." Iskifa took Shonta's hand in a gesture of friendship. "Your boys are good with their sticks. They seem like generally excellent young men."

"Thank you. They are great athletes, and I am thankful they have not yet been tested in war, but they make me very proud."

While Robert stayed behind to gather firewood, they walked out of earshot, where Shonta privately expressed some anxiety to Iskifa about the white man and his unusual animal, and even asked Iskifa if he wished for him and his sons to kill them. He knew wordmasters were not warriors and were not required to fight.

"No, with certainty, no," Iskifa replied, shaking his head emphatically. "The Creator has sent me to save this white man, and even though I'm not sure what will become of him, I am certain I am to take care of him. Do you think people will be scared and want to kill him?"

"He does not scare me," Shonta laughed, if a bit nervously. "He's a good athlete, but so pale and so alone. Is he now your son, Iskifa? Have you adopted him?"

"I had not thought of it that way," Iskifa replied, perplexed that Shonta might take such a notion. Still, he grasped Shonta's arm to guide him to the spot on the riverbank he chose for camp, and Shonta accepted Iskifa's invitation to join him and Robert for the night. Iskifa assured Shonta again that Robert represented no threat he could imagine, to them or any other people in his country. "Maybe I will adopt him," he affirmed, portraying enthusiasm for Shonta's sake, although privately he felt discomfort with the idea.

CHAPTER ELEVEN

CIVILIZATION

L IZBETH AMUSED THE STICK FIGHTER UNTIL SHE BIT ONE OF HIS fingers. The young man yelped, jerked his hand away, and shook it. All the men chuckled, including Robert, though he felt struck by how odd and new such humor felt to him. He could not remember the last time he laughed.

Afternoon shadows lengthened, and the stalky plants cast curious silhouettes onto the road. The air cooled, and Robert noticed the buzz of small biting insects, rhyming with a buzz of hunger in his belly. His companions looked tired also, and probably hungry, too. They seemed intent, however, on their goal and progressed steadily until they came in view of a hill in the middle of the fields. Atop it, to Robert's utter amazement, glistening in the orange light of approaching sunset, stood a great house as large, he speculated, as any on the boulevards of Dunfermline. Closer, he realized it stood on a shaped hill, level as water in a glass, its four sides sloping upward with geometric precision.

His hope increased at such a mark of possible civilization. It must be manmade, he thought. He had never seen such a hill, without any roundness or irregularity in its shape. It was beautifully landscaped with uniform grass on its sides. Colorful flower gardens and trimmed shrubs lined symmetrical stone stairways to its peak. Smaller houses, pens, a pond, and open sheds clustered around its foot. Apart from the oddness of the buildings, the layout reminded him of country estates in Scotland and England. The thought brushed briefly but painfully across recollections of his home and warmly familiar places there.

They drew near the hill, where children ran out to greet them. A young girl with yellow flowers in her long black braids dashed forth from the pack. "Grandfather, Grandfather," she cried in Shonta's language, leaping without breaking stride into his outstretched arms. She hugged him quickly and just as swiftly wriggled down for a better look at Lizbeth.

The stick fighter looked proud to hold the rope while the curious children gathered around the goat. He smiled broadly. Robert hadn't noticed until then that one of his former opponent's eyeteeth was missing from a fresh-looking socket. He felt a slight sense of remorse, mixed with a mumble of, "You shouldn'tav caused the stooshie, mate."

The children noticed Robert and became more reserved. They tried not to stare, but suffered difficulty at that.

Soon the men and goat moved forth again, a throng of chattering children revolving about them like flies around a sweet spot. The children sneaked up to touch Robert, one by one. He knew they did so out of curiosity, but the kindness of it almost caused him to cry. For an instant, he thought of Tain's and Wainwright's children, but contained the flow. It was the ship's captain in him, he supposed, that hoped someday he might deliver the sad news to their Scottish survivors.

He tried to take in details of his surroundings, but wandered amid distractions. He noticed what looked like a strange species of deer kept in a pen, and large, strange birds in another. An older girl-child deftly spirited Lizbeth away, cooing and luring her with a handful of sweet leaves and grain. The men stepped to the main stairs to take them up the sculptured hill to the house at its top, marching between purple, yellow, and blue flowers lining the upward path, all between trimmed shrubs. Orange-and-black butterflies flitted about the blossoms.

Pain returned to Robert's punctured leg and foot before they gained the summit, where the house burst into view, dumbfounding him with its scale. It looked, he thought, somewhat like the Scottish farm cottages—attractive use of logs, heavy thatching on the roof—but was so much larger. His eyes diverted to the sweeping view of fields and streams and the village surrounding the mound. The setting sun illuminated a thin layer of cloud above the horizon, splitting orange light into shades of pink, purple, and blue. The breeze felt fresh and cool with nothing to break it at this height, and the scent of the flowering vine from an arbor beside the path was nearly intoxicating.

At the house's entrance, he marveled at intricate carvings in the logs around the doorway, depicting detailed scenes of people and animals and the crops growing around the settlement, some dyed with various pigments, mostly light colors—white, yellow, and light green, with splashes of vermilion and purple.

Shonta stepped forward and called out. Iskifa adjusted his cap and mantle, stepped forward beside Shonta, and held his staff in what Robert supposed he thought was a distinguished posture. Robert stood back with the stick fighter and the fast dancer.

Several minutes passed, seeming like an impolite eternity to Robert. His legs and feet hurt, he was hungry, and he felt anxious about what waited inside the house. Finally, a large native with a severe chin, in colorful dress, with large ear ornaments and an outlandish hat made of what looked like the skin and fur of a black-and-white animal stepped through the open doorway.

"Shonta, my friend," the large man said kindly in Shonta's language. His expression changed as his gaze fell on Robert, who averted his eyes, then hazarded another furtive glance. The man looked frighteningly stern and his face contorted. He lifted his hands slowly up over his head, swept them down to slap his thighs, and let go a thundering laugh to echo out over the fields. Still chuckling, he stepped aside to let all pass inside.

His house was large and open with a high vault overhead. Several women inside tended to household duties, and three others sat cross-legged on woven mats, perhaps playing a game. They all stood, smiled, and greeted the men, soon turning to each other with excited whispers at the sight of the strange white man.

"May I present to you, the wordmaster of Chunuli, Iskifa Ahalopa," Shonta said, with a wave of his hand. "*Yukpan anompolichi ishto*," he finished with a flare of oratory.

"*Hallito*," the large man responded, bowing at the waist. "*Minti*," he said, obviously speaking Iskifa's language, sweeping his hand toward the interior of his home.

"*Yakookay*," Iskifa replied.

The big man led them to a corner where the open doorway permitted a flow of air, to offer seats on comfortable mats and furs laid on the floor. The lord of the house picked up a ritual tube from a low table between them. Robert assumed they were about to suck smoke together. The old men chatted in their tongue for quite a while. The younger natives spoke only when addressed by the older men, Robert noticed, and he was not addressed at all for some time.

Finally, Iskifa turned, extended his hands toward him, and said, "Robart." Turning to the big man, Iskifa said, "Chilantak *ishto*." Chilantak bowed his head gracefully toward Robert, who returned the gesture.

Chilantak opened a small pottery jar on the table, took out a tiny glowing coal, and set it in the top of the smoking tube atop a pack of dark-colored herb. He offered the pipe to Robert, who refused, holding his hands up palms facing out.

Chilantak bristled, glowering wild-eyed, and began to rise slowly, clearly angered. Robert recoiled, feeling the urge to flee, instantly realizing he had nowhere to go. Iskifa reached for Chilantak's forearm, gripped it, and tried to restrain him, but the big man continued to glare at Robert, still rising. Iskifa calmly spoke to Chilantak in his own tongue and must have found the right words, because Chilantak halted and settled back into his seat, still peering at Robert. His severe expression slowly softened while Iskifa continued to explain. Iskifa turned to Robert, repeated the gesture Robert made, and waved his hands in a level position, a clear sign that he should not have done so toward Chilantak.

"I am sorry, me laird," Robert offered, repentant.

Chilantak smiled and forced himself, or so Robert reckoned, to laugh, handing the pipe to Iskifa, who sucked the smoke. It passed to the stick fighter and fast dancer, who exhaled through their mouths and noses. Smoke coming from the nose of a human being looked even more amazing in daylight to Robert than at the campfire the evening past.

The women brought in fresh fruit, dried fish, and jerked meat in small portions for each man. They laid large, earthen bowls of water in reach, and drinking was accomplished by means of unusual-looking dippers. Watching guests seemed contrary to custom, but the women did not appear able to resist peeking at Robert anytime they came near him.

After long conversation with each other and occasional gestures and orchestrations of friendship toward Robert, the party moved outside, to the edge of the mound. There they looked down upon the village, at a large fire burning in a plaza between small dwellings and outbuildings to the east. People gathered there. Robert could see their forms by the firelight and the brightness of a nearly full moon well above the horizon. Some sat near the fire against chair-like frames set almost flat on the ground. Small knots of people scattered about the plaza, some smoking and resting their feet on pen rails, some sitting together on mats. The air felt mild. Despite the strong moon, bright stars shone in darker quadrants of the heavens.

The view looked splendid, even from no more than fifty feet above the river-bottom land spread around them. Robert could see the moonlight reflect off a wide spot in the river perhaps a mile east. They walked along the south rim, Chilantak speaking and pointing occasionally at specifics indiscernible to Robert, presumably giving crop reports, since they rose as far as anyone's eye could see. At the center of the south rim of the mound, benches sat under a shade arbor covered by sweet-smelling vines.

Robert stopped to rub his foot atop one of the benches and looked back toward the house. It reminded him a little of Scottish churches at night, but with more a personality of its own—something like what buildings might have looked like in Judea, he imagined, where Jesus walked.

They made the round of the west end of the elevation, passed another arbored bench, and started up the north rim, stopping near the middle to sit under the arbor. Chilantak picked several flowers from the vine covering the arbor and passed them about for the men to smell. They did not speak. Iskifa took his flute from his bag to play a slow tune while they all sat facing north. Robert surveyed the fields. The moonlight glinted off the shiny leaves of the stalky plants rustling in a gentle breeze. He thought about how grand it must be to be lord of such a domain.

Quietly they rose after Iskifa finished playing, to walk single file down to the village festival, with the fast dancer in the lead, the three elder men following him, and Robert and the stick fighter coming last. The women had gone ahead. Two took Chilantak by the arms as he came off the stairs, to escort him toward the fire. Another took Iskifa by the arm, and a fourth escorted Shonta.

An animal of some type roasted over the fire—probably a deer, Robert guessed, judging from its size. He was invited to sit in a place of esteem, and little children gathered around him at once, some handing him small dolls and other toys, which he examined and gave back, smiling and enjoying their affectionate attention. The older people acted polite, even if they tended to cluster anywhere they could have unobstructed views to watch him.

Chilantak stood, animal skin hat still on his head, while he flowed into a deep-toned oration, occasionally sweeping his hand toward Robert, Shonta, or Iskifa, perhaps introducing each. He was a massive, muscular man with a large belly, Robert observed, wearing pants and no shoes that evening. He, too, wore the characteristic vest of local fashion, his of subtle color.

One of the village men carved the meat, and a general sense of satisfaction seemed common to all while they shared it, along with vegetables and fruit warmed under the coals of the fire. The music of the children's voices was always nearby, comforting to Robert. They played with their little toys and with a round leather object they chased and tossed to each other, but they never became too loud or bothersome.

The men passed smoke-sucking pipes informally from time to time, along with a jug of a sweet-tasting, fermented drink. Robert enjoyed and relaxed with a drink, feeling pleased to see none took it to drunkenness. All seemed at ease with each other, and never did one raise his or her voice, which Robert found oddly comforting, even if unusual compared to Scottish gatherings, which he took care not to think too much about. His fears left him for a while. Iskifa and another man and a woman joined to play their flutes after the meal, while several others accompanied on hollow-sounding rawhide drums. Rattles joined in, and singers incanted strange, if pleasing, sounds.

When it came time to sleep, Robert, the stick fighter, and the fast dancer were shown to a small house with sleeping mats laid out. Iskifa and Shonta returned to the house with Chilantak. Robert lay down, feeling a concern for Lizbeth, but sleep swallowed him quickly.

The children had no reservations about sharing Lizbeth's milk with Robert the next morning. They were fascinated by the milking and wanted to help. Lizbeth flinched uncomfortably, apparently not much liking the way the children pulled on her teats, yet she seemed to glory in their attentions.

Stick fighter and fast dancer groaned and complained when Iskifa roused them and Robert awake early that morning. The dawn light was dim, and like Robert they probably didn't know what Iskifa seemed so eager about. He must have told them over fruit and boiled eggs served by Chilantak's women, because they nodded drowsy approval about something.

Iskifa unrolled his map for Robert, directing him to look at the six sun symbols between Chilantak's town and the next, signified by a cluster of houses. Robert reasoned it meant six days' travel to the next big town. "Six days walk," Robert pronounced to Iskifa, holding up six fingers and making a sweeping arc sign with his right hand cupped, as if to hold the sun.

"*Ii*," Iskifia replied, nodding and mimicking his six fingers and arc-of-the-sun sign.

Robert shuddered to think of walking six more days inland, but the options of staying alone and unguarded in Chilantak's town or trying to return to the coast by himself seemed yet more doubtful and frightening. As bizarre as it might have seemed, Iskifa was the only human being he could trust in this world.

Before long the troupe hiked down the road again. A swarm of children marched with them, taking turns leading Lizbeth. Iskifa stopped at an opening in the brush, bade the children to stay on the road and mind the goat, and led the men down to the river for a quick, restorative bath. They rejoined the children to continue about a mile before the little ones turned back at Iskifa's command. He smiled at them while he spoke, and every child hugged him and Shonta before they left. Some of the bolder children hugged the stick fighter and the fast dancer, and even Robert, a sensation that flared against his healing, if still tender, sensibilities. The children pranced away, some pinching their noses and singing, "*is-si ko-so-ma, is-si ko-so-ma*," and others singing, "Lish-bit, Lish-bit."

The people of Chilantak's village worked in the fields, cultivating and hoeing. A woman carrying a baby in a pouch on her back toiled beside her husband amid large, squat plants with big leaves and bright yellow fruits. She called them "*olbi.*" The man turned the leaves to expose their undersides, and she poured a dark green liquid on them, apparently to kill or repel small bugs clustered there. Iskifa took out a pouch holding the same mixture he burned in the smoking pipe and gestured to Robert that the natives used it to make the insecticide. Another field contained the plants from which they took the smoking material, or so Robert figured Iskifa's signs to say. He felt sure he had never seen anything that came close in Scotland, England, or France.

After a few more miles of small farms and crop fields, the vestiges of Chilantak's town disappeared, and they entered what Robert had to admit was the most amazing wilderness. Although perhaps not as pleasing to his eye as the Scottish highlands, the pine and hardwood forests and wetlands that gave way after a few days' walk to higher benches and woodlands nevertheless thrilled him with unique and mysterious beauty. Over the next five days and nights, the small group walked vigorously from sunrise until late in the afternoon, stopping to make camp and fish and hunt in areas of breathtaking natural splendor—waterfalls, oxbow lakes, and limestone caves. Robert gained strength each day and his fears gave way to the delights of learning from his skilled comrades the nuances of hunting and fishing in pristine wildlands.

They encountered an occasional isolated village where people were always eager to offer hospitality, but Iskifa and Shonta seemed intent on accomplishing a certain amount of distance each day. On the sixth morning, Robert noticed hills in the distance, east of the trail. The group turned onto a side road along a large creek leading toward them. They were still in the river bottom, and he thought he might see another manmade hill, although the shapes on the horizon looked too numerous and irregular to be mounds, he decided. Yet the closer they came, the more he realized that indeed they were mounds, with buildings atop them, like Chilantak's. Yet unlike Chilantak's, all were protected by a massive timber wall. The old men conferred a moment until they seemed to decide only Shonta and his eldest son would enter. They returned after a couple of hours bearing needed provisions. The group retraced the side trail and again took the river road.

Houses and small plantations of crops began to appear along the widening trail, and Robert sensed they approached a larger town. Various sorts of commerce—merchants in makeshift huts and small buildings gathered, sparsely at first, until they lined the road. The closer they came to another mound cluster, visible beyond them, the thicker the merchants became. Men, women, and children, all displaying varieties of headgear, clothing, and other wares too strange for Robert to identify, flowed from the roadside shops and booths to flock around him and Lizbeth.

Iskifa, Shonta, and the young men soon found themselves busy explaining the strange creatures with them. The young men especially seemed to appreciate opportunities to talk to any curious young women. They appeared, Robert observed, as if they tried to seem responsible for delivering their exotic visitors. The stick fighter pointed to bruises still visible on his face and showed one girl—who appeared to Robert to be a blossoming teenager—his missing tooth, all the while orating on the subject, nodding now and then toward the foreign white man.

Iskifa treated Robert's wounds with regularity, and his smaller ones throbbed less now. The deep wound in his leg no longer ached with every step. Still, some of his old misgivings began to return. He felt anxious to avoid another encounter like his misstep with Chilantak.

The throngs of people nevertheless provided entertaining diversion. Merchants held trade goods before him, trying to convert him from a traveler to a customer. He saw women who seemed dressed quite well and noted how they kept themselves from the press of the crowd. Generous tattoos on bodies surrounding him reminded him of stories of the ancients who warred against the Romans, called "Picts" because of their practice of tattooing elaborate pictures on their bodies. The church had outlawed tattoos several hundred years earlier, condemning them as "diabolical marks."

The children there, however, seemed particularly lighthearted and frolicsome, running about, spinning hoops on sticks, and chasing each other. They brought their dogs to join their chases in and out of the growing crowd. The dogs especially annoyed Lizbeth.

The scene around Robert filled him with a new mixture of hope and uncertainty. The people here seemed more civilized the more he saw of them, yet so strange in so many ways he felt sure they must be infidels and heathen. He now felt convinced theirs was a rich enough society that he could find materials to build ships with sails to take him back to Scotland. Their commerce was extensive. Shops of various degrees of sophistication sold fruits and vegetables. He saw tool merchants, jewelry shops, and clothing and footwear sellers. He saw strange-looking tents, tall and cone-shaped and covered with what looked like skins, some tanned white and others the color of a buck's hide. Log buildings with split-wood roofs and thatched-roof buildings with clay-daubed walls stood about. Outside some buildings stood thatch- and bough-covered arbors where old men sat drinking and playing games.

Meats and furs hung about, and pleasant aromas of cooked food filled the air, borne on smoke. Pottery of all types and elaborate art and jewelry made from shells hung on display, for sale. Large baskets full of bulky seeds and what looked like some kind of dried peas sat tilted to entice the customer on the road, alongside strings of dried vegetables of all colors, and dried and smoked fish. A tall woman, dark, slender, and immediately beautiful, walked up to Robert and hung a string of small shells around his neck.

Despite such distractions, he followed while they pressed through the crowds toward a vast fence around what Robert figured must be the main part of the city. Now and again he noticed tough-looking men who did not mix with the crowd and how they observed the people with stern sobriety. He could only compare them to authorities that might behave the same way in many ports of Europe—constables, perhaps, he thought.

He saw Iskifa turn aside to talk to some merchants they passed. Now and then the old native took something out of a pouch attached to his sash. It was hard, however, for Robert to focus on much besides the people pressing close to touch him and get better looks at him, until Iskifa came forth to beckon him into one of the roadside shops. Therein a woman slipped a simple sleeveless shirt over his head, without ceremony. It felt strange, but in the next moment, another woman pulled on his arm to bring him to sit on a stool, before which she laid out an array of pairs of sandals and without asking permission, tried each on his feet until she found a pair that fit. Robert stared at his feet, hesitant and anxious about his poverty, but the woman pointed to Iskifa, indicating he paid for them.

"Thank you," Robert said sincerely.

"Ah," Iskifa responded, impatiently nodding for them to proceed.

Soon they approached the great wall, which amazed Robert more than ever. It stretched almost as far as he could see in both directions from across the road, standing three times the height of a man, built of logs each a foot thick, set upright with ends buried deep in the ground, all bound together. Every fifty feet or so there stood a parapet, perhaps for guard stations, although he could see no sentries.

Its gates were open, however. People passed in and out. Still outside it, Iskifa stopped to unroll his map at the table of a woman who sold beautiful woven mats, chatting with her briefly and nodding, as if confirming his bearings. He smiled confidently at Robert, returned, and led him through the gates.

Inside the wall spread another city all of itself. Large flattop mounds, crowned with houses as big as Chilantak's, loomed here and there among smaller mounds bearing smaller, but still impressive buildings. The center of the compound, which spread across several hundred acres, as best he could estimate, was mostly open—a large plaza, he supposed. At the end farthest from the gate stood an enormous mound, terraced at several levels, supporting many small buildings on its lower terraces and a huge one at its paramount. Though dramatically different in style, to Robert they looked yet more imposing than the castles of the Scottish kings in Dunfermline or any structure he knew before. Besides the several flattop hills of varied elevations around the perimeter, Robert saw houses and mercantile establishments of different sizes and constructions clustered about, everywhere.

Iskifa's head bobbed between the sights of the city and the map unfurled in his hands. "Ah," he said, double-checking the map. "*Intannap*," he added, pointing toward the southwest corner of the city. "*Sayakaa.*"

A new throng of children and curious adults flocked to Robert and Lizbeth, making it hard for him to see where Iskifa headed—impossible, had the old man not moved with direction and purpose. Robert managed to keep Iskifa's colorful cap in sight from amid his turbulent sea of onlookers, and could pick up the sound of his flute. Odd timing, Robert thought, but then he must feel good about getting here.

Shonta and the young men stopped along the way among people who embraced them, uttering strange, high-pitched whistles and seeming genuinely pleased to see them. Iskifa ignored them, moving like a bee to the hive, leading Robert to a stairway leading to the top of one of the great mounds. He did not hesitate and began to trot up the steps.

"Sir," Robert called him urgently, to stop him.

Iskifa looked down with an impatient frown.

Robert held up Lizbeth's rope, his questioning posture matching the confusion on his face.

Iskifa marched back down the steps, took Lizbeth's rope, and tied it to an arbor post in a patch of grass. Robert dithered, still confused, not wanting to leave Lizbeth at the mercy of a crowd of natives, but Iskifa gripped his arm and coaxed him toward the steps. Robert balked and frowned, stubbornly.

"*Ishilaafowanna,*" Iskifa insisted, pulling his arm again.

Robert relented a little and let Iskifa tug him, if a bit off-balance, up the stairs. He glanced back at Lizbeth, whose attention had turned to children who gathered to pet her kindly and cautiously. Robert set aside his worries as much as he could.

Iskifa released his grip, and Robert followed up the landscaped stairway. The steps were made of hewn logs set into the steep slope of the earthwork. Green, lush grass covered the perfectly symmetrical slopes of the mound, and colorful flowerbeds lined their way.

At the top of the stairs a young, well-dressed native woman and an older man in raiment similar to Iskifa's greeted them.

"*Hallito! Ashali Iskifa,*" the young woman said politely, bowing slightly from the waist before abruptly, as one overflowing, rushing forth to hug the old man firmly, like a family member. "*Chipinsa sa-bannatok,*" she whispered, releasing tears that seemed to Robert to be from joy.

"Robart," Iskifa said, stepping back and nodding toward him. "Taloa Kinta," he said, nodding gracefully toward her.

Robert, struck by her beauty and compelled to assume the custom of the young men of his land and breeding, stepped forward to clarify the introduction. "Robert Williams," he said, adding emphasis to his surname, although for the moment he felt sure she could understand neither his words nor the propriety of his behavior.

"How do you do, Master Williams?" she replied in perfect English.

Robert gaped at her, speechless.

CHAPTER TWELVE

TRIAL

YOU DO SPEAK ENGLISH, MASTER WILLIAMS?" TALOA ASKED, now looking somewhat puzzled by his gaping silence.

"Yes … of course … " Robert all but choked on the words. "I just can't believe anyone does … I mean, you do," he stammered. "Taloa, is it?" he asked, thunderstruck after the shock of hearing English spoken and by the fascination of her simple beauty.

"Yes," she replied, "Taloa." She turned to speak to Iskifa in his tongue for a brief conversation—probably, Robert thought, to learn who he was and how he got here. The other old man, who had stood back while Taloa greeted and spoke with them, gestured with open hands toward Robert, appearing to notice his wounds, and offering a seat on a bench a few steps away, one that commanded a fine overlook of the city. It felt good to Robert to take the weight off his legs, and the magnificent view revealed in more surprising detail the vastness and bustle of the town—certainly not what he expected to see amid what seemed like a dense and untamed wilderness. Taloa and Iskifa finished talking, knowingly touching each other's forearms and smiling.

Keeping a polite smile, she turned back to Robert. "Master Williams, welcome to the great walled town of Anoli. The wordmaster has told me of your unfortunate shipwreck and the sad loss of your friends. I express my sorrow for your tragedy."

The soothing syrup of his own name on the voice of an English-speaking woman was almost more than Robert could bear—the sound of English, the sound of sympathy, the melody of this young woman's voice. His eyes began to fill, and he spoke to keep from crying. "Thank you," he said, straining the gravel from his throat. "How, pray God, do you know my language?"

She seemed pleased to tell him, if carefully so. "A man from across the ocean lived here in our city for several winters before, alas, he died. He came here at Master Anli's request, from a Delamac village in the far northern forests of *Taakchaka Bokota*. He lived with his Delamac wife and children as our honored guests, so we could regard and learn his language. I am Master Iskifa's apprentice, learning to be a wordmaster like him, and I was sent here by him to finish my learning under Anli Basha, wordmaster of Anoli." She stopped abruptly and blushed. "How crude of me," she said. "May I introduce you to the master?" She turned and with a sweeping wave of her arm bowed toward Anli. "Anli Basha," she said slowly, dignifying his name.

"Greetings, good gentleman," Anli said clearly, with a smile, although without Taloa's better diction.

"Good day to you, me laird," Robert said, again surprised to hear another native speak English. "And how do you do?" he asked incredulously.

Anli, a tall, very dark-skinned man, with stunning and sharp, but friendly features, tilted his head toward Taloa, maintaining a confident smile, and spoke to her in his language.

"Master Anli says he is well and happy, and he also welcomes you to the wordmaster house of Anoli," she translated. "He would with pride inform you also that a wordmaster house has stood on this mound for many generations, and that he is the thirty-first wordmaster of Anoli."

"I've never heard someone called 'wordmaster,'" Robert replied, bringing up a question if only to hear her speak more English. "What is a wordmaster?"

"There are many tribes in this great land," she explained, "and they speak many different languages. A wordmaster works hard all through life to learn many languages. That is a wordmaster's main purpose. Without trusted wordmasters to work things out, we would have a harder time trading with each other, and there would be more war."

"Taloa, is it?" Robert asked again, enjoying the sound of her name.

"Yes, Taloa Kinta," she replied, although he saw her eyes darken as if noticing a suspicious distraction somewhere behind him.

He turned to see two frowning men emerge at the head of the stairs. They were, he reckoned, the serious-looking fellows he saw at the edges of the crowds swarming around them on their way into town. They wore identical mantles. One looked stout, about the average size of natives Robert saw there, who tended to stand a bit shorter than him. The other was taller, also muscular. They spoke seriously, but politely, in their language to Anli.

Anli replied in kind, although with some indignation, as if protesting, and gestured at them. Taloa's smile vanished, and she stepped closer to hear what the men said.

The two men turned toward Robert, each seizing an arm. A flush of fear ran hot in his veins, and he tried to jerk away, but they were strong and determined. "What is this, Taloa?" he pleaded, resisting them. Iskifa joined Anli to protest.

"They are *apiisachi*—how do you say? Watchers," she explained while Robert stiffened, scanning for an escape route. "They watch for enemies and troublemakers," she continued, following as close as she dared while they pulled him toward the steps.

Remembering one of his better moves in his fight with Shonta's son, Robert twisted, pulling loose, fell to the grass, and launched a sweeping kick toward the shorter one's ankles. The watcher, caught by surprise, took the blow and fell hard on his left shoulder. Robert sprang to his feet and darted toward the steps to escape, but the taller watcher dived for his shoulders to grasp him and jumped on his back, sending Robert to his face. He knelt on Robert's back, grabbed his right arm and twisted it up toward his shoulder blade. The other man jumped back to his feet to help his partner hold the white man down.

Robert stopped struggling, and they drew him up to stand, their strong grips digging into his arm while they pulled him toward the steps again.

"We will help you, Master Williams," he heard Taloa call after him.

Robert felt numb again. He had suffered so much astonishment and pain it began to seem normal. He tried vainly to jerk loose, but they made their grips still tighter.

The townspeople frowned with disapproval at the watchers while they dragged him off the last step and stopped so the smaller man could untie Lizbeth, although he had to push his way through a flock of scowling children to get to her. Still, no one among them protested—the children and the adults seemed to know better than to speak against the watchers, however much they disliked what they did.

The one left holding Robert's arm seemed disturbed and distracted by the other's difficulties with untying a stuck knot in the strange horned creature's rope. Robert felt his grip relax a little and broke away to bolt through the crowd. He almost got away, but the sheer number of onlookers slowed him, and the big watcher tackled him, punching him in the face so hard he lost consciousness for a moment. The watcher stood to wait for Robert, who dabbed blood from above his eye. Robert rose to a knee before lunging for the big guard's legs and taking him down.

The watcher hit the ground hard, but used his strength and the momentum of the fall to roll backward and flip Robert onto his back. Robert felt the wind go out of him, like his lungs were stomped by a horse. Run, he thought, run—but he could not move. Gasping mostly dust, he struggled to his feet. The watcher patiently allowed Robert to stand and drew back his fist, but a quicker hand stopped his.

Iskifa held the athletic Anolian's fist, speaking calmly to him and then to Taloa, who had come forth from the crowd. She nodded to him and spoke to Robert.

"Master Williams, you should go with them. They are two of the fastest and strongest men of the city. You cannot get away," she said "We will argue for you. If you don't go with them, they will arrest us also."

The watcher retreated a half step. Robert stood and brushed dirt off his breeches. "I can't believe this is happenin'. Have you people no backbone?" he grumbled.

"Some things we cannot change," Taloa replied, staying composed. "You must trust us and go with them."

"You're makin' a big mistake," Robert retorted. "These people mean to kill me."

"Just go with them, Master Williams," she said, imploring. "We will get you out of this."

Her sincerity persuaded Robert to relax. She pressed his shoulders between her hands, darting glances at his face—if never in his eyes, he noticed—and nodded to Iskifa.

"*Hachibaaya'achi,*" Iskifa told the watchers. They frowned, but did not take Robert's arms again.

"Master Iskifa told them that you will go with them now," Taloa translated to Robert, her hands still on his shoulders.

The smaller of the watchers led Lizbeth, with a group of solemn and distrustful children close behind. The bigger fellow stayed near Robert, although not touching him. The parched summer air and the scuffle created a mighty thirst in Robert, his leg hurt and the new sandals had rubbed a blister on his foot. Taloa and Iskifa followed a few steps behind.

Robert observed a significant crowd of people moving with them, apparently curious to see what would happen to Anoli's strange visitors. All marched across the large plaza, passing a large, grassy, rectangular field that, he noticed, no one walked on. It appeared to be a sort of commons or playing field, perhaps, empty of people while the sun peaked in the sky, without a cloud to shield it. When the walking rhythm became regular on the hike across the plaza, the children began to sing, lightly, "*Is-si ko-so-ma, Is-si ko-so-ma.*"

Robert rubbed his ribs, feeling confused. "What are those children saying, Taloa?" he asked over his shoulder.

"Stinking deer," she replied. "The children have named your animal the 'stinking deer.'"

Robert could see the humor, but did not feel like laughing. He kept massaging his ribs, assuaging the pain and noticing how much fat he had lost since he left Scotland. He felt weak and exhausted. They came to another mound standing near the timber wall and proceeded up the steps. The watcher started to take Robert's arm again, but he jerked away and stayed a step ahead of him. He stopped halfway up, panting, looking out over this city from that high vantage point, still amazed by its scale and population. The great mound in plain view struck him as surely the largest structure he ever laid eyes on. The huge building atop it looked spectacular, as impressive as any castle.

The watcher prodded him from his brief reverie. Lizbeth bawled her complaints against climbing the incline, but was pulled firmly by the other escort, who exhibited no amusement with her.

Before the building at the top, under an arbor, sat a large man in colorful clothing, wearing a black cap and a wide brown sash girdling his rotund midriff. Sunlight reflected off his large copper ear spools while he spoke to the watchers, then rose, beckoning all to follow inside.

A sunken fire pit, circled by benches, sat in its broad interior. The back wall of the room comprised a large, carved mural, like the carvings around Chilantak's doorway, depicting the view from the top of the mound, its pigments and stains lending vibrant color to the grass, the mounds with their large shadows, the clouds, the sun, and other features for a striking image of Anoli.

The large man pointed to water pots and dippers on either side of the doors, and all drank except the watchers before they found places on the benches. The watchers came to stand on either side of Robert and Taloa, who sat together so she could translate.

The fat man spoke in his language, in a tone of oratory, and his men replied. He looked at Robert and said something.

"He wants to know your name," Taloa whispered.

"Robert Williams," he answered, clearly but tensely.

The headman spoke again, and Taloa translated. "He says he is Apesa, judge of Anoli, appointed by the Creator and approved by the people."

"Pleased to meet ya, I'm sure," Robert replied, surprising himself with his tone of Scottish cockiness, still kneading his ribs.

Apesa spoke and Taloa translated. "He says you are accused of being an enemy spy, and the penalty for this crime is death. What do you have to say for yourself?"

A quiver of fear started to come over Robert, but he prayed silently for a moment, stopped rubbing his ribs, and replied, minding his tone, "I am no spy, me laird." Taloa translated.

"Why should I believe a man whose skin has lost its color?" Apesa asked.

"Because I do not lie," Robert responded through clenched teeth, slipping into the Scots' vernacular, "and I was born from me mother with this skin."

"If I killed you, would you die?" Apesa asked, seeming either contemptuous or incredulous; Robert couldn't tell. "Or are you a *hattak okpolo*, an evil one?"

"I am no devil, your highness. I am a child of God, and He is my witness."

With a frown, Apesa got up to examine Lizbeth, who stood tied to a wooden column behind the circle of benches. "What is this foul-smelling beast, pale man?"

"It is a domestic animal. I brought it with me across the ocean. It belonged to the king of my country. Its milk was his medicine."

Apesa screwed up his mouth in disgust after Taloa's translation. "Why would a grown man drink milk, bloodless fellow? Does he still suckle at his mother?"

"It is medicine for his stomach that burns."

"Have you no mint?" Apesa asked, as if amazed.

"We have mint, but the king favors the goat's milk for his stomach," Robert replied, doing his best not to seem as weary of the subject as he felt.

"I don't believe you. I think you are lying. And lying is punishable by death. It is a worse crime than spying, because it is a crime against yourself."

Robert flushed, losing patience, but elected to maintain calm. "I speak the truth, me laird."

"Why are you here, white man?"

"I am here because me friends brought me here. I 'ave only one desire, and that's to find some boat builders who can help me return to me home across the ocean," he pleaded, putting sincerity into his voice.

"Who is this old man with you?" Apesa asked.

"This is the man, Iskifa, who found me on the beach. He is a wordmaster," Robert said.

"Iskifa Ahalopa," Iskifa interjected, not looking up from cleaning his fingernails with his small stone knife.

"I have heard of you, Iskifa Ahalopa," Apesa said, turning his round face toward the lithe Iskifa. "Where are you from, and how many languages do you speak?"

"I am from Chunuli, fifteen days' walk to the west, and I speak nineteen languages." His reply sounded curt, indicating to Robert that he held no more patience or respect for the fat judge than he did.

"How did you come by this white man, Iskifa Ahalopa?" Apesa asked.

"I first saw him in a dream, through which *Aba Binnili* instructed me to find him. I recognized the ocean as the eastern sea. I found him, as I expected, near an Onnaha fishing village eight days' walk from here. His ship wrecked, and he was the only survivor," Iskifa answered with monotonous calm while Taloa translated the exchange to Robert. He asked Apesa, "Why are you concerned about him?"

"As you know, the *Yamohmi* is going to be played soon in Tochina, far to our west," Apesa began. "There will be one hundred players on each team."

"Yes," Iskifa responded, dryly.

"The final qualifying tournament to determine the Yukpan Confederacy team will be held here this very evening," Apesa went on, gaining enthusiasm. "There are judges here from all around the region, and the best athletes in the east are coming into Anoli as we speak, hoping to be selected to play for the confederacy in the *Yamohmi*. Iyapi and Shakba will be here. They are considered the best."

Taloa couldn't quite keep up in her translation, so she whispered brief facts to Robert about the *Yamohmi* and the qualifying event in Anoli.

Iskifa seemed not at all as excited as Apesa. He removed his cap and shook his head, as if to cool his hair, sounding bored with the matter while he asked, "And what has that to do with my friend, Robart?"

"Everything, wordmaster," Apesa declared, as if to make a point. "People, including myself, have been making ready for the *Yamohmi* for several winters now. Large sums of shiny metal, furs, jewelry, bison, hunting and fishing rights, and other valuables are being wagered on the contest between us and the Allahashi. This is Yukpan wealth at stake," he concluded, with emphatic, oratorical flair.

Taloa translated as well as she could, but the older men were taking shorter pauses. Robert feared they might lose their tempers and knew who would likely be the loser if they did.

"Thank you for reminding me of the foolish betting going on, Apesa, but you still have not told me what this has to do with one white man who washed up on the beach."

"I have heard you are stubborn, Ahalopa, so listen carefully. It is no secret that Yoshoba is a snake of the subtlest stripe. You know what's going on in his 'kingdom,'" Apesa said, huffing with imperious disapproval at the mention of the Allahashi headman. The sweat beading on his forehead worried Robert.

"I know, of course, my well-fed friend. That is precisely why I advise my people, and I would also counsel you, not to go to the *Yamohmi*. It is a feast of the dead," Iskifa rejoined bluntly.

"Your position is not unique. There are those here who are afraid of it. But we need the trade with the west if we are going to continue to prosper." He stopped and exhaled briskly, fluttering his lips with frustration. "Yoshoba, it is believed, is sending spies and agents around to the confederacy towns. He wants to buy off our best athletes either to come over to the Allahashi team or to throw the game."

"You are crazy if you think my white man is Yoshoba's agent," Iskifa replied bluntly, frowning.

"You are the fool, tiny man," Apesa retorted. "One of their favorite tricks is to create a decoy, like a strange person with a strange animal sent into a town to distract everyone while the agents make their offers to the athletes. They even travel with groups of players or storytellers and operate while the shows draw others away." He wiped his brow and gestured toward Robert. "I have watchers out right now, and I think your white man is just such a ruse."

"Do you think I lie to you, Apesa?" Iskifa said, rising to stare gravely into the fat man's eyes. Taloa struggled to keep up, still whispering abbreviated translations to Robert.

"It would be unwise of me to accuse a Yukpan wordmaster of lying, my small friend, but who is to say you were not duped, and that the scene on the beach was not staged just for you?" Apesa said, folding his hands upon the brown sash around his enormous belly, exposing to Robert the hilt of a large knife.

"How would you explain the animal, thick one?" Iskifa asked.

"The stinking animal is hard to understand, my bony brother, but you do not expect me to believe it came over the ocean," Apesa blustered, appearing even to Robert to be taken off his guard. "The animal makes your white man more suspicious. I have heard they have strange animals in the great mountains west of the *Misha Sipokni*, the River Beyond All Age, and Yoshoba lives much closer to them than we. I think I should just recommend to the council that we kill this white man, and then we will know for sure that he can do us no harm."

"Let us just kill everyone we meet and do not know," Iskifa retorted, sneering with sarcasm. "Then they certainly cannot hurt us—in this life."

Apesa stared with bitter intensity at Iskifa, at Robert, and again at Iskifa, but did not speak.

"So, you do not believe my dream and that *Aba Binnili* sent me," Iskifa continued with a snarl that even without translation sent a shiver up Robert's aching spine. "You think I was just walking on that beach for my health, so far from my home?" His brow narrowed, and the look he shot at Robert unnerved the young Scot, who had seen enough confrontations among men to conclude, with great anxiety, that the old men looked tough and resolved, and that neither would budge any closer to the other's position.

Apesa rocked back on his bench, cast his eyes toward the fire pit, pressing his hands upon his massive knees, and his lips together.

Robert felt his nerves rise to a jangling chorus while the pause lengthened.

At last Apesa turned to Robert. "I think I want to kill you and solve my problem with you. I have more important matters to deal with." Taloa, with halting reluctance, translated his pronouncement to Robert.

He shuddered.

"You wait here, white man. I will go to decide your judgment," Apesa said. He got up to walk outside the house. Iskifa followed, leaving Robert with Taloa and the watchers.

Robert dismissed the sirens of isolation and fear and turned cool, as he was trained to behave during crisis. He centered on anger, especially at being put upon and set on display as the foreigner, the man of the wrong color, for the entertainment and disposal of godless and ignorant savages. He rose to pace about the fire pit, noticing the watchers bristled when he stood and hardly caring that they did. "Is it too much to ask or too hard to believe that I jest want to go home?" he asked no one in particular.

"Your feelings are understandable, Master Williams," Taloa answered, sympathetically.

He sighed. "Would you call me Robert, please?"

"Master Bannet, the white man who just died, told me to never call an Englishman by his first name," Taloa said.

"Of course. But I am a Scot. Besides, I think Master Bannet meant you should call elder men by their last names. I think we're about the same age, aren't we?" He turned to look at her while he asked and noticed the exquisite line of her face. Perhaps she was much younger, he thought, but still, she spoke with maturity.

She diverted her eyes from him. "I was born nineteen winters ago," she replied.

"Ah. Then I am but six years your elder. Not enough to call me Master Williams." He managed a faint smile, studying her since she would not look at him. She wore a dress the color of straw, sleeveless with a closed collar, and a delicate and colorful beaded necklace matching a heavier beaded belt at her waist.

"All right … Robert," she conceded, with a tentative smile. "There are well-known boat builders on the coast, north of the Onnaha villages that Master Iskifa spoke of."

This information flushed Robert with quick hope. "Kin they build ocean-going vessels?" he asked.

"Master Bannet said he thought they could," Taloa recalled, sounding a bit cautious. "They sail up and down the coast, fishing."

"Have any of your people ever crossed the ocean?" he asked, intrigued by such an unconsidered possibility.

"Not for many, many winters," she said. "We have many stories of our people in the long times crossing the ocean and stories of strange people who crossed from there to here," she continued. "They say there are white people living far north, also, and a clan of purely black people from a faraway land who married into a tribe on the wide prairie west of the great river, before the great mountains. Traders from the south tell of large tribes of black people on the seacoast south of the Mayapan. They say they came from the other side."

Her words were like honey to his ears, but the sight before his eyes drew most of his attention. Her copper-colored skin was hard not to look at, and her coal-black hair lay long and shiny, gathered in back and tied with a delicate leather band. Despite the jeopardy of the moment, he felt attracted to her, until he remembered Celia for the first time that day and checked himself with a jolt of guilt. He turned to look out the doorway. "What is that on the big mound, there? Is it where the king lives?" he asked.

"That is the grand meeting house of Anoli, the most famous location in this land," she replied. "Like us, they call their king *minko*, which means 'leader.' He lives there," she said, walking closer and pointing to a smaller building on a lower mound just beyond the great one.

"What kind of meetings do they have in the grand house? Are they like church?"

"Master Bannet told me about your religion and your churches," she answered. "We worship the Creator—not in large groups, but in our hearts, all the time. We have religious ceremonies each season. We use the grand house for dramas, talks, dances, and sometimes for large town meetings in winter. We think of all these as ways of worship. There will be dancing there tonight after the stickball tournament."

"Is the *minko* absolute in his authority?"

"No. He must have the support of the Council of Elders, mostly thinkers and men of knowledge. They are selected by their clan mothers to make decisions when they are needed. Women are called into council when they possess important knowledge."

He studied her demeanor—confident, but not aggressive. A ray of sunlight through the smoke hole high above them in the roof lay in a bright oval across her lap, illuminating her capable-looking hands folded there. "Are you one of those women?" he asked.

"No, I am too young," she responded thoughtfully. "But I will be when I am older and wise enough, because I will be the wordmaster of Chunuli. Most women do not choose these disciplines. I will limit myself to only one child, if I marry."

Robert changed the subject with a nervous sigh. "Might they really kill me?" he asked.

"It seems unlikely to me," she replied.

He still noted her lack of confidence in that opinion. "Do they kill people?"

"I have never seen an execution," she responded, as if choosing words carefully, "here or in Chunuli. But we have laws that carry the penalty of death if transgressed. And I have never heard a Yukpan joke about death or make an accusation without belief."

Such facts returned flaring unease to him. He had thought maybe Apesa was just finagling to see if he had any money, like English magistrates did to Scottish seamen in port towns. He sat down beside her to whisper, "Do you think I should try to escape?"

"That would be most foolish, Robert," she answered. "Yukpans have a high regard for the law and believe transgressors should never flee its judgment. It is the worst kind of disgrace."

A cramp shot through the muscles in his back. He was at the mercy of the fat native, who at that moment probably toiled over a pot to boil him in, he reckoned. Still, he trusted Iskifa and Taloa. He had to. As anxious as he felt, he found her words comforting. Her polite, direct manner was unlike any woman's he met before. "Why won't you look at me?" he asked.

"It is not proper, Master Wil ... Robert," she replied.

"Not proper to look me in the eye?"

"The eye is the window of the soul, Robert. It is one of the most intimate contacts between people," she said.

"What if I ask you to look me in the eye? Then is it all right?" he asked.

She flustered a moment. "I don't know. No one has ever asked me."

Robert retreated into proper embarrassment at his own prying, but before he could apologize, Apesa strode back in, followed by Iskifa. They took their places in the circle of benches, their faces without expression. Taloa straightened, preparing to translate.

Robert sat silent with anticipation.

"Robart Williams," Apesa said, "stand up."

Robert rose to attention, Taloa beside him.

"In my authority as thirty-fourth judge of the people of Anoli," he said, pausing so Taloa could translate, "I find that you are not a spy or an enemy."

Robert's shoulders sagged and his head drooped with relief. His thoughts ran to the boat builders on the coast.

"But, to ensure that the interests of the Yukpan Confederacy are fully protected," Apesa continued, again pausing for translation, "you are released into the custody of Taloa Kinta and the wordmaster house. You are not to leave their sight until after the *Yamohmi*, after which you may go where you please."

Taloa translated, noting Robert's mixture of confusion and disappointment. She turned toward Apesa. "Honorable Apesa," she said, first in their language and then in English, "May I speak?"

"Yes, you may."

"Anli Basha and I have promised to travel to the *Yamohmi* for an important language council there."

"Then you will take the white man with you. He will make for you an impressive exhibit. But do not let him out of your sight until after the contest," Apesa declared, rising to stand with an air of conclusion. "This is my judgment." He and the watchers walked out.

Taloa finished translating, watching Robert slump down to sit on the bench, lean wearily on his knees, and stare blankly at the floor, struggling to comprehend.

HOLISSO TOKLO

BOOK TWO

CHAPTER THIRTEEN

POWER

Y OSHOBA'S EMPIRE GLITTERED BEFORE HIS EYES. A MORNING thundershower had drawn him to the portal of his palace, and he had just watched a lightning bolt strike near the great river. He felt like he stood even with the gods. He could see the northern tribes' long canoes and colorful river craft clogging the tributary creek into Tochina. The moveable villages of thousands of diverse peoples stretched toward the river and as far north as he could see.

Two young women lay asleep in his bed, but he knew it meant death to the powerful to surrender to luxury and rest on achievements. I must advance, he thought, turning east to watch the bright orange sun break the horizon beneath lifting clouds.

He stood atop the palace mound of the Allahashi, the greatest structure in the northern world. Not since his great-grandfather came up from the south, pressing his campaign to convert the simple Nayimmi people to sun worship, had anyone dared to challenge the authority of the Great Suns, the rulers of the Allahashi. Since then the Nayimmis' foolish Creator religion had been all but erased, and great progress propelled their civilization.

Illustration on previous pages by Michael Freeland, courtesy Chickasaw Council House Museum

Yet ahead lay what promised to be the grandest of days in a grand, modern history. The Allahashi would dedicate the largest and most modern athletic structure of all time. Delegates from everywhere in the territory would come for the *Yamohmi*, and all would acknowledge him as the greatest leader the world ever knew.

"Did you miss me?" Ilaponla asked, silently wrapping her arms around his waist from behind.

He felt instant irritation at being jarred from his royal reverie by her uninvited entrance and impudent, stealthy approach. He gripped her wrists to remove her embrace. She held in her hand a prairie rose with a long, ragged stem. "No," he replied flatly.

"You mean I'm not as good as those children you sleep with, Rising Sun? I thought you preferred the touch of understanding in your dreams," she cooed, sliding around to face him, holding the rose to her lips.

Her radiance while she stood in her nightdress with the first rays of the sun firing silhouettes through her breeze-blown hair all but diverted him. Ilaponla was well past the blush of youth, yet her beauty was rivaled only by her cunning. "I prefer untrained passion to the yawn of mastery, if that's what you mean, squash blossom," he replied without smiling. "Is the morning meal ordered?" he asked, changing the subject.

"Yes, of course. They will have it for you and the headmen when the sun's at a sixth," she answered. "Do I get my reward for good service?" she asked.

"Serving the Great Sun is reward enough. Go. Make sure the meal is right. I want it on the east terrace. Everything must be fresh. The day of supreme glory approaches. Go!" he repeated, as forcefully as he could manage. He felt difficulty at resisting her, and it irked him.

"Yes, my master," she hissed through her teeth, but took his hand to puncture his thumb with a thorn from the rose stem. A trickle of blood sprang from the tiny wound. He neither flinched nor took his eyes off hers.

"Go," he said calmly.

She turned and walked away slowly. His eyes followed the sway of her lean hips until she dropped the rose, and his mind returned to the plans he laid so long ago.

Yoshoba's advisors assembled punctually for the morning meal under the arbor on the terrace on the sunrise side of the palace mound. The air felt fresh after the lightning storm, and the blue-skied morning fit the occasion to put finishing touches on Yoshoba's plans for the *Yamohmi*, the "fashionable event."

"How is the team shaping up, Oppoloka?" Yoshoba asked his star player.

"Quite well, my master," Oppoloka answered with the brisk, hefty voice of an athlete. "All but a few players have arrived, and our workouts have been spirited. The Chepoussa and Chinkoa are not here yet, but they are nearby."

Yoshoba saw how the morning sun highlighted the contours of the superb stickball player's muscles. Oppoloka was not tall, but proved himself the fastest known in the domain, and all the Allahashi agreed his agility and strength made him perhaps the best athlete in the world. "Are you prepared to take out Iyapi and Shakba of the Yukpans?" Yoshoba asked with a grin.

"We are prepared to take on the best the Yukpans have to offer, Great Sun," Oppoloka replied with an athlete's sportsmanlike confidence.

Yoshoba regarded such confidence as arrogance, even if characteristic of athletes, and that, besides their popularity, irritated him. Still, he knew he could not afford to offend their temperaments, at least for the time. He handed Oppoloka a plum with a smile. "Of course, my son," he said. "Just remember that great wealth will change hands with the results of the *Yamohmi*. You will bring honor or shame to thousands."

"The victory will be ours, my Sun," Oppoloka said, repeating his confidence.

"Are the rooms ready for our guests, Anunka?" Yoshoba asked after he had raised his cup and a bowl of food to the sun.

She began to answer in a soft voice.

"Speak up," he prompted, sharply.

Anunka finished her bite of fish with a hard swallow and touched her lips with her fingertips. "Yes, Great Sun," she said after clearing her throat, "they are outfitted comfortably on the honor mound with fresh mats, bedding, water, and food, and the servants have been taught what to do to make our guests comfortable." As if on cue, a young servant coming around the group offered Anunka a choice from a platter of boiled eggs, plums, grapes, strawberries, and smoked fish.

Anunka was efficient, but forgetful. She was Yoshoba's mother's youngest sister. "Don't forget fresh cut flowers, tomorrow morning," he reminded her.

"Yes, master, anything else?"

He ignored her question and turned to Toksali, the stadium architect and workforce taskmaster. "Is the arena ready?" he asked.

"Everything is on time, Great Sun," he replied. "The playing field is in perfect condition. The grass is beautiful and thick. The spectator mounds are cut and prepared. The new wells are dug and settled. The boys who will carry water to the spectators are trained and practiced. The food merchants are ready. Let us look," he said.

All stood to walk to the edge of the terrace, from where the arena and facilities lay in view. The panorama would have pleased rulers of any age. The sprawling, walled city with its sacred mounds, public plaza, ball fields, and ceremonial sites, and its surrounding community of houses, merchants' buildings and huts, ponds, pens, granaries, and crop fields looked impressive enough, but the new mounded arena was its crowning achievement, Yoshoba thought—the zenith of an old civilization grown rich. And sustaining this great city, he reflected with pride like that of an owner of a precious object, was the great river— the river beyond all ages.

"We are looking at the greatest city north of Tajin, my friends," Toksali proclaimed, arms outstretched. "I believe we have thought of everything. The public privy huts are finished and supplied with straw, and the crews are well taught. The campgrounds at the *Misha Sipokni* and at *Bokoshe Quexa* are well provisioned and working well."

"How many people do we expect?" Yoshoba asked.

"The measurers and wordmasters have been counting as many ways as they can," Toksali continued. "They say we might see as many as sixty thousand from the Allahashi Confederacy and as many as forty thousand from the Yukpan Confederacy and others. Most of the tribes have arrived, since the *Yamohmi* comes during the green corn celebration."

"People are here from the *Taakchaka Bokota* in the far northeast," Holabi, the high priest, interjected, "and great numbers have arrived over the past fortnight from the river of the big canoes. Some have come from the great western mountains. They bring fine furs, wood and horn carvings, beadwork, precious stones, and shiny metal for trade."

Their report filled Yoshoba with pride. His plan, which he began twelve winters ago, was about to pay off. "Excellent!" he said. "I hear excellent news. This is how an empire is built, my friends. We will not need to conquer. Others will join us voluntarily, and we will be the richest people in the world. What about the ceremony, Holabi? Have all arrangements been made?"

"Everything is ready," Holabi reported, his voice beginning to meander with reluctance, "except the crown, Great Sun."

Fire shot through Yoshoba's ears. This can't be, he thought. "You are telling me the most important part of my costume is not ready? What do you mean?" he fumed.

"I mean it—it never arrived, Great Sun," the priest stammered.

"Why not? We sent our best runners a moon ago. I cannot believe this," he snarled, grinding his teeth.

"One runner returned yesterday with his ears cut off. I tried to tell you not to trust the Aranamas, Yoshoba."

"But the meeting was set up by a trusted Aranama—what was his name, again?"

"Effran," Holabi said.

"Yes, Effran—he's helped us trade with the Aranamas for twenty winters or more. You mean the long-eared skunk betrayed us?" he asked, eyes wide with shock.

"I'm afraid so, Great Sun. It seems he can be trusted with corn and peyote, but not with gold from the south," Holabi replied, still abashed.

"Ears cut off?" Yoshoba muttered, catching up with that detail.

"It looks like they wished not only to rob us, but to insult us, too. They could have killed him, like the others, but they wanted us to know they got the best of us," Holabi explained, glumly.

Yoshoba long ago grew weary of betrayals like that, even while he conceded they seemed to accompany such power as his. The more he accumulated, the more people seemed to steal from him and betray him. "They will be punished," he declared matter-of-factly. "They cannot always hide in darkness; they cannot escape the path of the Sun. The dogs." He gathered his wits. The Aranamas' insult would not be forgotten, but revenge would have to wait. Surely none would show up at the *Yamohmi*. If they did, they only would make his revenge sooner and sweeter.

"Let us walk down to the field," Yoshoba said, shaking off frustration. He clapped his hands and young servants came with large bowls of water and towels so the guests could wash before descending off the terrace toward the mound rim, where he stopped to survey the bustle one hundred forty feet below in Tochina, the great city continuously inhabited for at least seven hundred winters. New buildings still went up, as well as huts, pavilions, and arbors erected by scores of merchants, gamblers, and others arriving for the *Yamohmi*. It exhilarated him to be at the center of so much human desire.

They descended one of the four long stairways down the sloped sides of the flat-topped earthen pyramid, palace bodyguards falling in before and behind them. A great throng of people already clogged the merchants' huts and dusty streets.

Yoshoba's personal guards were trained to observe every movement the Sun made, but to stay away while he was at home. They were elite warriors, empowered with full legal right to kill anyone they deemed a possible threat to the Great Sun. They carried bows, arrows, long knives, and short throwing spears, the most deadly of their kind. They wore shiny metal armbands, metal belts, and sleeveless vests of tightly connected, small-diameter oak limbs to protect their chests and abdomens. Yoshoba felt secure among them, for they were greatly feared.

"Shatanni," he turned to address his highest military aide and oldest friend, "I have special arrangements to discuss with you." Shatanni was most feared among all palace and temple guards. He was captain and supreme leader of the Warrior Society that included, by Yoshoba's decree, every fighting man in the Allahashi territory, and he ranked second in command only to Yoshoba. Unlike other nations, Yoshoba's society relegated judges to minor positions in the administration of local affairs. No priest, no house master, no elder outranked Shatanni—not even Holabi, who also could claim a great deal of power.

The two great men of the Allahashi inherited their positions. Yoshoba was the third-generation Great Sun, and Shatanni the third-generation captain of the temple warriors and his ruler's first cousin. They grew up together, scuffling and fighting as boys, and trained in athletics, hunting, and weapons together, always close friends, but also rivals. Both fell in love with Ilaponla as teenagers. Yoshoba won out.

Yoshoba indicated he wished to discuss finer details of the *Yamohmi* with Shatanni, who had returned from meetings with commanders in outlying regions as part of his charge to keep lines of communication open and military agreements alive with other towns and tribes, particularly those farthest from Tochina.

"Shatanni, you and I will go look at the vaults under the arena mounds," Yoshoba announced, sounding casual about it. They parted from the others to walk toward the arena and through the practice plaza, where athletes practiced their game.

The players buzzed to see the approaching Sun and his guards, and their pace accelerated. They practiced inside a great circle of forty-eight poles, set nine paces from each other to make a field of one hundred and thirty-five paces in diameter. Half the athletes stood at poles on the perimeter and the other half evenly circled a pole at the circle's center. The practice was to throw and catch the *towa*, the ball, with their *kapocha*, sticks, and come as close as possible to the poles. The *kapocha* were flat sticks with leather thong pockets in their looped ends.

The object of the game of *toli*, stickball, was to advance the ball and cause it to strike the goal post at the opponent's end of the field. This was usually accomplished by strategically passing the ball on the run. The most spectacular scores were long-distance throws. The great *Yamohmi* would be a stickball game with a hundred players on each team, competing on a field almost a mile long and a half-mile wide.

"Remember the championship against the Chikashas in the eighth winter after the great flood, Yosh?" Shatanni asked while they passed the practice field.

"I do. They still talk about your pass at the end of the game and my score," Yoshoba replied with a wistful grin. "They say my scoring throw was a hundred paces and your pass was nearly a flight. I am pleased to hear how time improves our heroics." Yoshoba also remembered that was the same season he wed Ilaponla, but did not mention that.

They came to the vaults, where Yoshoba's guards checked inside before letting them in and stayed outside so they could speak alone. The two entered under the west-side spectator mounds, gently sloping earthworks about forty feet high and flat on top. The morning sun shed some light inside and faded the farther they walked.

"Very clever," Shatanni remarked, surveying the large room and its vaulted ceiling supported by heavy cedar timbers. As far as the public was concerned, the vaults were built to accommodate burials for Tochina's growing population, ready to hold several generations of prepared dead before the earth would reclaim the timbers and the mounds would settle into rounder shapes, ready for finished contouring. So the people thought.

"What did the other commanders think of my plan?" Yoshoba asked Shatanni after they moved out of the guards' hearing.

"You know I don't like your plan, Yoshoba," Shatanni said.

Yoshoba bristled. "Whether you like my plan is not my question. Did you take it up with the other war leaders?" Yoshoba demanded, squeezing his stone scepter, the Allahashi symbol of royalty he carried.

"Of course, I told them, as best I could," Shatanni replied, glowering with displeasure.

Yoshoba's neck stiffened. "As best you could? As best you could?

What in the name of *Hashi* does that mean? Did you tell them or not?"

"I told those nearest to us every detail. Those who live farther out or closer to the Yukpans are not as strongly in favor of our alliance as the ones closer to Tochina," he explained.

The Great Sun's blood began to boil. "Since when are you charged with making political interpretations of my rulings and my plans? You idiot. I never should have trusted an important diplomatic mission to a warrior."

"You're the idiot, Yoshoba," Shatanni barked back. "You're not satisfied with anything. You never have enough wealth or enough power!"

Yoshoba grabbed Shatanni's mantle, whipped a slender stone dagger from his belt, and held it to the warrior's throat. "I should kill you like a tick, Shatanni, for your insolence."

Shatanni's hand rose reflexively for his own knife, but stopped. "Go ahead, Great Sun, and see how far your plan advances," he whispered, without so much as a quiver in his voice.

Yoshoba's anger withered, and he released Shatanni in chilly realization of his disadvantage. His whole grand plan depended on the military leader's intelligence network. He needed to change his tone. "I could have you publicly executed for naming me disrespectfully."

"Your power is supreme, Great Sun," Shatanni murmured, sounding more resentful than deferent. He jerked his mantle back into place and stepped away, turning his back.

"I have conceived every detail of the plan and polished it for many winters, my old friend," Yoshoba said, trying to repair the damage. "I am sorry to lash out at you, but you must understand my frustration."

Shatanni did not respond.

"The Chahta, the Chikasha, the Chalakki, the Mabila, the Alabamha, the Mvskoke, and the other Yukpans have controlled the southern and eastern trade routes for as long as anybody can remember," he said, still trembling, trying to marshal his calm. "Their damned religion and their old customs are an eternal pain. Our empire has expanded in every direction, but we are stifled by the Yukpan Confederacy."

Shatanni turned to plead with him. "If our empire is not big enough, then let us expand it to the west, Yoshoba. There are lands and peoples we barely know on the other side of the deserts and the big mountains. We can trade with them—or fight with them, if it is blood you crave."

Such words irritated Yoshoba. How many times had he heard them from the foolish and shortsighted? "If we expand to the west, we will be weak to the east, and the Yukpans will see the advantage and conquer us. Don't you see? We have no choice. We need to strike first and take the advantage."

"I see that you have made yourself believe that, my friend."

"It is the truth. My father saw it and complained about it, but he never did anything about it."

"Your father was a wise man, bear cub. He was the one who established the Allahashi," Shatanni pointed out.

"My father was an old woman when it came to big decisions," Yoshoba retorted coldly. "So tell me, what did the others have to say? How about Makali to the far north? He has no love for the Yukpans."

"He, of course, liked your plan. His elders still talk with venom of how they were driven from their homes by the Chikasha."

"Good! Good! What about Ashwa and the Ojibwe?" Yoshoba asked, foreknowing the probable answer.

"I was general in my questioning of him, just to feel him out on the general idea of going to war," Shatanni reported. "Ashwa, as you might suspect, is comfortable in his fields and wants no quarrel with the Yukpans."

Yoshoba panicked at a thought and asked, "You did not contact the Lenape, did you? I did not warn you, did I?"

"No, you did not, and yes, I did contact them. I had a very cordial visit with Hofka-Hili."

"Oh no. You fool. I do not suppose he told you that one of his daughters just married the son of a Yazoo holy man."

"Well, no, he did not."

"Of course, he did not," Yoshoba mourned pathetically, wringing his hands. "He's an old fox and you are a goose," he complained, pacing and kicking the dirt.

This time Shatanni bristled and jumped toward Yoshoba. "Listen, Yoshoba, we have known each other a long time, and I'm running out of patience with your insults."

"Your head is solid stone," Yoshoba countered, too distraught to react to him. "How long must a man be a warrior before he learns to recognize an enemy?"

Before Shatanni could speak again, they were interrupted by a call from the doorway. "Great Sun!" It was one of the guards. "Holabi says the delegates are assembled to practice the dedication ceremony. Can you come now?"

"I am coming," Yoshoba shouted out through the vault entrance. He turned once more to Shatanni. "We will take this up further after the ceremony practice. We have too much at stake to permit any stupid mistakes. Come, you will be at my right hand." He turned toward the doors.

Shatanni fell in step. "There will be no mistakes, *Yolcatl Mictiz*," he said, gravely addressing Yoshoba by his childhood nickname in the old language. The nickname meant "skunk killer," taken from a humorous hunting incident they shared as boys.

They stepped out of the darkened enclosure, shielding their eyes from direct mid-morning light. Yoshoba worried that something might spoil his finest hour. But if he could not trust Shatanni, whom could he trust? Certainly not Holabi, he thought. He still showed signs of sympathy with the foolish religion of his forefathers.

It was his grandfather's mistake to allow the same old priest class to continue in the new, true worship of the sun god, the giver of life. Their childish superstitions, Yoshoba felt certain, were the enemies of true justice—a justice that would allow superior minds like his to craft a culture of enlightenment and progress.

He filled his chest with the cool air and admired the playing field around him, recalling with prideful satisfaction how much of the labor to build the spectator arena mounds was accomplished during the past several seasons using slaves taken from the west. They might have gotten a few Aranamas, he mused.

The slaves were always thoroughly interrogated, at his order, and told their families would be killed if they tried to escape. None did, although a few died under the hardships of labor. A brilliant working plan, flawlessly carried out, he judged. He looked forward to using Yukpan slaves the same way.

He started toward the temple mound, confident of his destiny.

CHAPTER FOURTEEN

JEALOUSY

TALOA STARED IN SILENT SHOCK, WATCHING APESA AND HIS *apiisachi* vanish through the doorway.

Robert sat confounded. Just as he thought he might be headed home, chopped down. Going to the *Yamohmi?* What was a *Yamohmi?*

"Where is this ... *Yamohmi?*" Robert asked her, sounding as stunned as he felt.

"About fifteen days' walk to the west," she replied, as if by reflex. "I've got to talk to Apesa," she blurted and ran out. Iskifa followed her.

Alone and at a loss, Robert could hardly muster the will to stand. Here he sat on a man-made, earthen pyramid in a river bottom on an island or a continent, among humans completely foreign to any he could imagine before. The weight of his loneliness sank in his mind and body to mix with fear, confusion, and pain. Competing with his anguish, at least, was a bit of relief at having escaped the threat of death by whatever barbaric means they used here. But, after all, why should he not have? He had done nothing wrong.

He tried to remember what day it was. Keeping the day and date was something he compelled himself to do aboard the *Manannan* to pre-

serve sanity. It disturbed him to lose track. So much had happened—
the shipwreck, Iskifa's doctoring, burying McLaren, rescuing Lizbeth,
the stick fighter, Chilantak's town, the wordmaster's mound, amazing
things in between, and now this. He counted the days and nights.
"Tuesday, the eighteenth instance of Junius, 1399," he whispered.

On the brighter side, Iskifa—his friend, Iskifa—argued well for
him. But Apesa's verdict—go to the *Yamohmi* or die, through chal-
lenging country among people who might kill him at any moment for
any reason, as the fat judge very nearly did. "I don't know if I'll ever get
home," Robert murmured. He rose to shuffle to the doorway and look
across the commons at the enormous mound with its grand meeting
lodge and the lesser, yet still impressive, *minko*'s mound on its flank. It
almost took his breath away to see them again. From this high point,
the mounds and their picturesque buildings blended so beautifully
with the rest of the city around them and the green crops and lush
forests beyond the immense wall of tall, thick timbers.

He turned to another doorway on the opposite side, his fascination with such marvelous sights obscuring his gloom for the moment.
He watched the small, fleet-looking boats, the river craft, and larger
vessels outfitted for freight and passengers. People, some in colorful
clothing and strange, feathered hats, looked busy in every part of the
city. As soon as he focused enough to discern the business of one interesting scene, another would attract his eye.

Unbidden memories entered to parade through his thoughts, of his
astounding experiences walking up the river valley, seeing the long-
boat natives, the big crops in the wide valley, and the monstrous-head-
ed cattle in the box canyon. He shuddered to recall how he offended
Chilantak. His thoughts slipped back through the encounter with the
stick fighter, the insect song and dance, and before that, digging Mc-
Laren's grave and rescuing Lizbeth from the wolves. He had to check
himself before his mind could slide back into the torment of the shipwreck. Remembering the endless voyage and the whirlwind were almost more than he could bear. The nine days he spent on these shores
seemed more like nine lifetimes.

Lizbeth, still tied to a column nearby, bawled for his attention. He turned to her, his strange friend and all that was left of his previous life. He had been delivered to a strange purgatory with the king's goat. God must have a twisted sense of humor, Robert thought. He got up to pet her, wondered whether he should take her out for some grass, but decided instead to take a moment to think, to plan. He fetched a dipper of water for himself, then for her, and began to pace, thinking.

"What are me choices?" he asked himself aloud. "I can try to escape and find the boat builders," he mumbled, glancing out the doorway at the river craft, "but none can speak me language, except Taloa, and I have nothin' to trade, except labor. And it will be hard to trade if I don't speak their language or they don't speak mine. So that's not a very good choice."

Hearing himself lapse from the proper English of trade into his homier Scottish brogue nudged his confidence. "Maybe I could get Iskifa to pay for a boat and outfit it for ocean-going," he said. "But, even if he could afford it, why would he want to send his money across the ocean?

"That won't work," he decided.

He let himself think what was unbearable to admit a few minutes earlier. "Lizbeth," he said to her, "If Taloa and Iskifa can't change their minds, I'm just going to have to make the best of it. She can translate for me and probably teach me their language. I'll just have to get me a boat the way I got the last one, by working me tail off."

"What did you say?" Taloa asked from the door.

Her entrance surprised him, but he was glad to see her. "Nothin' really," he replied.

"Apesa would not change his mind, Master Wil...er, Robert," she explained, weary from what must have been futile negotiation. "You must be kept in the custody of the wordmaster house, and the wordmaster house must present a report to the general council of wordmasters at the *Yamohmi*."

Robert slapped his forehead and tried to keep his voice down despite his frustration against such authoritarian mindlessness. "I can't go so far inland; it's several hundred miles isn't it?"

"Yes," she answered pointedly, showing frayed nerves, "but can you not see you have no choice?"

"I kin see I need to stay near the coast and find some boat builders or I'll never make it back home."

"You have no choice Master Williams," she insisted. "Homesickness is better than death. If you defy Apesa's order, you will most probably be killed."

Robert peered at her, absorbing what she said and remembering his own conclusions. "If that's the way it has to be," he said, "then, so be it." Within himself, he thought, I'm a ship's captain. All I can do is look for opportunities to build or buy a boat. These people are generous. I will get to know them, and perhaps they will help me.

"I know you are disappointed," she conceded. "I saw the way your eyes glowed when the talk about the boat builders came up. It must be terrible to be so far from home. Master Bannet talked about that often," she added.

"At least I'm alive. And that matter was in doubt a little while ago."

"Come along, now. Let's take your—how do you say?—*goat* back to the wordmaster house."

Robert untied Lizbeth to follow Taloa down the impressive stairway. At its bottom spread a crowd of at least a hundred gathered, he presumed, to slake their curiosities about the white man and his goat.

Robert, Lizbeth, and Taloa soon sank into the curious throng. "You are quite an attraction, Robert," she remarked while their eyes briefly met among the people who touched and laughed, some offering small tokens and gifts.

"Never thought a body could get famous by jist bein' different," Robert muttered, not altogether comfortable.

Taloa smiled as a little girl tugged her away to show her something. "It's on the way to Anli's mound. I won't lose you," Taloa called back to him.

"Jolly good," Robert said, at last opening himself to allow the crowd's relentless friendliness and enthusiasm to buoy his spirit. "Jolly good."

Iskifa and Anli Basha sat in conversation, heads nodding, palms opening and closing, when Robert and Taloa entered the wordmaster house. Taloa told him they argued about the *Yamohmi*, that Iskifa felt sure it would be a mistake to have anything to do with the Allahashi and their ways, while Anli took the opposite position, insisting Tochina was an ancient center of knowledge, and the vast exchange of wisdom found there would benefit all Yukpans.

Taloa made a dinner and set it outside under an arbor overgrown by a prolific vine. Robert realized he was famished. The jerked meat, fruit, and strange, nutty-flavored blue bread, like a grainy cake, tasted delicious. They enjoyed a sweet berry wine, truly satisfying after such a trying midday.

The tumult of city life seemed to Robert to recede below the plateau of the pyramid while they sat quietly. A breeze played with a few loose locks on Taloa's forehead. Robert looked past her to the east, to consider the playing field in the center of the commons. He thought it might be planted with a different kind of grass, from elsewhere. Athletes sprang about upon it, some running, some throwing small balls to each other with strange-looking sticks, and others in the center of the demesne, heaving thin spears at unseen targets.

Iskifa began to tell a story about Anoli, the great teacher and namesake of the walled city, born almost a thousand winters before. Robert relaxed into the musical harmony of his mellow voice, accompanied in rhythm by Taloa's softer background echo of translation.

"The man was irrevocable," Iskifa began, "in the *Hina Aalhpisa*, the Forward Path." He paused, holding his hand before him as if pointing with all his fingers in the vertical plane, looking out over the city. "His life is an example to us all. He was a musician, an athlete, a scholar, and a teacher, who revered *Aba Binnili*, creator of all, with his every waking breath. He lived on the *Chakchak Bok*, the Woodpecker River, in a house of timber."

He paused to withdraw something from his pouch and opened his hand to show everyone a few seeds. "He cultivated some goose foot plants and some roots for food, as well as an early variety of *tanchi*." Taloa quietly reminded Robert that *tanchi*, corn, was the stalky plant from which they took edible grain.

"He and his wife hunted and fished and lived a simple life, outside of Chakchak Town, which stands today. It was in the early days of Chakchak. It is said he and his wife elected to have no children so they could devote themselves to *Aba Binnili* and to helping other people.

"They were Yamasee people and lived at peace with their neighbors. It was a prosperous time, and trade was common all over the eastern and western worlds. People from the west had forsaken *Aba Binnili* some generations before and worshipped other gods, even material things. They came to think of the old ways as foolish and not modern enough." He paused again to accept a pass of the pipe from Anli, who lit it after Iskifa began. "They became friends with the Hokays, who no longer live," he continued. "The Hokays learned a new religion from people far south and west. Remember the little figurine I pointed out on Anli's shelf when we got back here after the trial?" he asked Taloa.

"Yes, quite well," she replied. "The funny little fat man with his hands raised."

"That is the Hokays' god, Etzaal, the god of mirth and happiness. They prayed to that idol for happiness. The Hokays were lazy people. That's why they are gone."

While Taloa translated, Robert's mind followed his eyes to wander and spied crowds beginning to gather around the playing field, setting up shades, and casting down mats and seating to face the field.

"Anoli again and again warned the Yamasee not to join with the Hokays, but the people did not listen," Iskifa continued, Taloa echoing close behind. "The Hokays had loose morals and thought it all right to raid, rob, and murder people for their own gain. As it turns out, the Hokays befriended the Yamasee for only one reason—to murder and rob them. The Hokays attacked Chakchak Town and burned it to the ground. They made slaves of the surviving Yamasee and made them dig up the graves of their ancestors and rob the goods. They desecrated their mounds and left their graves open.

"Some Yamasee escaped. They fled south under the leadership of Anoli and hid until the Hokays stopped looking for them. Eight winters later, Anoli, a teacher turned warrior, led the Yamasee against the

Hokays' main town and captured it. They freed the Yamasee slaves, executed the Hokay leaders, adopted their children, scattered the surviving adults, and made sure they stayed scattered, until their tribe was no more. Anoli and the others rebuilt Chakchak and began the Yukpan Confederacy, and so it has been ever since."

Taloa seemed absorbed by his story, Robert noticed. He watched her while she translated, and how she focused on Iskifa, her dark eyes twinkling, and her combination of innocence and adult femininity, all collecting into a volatile effect on his emotions. He had to look away, often. The more he watched her, the more the fondness and warmth spread over him.

"Why do you tell us this story, Master Iskifa?" she asked, in both languages.

"Because I believe it is all happening again," Iskifa replied, his voice soft.

She began what sounded like a disagreement with Iskifa on the subject, in their language, in such an abrupt and intense manner their conversation seemed to Robert to take on the character of a squabble, if a quiet and respectful one. He took the moment to stand quietly and excuse himself in the name of proper discretion and, mostly, to take a survey from their vantage. He spotted the clear path cut through the trees to the big river to the south, the same one they walked into Anoli, and once again he thrilled at the sight of a few large boats and dozens of smaller ones, landing and tying up along the banks. Another small flotilla navigated a tributary creek to the west. They were all riverboats, however, and even if oddly built, not altogether different from the river craft of Scotland and England. Still, he could not resist speculating that if they could build riverboats, then they also could build seagoing vessels, surely.

Iskifa ended his talk with Taloa—without an air of satisfaction from either, Robert noticed—got up and walked slowly away along the edge of the mound. Taloa sat thinking before she turned to Robert. "Pardon me for ignoring you, Robert, but I was carried away into Master Iskifa's talk."

"It looked like you were in a stooshie with him, or with what he was sayin'," he observed.

"A 'stooshie?'"

"A fuss or an argument."

"I think you are right," she replied, looking regretful. "He says he sees dangerous parallels between the Anoli story and our own."

"So he thinks the Yukpans are in danger of being taken over?"

"Yes, by the Allahashi."

"But what do you think?"

"I am confused. I find I am torn between his opinion and the opinion of Master Anli Basha," she said. "I, of course, must form my own thoughts, but these two wise men have never disagreed on anything so important before, that I can remember."

"Does it matter which one is right—I mean, now?" Robert asked, trying to be sympathetic to her divided loyalty, touched by her youthful affection for her two teachers.

A strand of hair pulled loose from her hair band in the breeze. She pushed it out of her eyes while she answered. "It matters a great deal if Iskifa is correct. If he is correct, this fashionable event, this *Yamohmi*, could be the beginning of the end for the confederacy."

"He thinks it could be that serious?"

"Yes. Certainly, he says, our society is more complex now. As our needs for trade and exchange with other peoples increase, so does the importance of the wordmaster's job, to understand and respect the languages and beliefs of other people." She paused, seeming to contemplate what Iskifa said.

"Please, go on," Robert said, his interest aroused.

She swiped the loose strand of hair again. "But the Allahashi, he says, worship strange gods and have given up morality for gain. He says they care more about shiny metal, trinkets, and their own ideas than about their families and other people."

"And how does that make any difference to Yukpans?" Robert asked.

"It matters, Master Iskifa says, because men concerned with personal gain and personal glory, like Yoshoba, are soulless vessels, eternally empty. So they constantly seek to be filled." She paused again, the afternoon sun glowing around her shining black hair.

"And?"

"And the only thing that stands between the Allahashi and conquest of the entire northern world is the Yukpan Confederacy. He thinks they want to devour us, and that the *Yamohmi* might be the bait he uses against us."

"So, you are afraid?"

"No," she answered, if not persuasively, Robert noticed. "I think he is probably wrong. He is so backward in his thinking about certain things. He is a joy when it comes to music and artistic things, but he is very reserved about mixing with other peoples. He respects them and wants to know them, but he always draws a line."

"Anli is different?"

"Master Anli is more in tune with civilization. He appreciates the excitement of diversity and trade in the larger towns and cities. He thinks there is much to be gained by social gatherings like the *Yamohmi*. He says they advance the arts of humankind." She seemed to relax while presenting Anli's views. The breeze fanned that strand of hair again. She lifted her hands to untie her hair band and re-gathered her wandering locks.

Robert felt a sense of increase for having her as a friend. "Let us not worry too much about it," he counseled, offering a smile.

"Worry is bad for the digestion," she agreed. "Master Iskifa says that, too."

She looked at him and stood to walk toward the rim of the word-master mound, where she looked down upon the throng collecting around the field. At once she broke her contemplative mood and came to attention to scan the field intently. She clasped her hands and jumped, once, like an excited girl. "The best athletes are here. This will be a great game," she gushed, her gaze fast upon the field.

Her burst of enthusiasm surprised Robert, who had come to think fondly of her as studious and reserved. Worse, he sensed something more than the love of a game in her—something he suspected might be deeper and more personal. He walked up beside her and tried to follow her eyes. "What's so interesting?"

She did not answer, still searching. He felt as uneasy in her attention's absence as he had felt comforted within its glow.

The wordmasters joined them to look on the crowd below which, Robert guessed, had to number several thousand. Canopies and colorful clothing glittered in the sun, and merchant huts popped up behind the crowds.

Lizbeth bleated from her grazing at an arbor post nearer the west rim of the mound. Robert saw she would need milking soon.

"Have you seen Iyapi?" Anli asked Taloa in halting English, his eyes darting between her and Robert, apparently taking pains not to exclude him.

"Yes, he is on the field," she replied, her enthusiasm infusing her English with a much more natural flow.

Jealousy at once stung and deflated Robert. Taloa has a boyfriend, he thought, grieving inwardly. Or perhaps she only admires one of the ballplayers, he rationalized, just as quickly. He waved a hand in front of her eyes to draw her attention to himself. "Who is Iyapi?" he asked.

"Just maybe the best stickball player in the world," Taloa answered, annoyed. "He lives in our hometown of Chunuli, and people there say he is the best ever from our town. I have not seen him for three winters."

Robert felt instant embarrassment at behaving on impulse like a jealous teenager, and that with a girl he barely knew. Besides, as he reminded himself, he was betrothed. Still, at the moment, he felt more bewildered by the confusion he felt about women than the strange spectacle below. He took a step down the slope, intending to defy her custom of avoiding eye contact. "What's so special about him?"

She folded her arms. "'What's so special about him?'" she mimicked, even capturing his accent with a stinging precision. "Everyone knows Iyapi and Shakba are the best *toli* players in the whole Yukpan Confederacy and maybe in the whole world. They are our best chance to beat the Allahashi."

Robert felt shocked. The edge on her words bit at him, and he lost ground at controlling his emerging feelings of affection, now clouded by unwelcome jealousy. He frowned and folded his arms. "What's so blasted special about *toli*?" he retorted.

Her face radiated amazement at such ignorance, but she did not answer, again craning to look past him.

He cringed. He knew he made a fool of himself, but his dander was up. A ship's captain, he thought, can never be thrown over, especially by the likes of a ball player. He gestured toward the field and started to speak, but the loud blare of a conch shell horn, blown by a man standing in the middle of the grass, interrupted. All the players moved toward the man. It seemed the game was about to begin.

Robert stewed, coming to believe his foolish decision to sail west after the gale would become one he would eternally regret. He felt trapped in a world unknown, and now his inner voice condemned him in irksome ways he hadn't imagined before, all to do with women, mingling with his brother's grating doubt about his fidelity. He sat on the bench, doing his best to seem dignified and detached as a captain should, pretending to watch the events unfolding below with propriety and objectivity, vowing to keep silence from there on.

By their costumes, he figured there to be two teams, each forming a line to face the other. They laid their playing sticks between them while the man calling them to action spoke, almost loudly enough to be heard all the way to the top of their mound, many yards west and perhaps a hundred feet above. Loud whoops burst from the players, and they huddled around the game master, save one from each team who retreated toward goals at either end of the field. The master tossed up a ball not as big as a man's palm, and a furious, noisy scramble erupted as players competed to get and control it. Soon a player emerged and flung the ball two-handed with his sticks, toward the nearest goal.

"Iyapi, Iyapi," Taloa squealed, jumping up and down.

The sound stung Robert. "Iyapi, Iyapi, indeed," he mumbled. Still, he watched the field where the thundering men, stampeding and whirling back and forth like herds of deer, amazed him. There must have been fifty to each team. The crowd cheered, moaned, fell quiet, and cheered again. Anytime one team neared the other's goal, a low roar seemed to boil up from them.

He had to admit he had never seen anything on such a scale before, but could not resist his disquiet. He turned to watch her, a raven-haired beauty standing on tiptoe at the rim of the mound. "What's the object of the game?" he asked, raising his voice to be heard, although suspecting he might know the answer, having seen many brutal matches of Irish hurling. No response. A ship's captain expected immediate attention, and her silence annoyed him. He leaned toward her. "Taloa!" he shouted.

She shot him a quick, aggravated glance. "To carry the ball and touch the goal, or to throw the ball and hit the goal," she replied. She clasped her hands and yelled, "Iyapi! Shakba!"

Robert turned to see one player break free from a gang of pursuers and race downfield. Just as another sprinted away from a smaller group of defenders at the other end, the man running with the ball let fly with a long throw. The second player leaped amazingly high to snag the ball in the narrow thong of his stick, landed, ran a few steps, leaped again, and fired the ball into the top dead center of the goal post from about thirty paces away. The crowd on the far side of the field cheered madly, jumping, dancing, embracing each other, and throwing things into the air. Taloa and Iskifa also jumped in a little circle, embracing each other and laughing and cheering, "*Okaamahli! Okaamahli*!"

Robert watched it all, feeling wonder at the customs of this new world mix with a detachment chilled by his new inner conflict over Taloa. Below him the players rested for but a moment, reassembled at midfield, and the melee resumed. Play continued for hours until the team Iskifa and Taloa cheered for finished with the victory, or so it seemed to Robert.

Taloa glowed more radiantly than ever, exclaiming at length in her native tongue until, in apparent and perhaps regretful afterthought, she turned to Robert. Robert knew he looked pitiful. He felt lost, understanding little. Taloa, looking sympathetic, said, "Robert, it is a great day for the South. Iyapi and Shakba were magnificent."

The crowd on the far side echoed the sentiment. "I-ya-pi, Shak-ba, *okaamahli, okuamahli*, I-ya-pi, Shak-ba," they chanted in unison. "I-ya-pi, Shak-ba, *okaamahli, okaamahli*, I-ya-pi, Shak-ba!"

Robert struggled to muster an intelligent question. "What is *okaamahli?*" he asked quietly.

Taloa smiled. "It means, 'the south,'" she replied.

Robert shrugged and smiled wanly. A confusing new sense of loss touched him deeply, and he felt unable to explain it, even to himself.

CHAPTER FIFTEEN

HOSPITALITY

I AM ONTO YOUR PLAN, GREAT SUN," ILAPONLA WHISPERED SLYLY, brushing Yoshoba's arm with her fingertips while she passed behind him near the edge of the palace mound from where he again surveyed his city.

"My plan is well known," he replied, remaining calm despite irritation with her.

"I mean the real plan," she said, coming around to his side and cupping his bicep in her cool hands. "The welcoming festival for the Yukpans," she added.

Yoshoba felt a flare of suspicion and a quick flush of anger. He turned with a glare, clamping her wrist. "That's dog talk, squash blossom. The wind speaking to the dust," he chided tightly. "Or you overestimate the safety of your position," he continued, squeezing her wrist.

"Ow! You're hurting me," she protested.

"What do you think you know of my plan?" he demanded, gritting his teeth.

She twisted, sagging from the pressure on her wrist. "All I know is that you have public meetings with the high council members, and then you have your midnight talks with Holabi and councils with

Shatanni. Then Shatanni leaves for long periods of time and comes straight to you when he returns," she blurted, wincing. "It looks to me like you are setting a trap for the Yukpans."

His eyes brightened with rage. He twisted her wrist upward, crumpling her to her knees. "You know nothing, woman," he hissed, glaring down at her with seething emphasis on each word. "And you have seen nothing."

Her head hung for a moment before she slowly turned her face upward, narrowing her eyes while she spoke. "You are going to slaughter the Yukpans and enslave the ones you don't kill," she said coldly. "And no one will know, unless I expose you."

He grabbed a handful of her hair and pulled her up, releasing her wrist and grasping her neck instead. "And why would you expose me, my queen?"

She did not struggle. In spite of her pain, she looked defiant. "Our law says the Great Sun must serve the good of his people," she said, almost choking. "And it is a headwoman's right and responsibility to remove you from power if you abuse your privileges."

Yoshoba considered killing her on the spot, but quickly dismissed the idea for the turmoil it would certainly cause. Ilaponla was the most powerful woman in the nation, from the most powerful clan. He released her and stretched his hands, palms out, toward her. "You always oppose me, woman," he said, turning his tone toward conciliation. "I keep the best interests of the Allahashi people at heart." He turned to pace back toward the rim of the mound. "If we defeat the Yukpans, especially when they are most vulnerable, it will be a great moment in our history. We can do so with a small payment of our own lives." He waited for a response and heard none. "In the time of the great famine, did they come to the aid of Tochina? No, of course they did not. If we subdue them, the whole northern and western world will join us, and we will never want again for food and trade. We will be strong enough to defend ourselves against or even to attack the Nahuas." He hoped the mention of the powerful and dangerous Nahuas might excite some loyalty in her.

He turned to her. She had composed herself to appear unaffected by his handling or his words. Her beauty painfully moved him, and he felt sorry, however little, for hurting her. He checked his impulse to rant, choosing rather to calmly enumerate his reasons. His pause, he felt, would give her a chance to focus for a moment on the great civilizations to the south. "I am sure you recall that before Effran the Aranama skunk turned on us, he told our traders that tribes on both sides of the canyons river in the far south were in fear of the Nahuas and preparing for war against them. If we don't conquer the Yukpans now, we will always have their pressure to the south and east, and our nation will become stagnant and die. Would you rather in your life-time see the Yukpans become our loyal subjects or see them become allies of the Nahuas?"

Ilaponla's scowl did not leave her face. "Our people don't want war," she countered. "They will not stand for such treachery."

"Will the people be content with our decline?" he asked.

"There are other ways to improve our condition without attacking the neighbors we invite as friends and guests."

Anger flared inside him again, but he kept his composure. "You are weak, woman, and foolish. If you try to reveal my plan and try to spoil my festival, I will declare you a witch. I know things about you, also—convincing things. I can have you gutted at the public altar and burned." His focus upon her grew tight, and his expression sullen.

She glowered back at him. He could not tell if he convinced her to relent. She said nothing.

"Get out of my sight," he ordered.

"Yes, Great Sun," she replied without heat and walked backward many strides before turning to vanish down the mound steps.

He felt frustrated. He questioned whether he should have married her, even if it solidified his position with the Wolf Clan and guaran-teed his rise to power. He could not let this Wolf woman stand in his way. He called to one of the servant boys for his pipe and sat alone un-til the sun set, considering her and her threats. He reasoned she could not successfully expose him and would regard his promises of swift retribution with all the weight he gave them. She also understood the threat of invasion by the ambitious Nahuas was real. Ilaponla could not oppose him and succeed, he concluded, without jeopardizing her own position of power. Still, he cautioned himself to keep watch on her.

His thoughts turned to the final preparations for the *Yamohmi*. He sent a runner to send word to Shatanni and Holabi, who appeared not long after, clad in commoners' garments to disguise their visit. Their positions of authority were such that nighttime councils with the Great Sun might raise suspicions if noticed by others. They did not remove their disguises even after entering the palace.

He confided Ilaponla's crazy threats to them, and they seemed shocked. They discussed precautions, including having her assassinated, but agreed merely to keep an eye on her.

"Have you given the temple warriors their instructions for the *Yamohmi*, Shatanni?" Yoshoba asked, watching him while he asked.

Shatanni seemed to hesitate, but replied, "Yes, Great Sun—they know only their stations, nothing more."

"How about you, Holabi, do you understand what you are to do?" Yoshoba asked, turning to the cloaked priest.

"I am prepared, Great Sun. I will have the Yukpan headmen and priests together as guests of honor, kept away from their warriors, as you instruct," Holabi affirmed.

Formless, whirling doubts gathered in Yoshoba's mind to plague him, and he fought not to show suspicion or indecision. "Good, then. We shall need no more meetings until just before the tournament," he said, minding his tone to sound confident. I need to hold them together just a little longer, he thought, and my destiny will be fulfilled. "Go your way, now, my old friends," he said, straining for eloquence. "The time of Allahashi glory and honor approaches."

○ ○ ○ ○

The two visitors left by separate paths. Shatanni, an expert in infiltration and undetectable movement, returned unseen to his house near the main gate.

olabi walked to the temple mound in the geographical center of

Tochina. He extinguished the torches in his quarters as soon as he entered. It was near midnight. He crept to peer through every opening in the temple during the next hour, surveying the grounds around the temple mound with great care and suspicion, until he felt sure Yoshoba's watchers had not followed him.

He changed into the breechcloth and coarse cape of a temple novice and slipped out the back door to step down the grassy rear slope of the mound, illuminated only by the crescent moon. He made his way to Ilaponla's house on the southernmost mound in Tochina, crept silently up the back stairway, and slipped inside. Ilaponla welcomed him, expectancy in her voice, to her bed.

"My true love," she whispered, as she enveloped him.

CHAPTER SIXTEEN

HOME

ISKIFA FELT SOME LOSS WHILE HE WATCHED HIS NEW AND OLD friends walk away north of Anoli—an interesting and colorful group, he thought. He wondered whether he might see Robert again, the strange and fascinating white man he saved and preserved for his first two weeks in a world new to him. It felt good to see his apprentice Taloa again, as well as his old friend, Anli Basha. He considered Basha as one of the most skilled and accomplished wordmasters in the confederacy, notwithstanding his foolish enthusiasm for the *Yamohmi*. He took comfort in knowing their traveling party included many athletes, older warriors, and their families, all of whom could protect them, especially Robert.

The moist wind blowing through the heavily leaved trees shading the road seemed to call his name. "*Is-kiff-aah, Is-kiff-aah*," it breathed while he coursed the road west along a tributary creek with a strong and constant flow, one whose name he had forgotten. Iskifa could have chosen any of several routes that might interest him, including traveling with Anli's group north toward the big town of Italwa, then turning straight west to Chunuli. He chose rather to start west at once because it interested him most to see his old friend Hushihoma, wordmaster of Tashkalusa, who also trained as an apprentice to Atanapoa.

Iskifa enjoyed the solitude and beauty of this part of *yaaknishto*. He liked traveling alone, and it pleased him in some ways to leave the complex of Anoli and the complications of life that could snare men there. Many winters had passed since he traveled the bottomlands he now walked through. Their verdant creeks and rivers flowed down from the mountains his Chalakki friends called *Shaconage*, mountains of the blue mist. Their woods were full of squirrel, turkey, rabbit, fox, deer, elk and, not uncommonly, wolf and bear.

He would skirt the big hills to the south and east to follow the creek that would become a river before crossing it to head due west to Tashkalusa, twelve strong days' walk if the weather held. From there it was only a few more days' travel home to Chunuli. "*Inchokka … inchokka*, home." He spoke those words aloud, his and the one Robert used, feeling the pure delights of the notions nestled in each.

Waiting for Taloa, Anli, and their friends and attendants to prepare for their long journey to Tochina had given him time for valuable rest that in turn gave him energy to walk without tiring until midday, stopping only to drink from an occasional spring, enjoy an unusual bird's song, or study an exotic herb, flower, shrub, or tree. Once, he stopped for a quick meal of dried fish and cornbread Taloa packed for him. He settled underneath a canopy of wild grapes, their vines sagging close enough that he could pick from them while he sat.

The people along the road were farmers, and their towns and planted fields grew smaller the farther he walked. He would not waste time talking and visiting with new acquaintances, no matter how interesting the people or their dialects were, and planned to indulge in at most a night or two with Hushihoma. He would not delay his reunion with his blessed Nanitana and his homeland.

He mused while he walked on the blessedness of his life, thanking *Aba Binnili*. The gifted accuracy of the dream the Creator sent to him once again engulfed him with gratitude. It turned out just as he saw it—the ocean, the beach, the pale-skinned man. His faith once again proved true.

Now and then thoughts of his beautiful Nanitana swarmed upon him like buzzing bees at blossom time. How sweet it would be to see her, enjoy her gaze and conversation and the strength of her skin. He laughed to himself as he recalled his advice to younger men who sought his counsel, which had accumulated the savor and standing of proverb in his oratory: a man needs three things to be truly happy—a good woman, a good fire, and a good dog.

That would make him think with a smile of Chola, his faithful old hunting dog, all but realizing the ticklish sensations of the greeting Chola would give him. The fat fires of feasting would soon warm his skin and germinate the words of song and story. Oh, what a pleasure, the breath of life he breathed, he thought, and what a pleasure the work. His understudies in the knowledge of woods would be eager to hear of the orange-hearted lumber the fish eaters used for their docks and for the ground courses of their log houses—woods that water would not rot and bugs would not eat. Every thought he imagined of home brought him a wave of pleasure. The grandchildren of his community would fawn over his stories of faraway places and covet the unusual dolls and toys he brought home.

Such thoughts propelled and sustained him, and the twelve days passed quickly. The journey to Tashkalusa, despite the fatigue of almost two moons away from home, seemed almost effortless.

He pushed for extra distance on the tenth and eleventh days of his walk to guarantee his arrival before dark on the twelfth day. The sun was still two-sixths above the horizon when the mounds of Tashkalusa appeared. Word of his arrival preceded him, and the first to meet and greet him on the road was an apprentice of Hushihoma, who offered refreshments before leading Iskifa to the wordmaster's mound.

"*Hallito*, my old friend," Hushihoma greeted him at his house atop the mound. "Where is your white man?" he asked, his voice lilting with playful sarcasm. "Didn't I say you were crazy to follow such a preposterous dream?"

"You underestimate me," Iskifa retorted, feigning indignation, "and worse, you underestimate *Aba Binnili*."

"Don't we all?" Hushihoma asked rhetorically, but looked about, appearing genuinely chagrined not to see a white man with Iskifa. "Again, where is he?"

Iskifa took a seat to tell the story. "Apesa, the judge at Anoli, suspected the white man of being Yoshoba's spy," he explained to a shocked Hushihoma. "He ruled the white man could not leave the custody of Anli Basha and my apprentice, Taloa Kinta, who are on their way to Tochina—" Iskifa paused, but Hushihoma, hand on his chin, did not interrupt, clearly held rapt by his story "—like several of the foolish people I ran into around your town on my way here."

"Yes," Hushihoma agreed with a frown, "several have left or passed through here on their way to the *Yamohmi*—but tell me more of the white man."

Iskifa proceeded to fill in Hushihoma on the details of finding Robert. Hushihoma interjected many questions about Robert's appearance, his strange animal, how Iskifa nursed the man back to health, their journey to Anoli, and the trial.

After his lengthy curiosity about Robert appeared to be satisfied, Hushihoma returned, if grudgingly, to the previous concern. "You know that I am as suspicious of Yoshoba and the *Yamohmi* as you are, Iskifa," he said. "I was taught at the feet of Atanapoa, just like you. I also worry for your white man, because he got drawn into it."

They shared all their news and the latest shadings in their language studies. Iskifa enjoyed Hushihoma's hospitality and friendship as much as anyone's he knew, but after two days of rest, he was ready to start for home. It took him three more days of walking and catching canoe rides on the Tombikbi River to arrive in Chunuli. As he expected, a gang of children met him on the edge of town, laughing and calling out "*Afosi falama inchokka*! Grandfather has come home!"

"What's in the bag, *Afosi* Iskifa?" the chorus rang out as soon as the hugs and kisses were over with.

In his great joy to see them he felt tempted to give them their gifts at once, but he elected instead to tease. "I have nothing in my bag but food and necessities," he pretended to protest. "Do you think I'm a sled, and that I have room to carry toys and foolishness on a such a long walk?"

His grandchildren and their friends frowned, all well spoiled by his habit of bringing all manner of toys and curiosities from his journeys.

He chuckled. "I'm only teasing, but you must wait for tonight's fire," he admonished, "or the younger children will cry as soon as they see your gifts."

"Yey! *Yakookay!* Yey!" they chortled. "*Afosi! Afosi!* We love you, Grandfather."

They drew near to Chunuli, and his friends and neighbors came out to greet him while he passed their homes. "*Chokma, ankana,*" they said, "Welcome home, good friend." Some pressed his hands, some kissed him, some bowed in his honor. "Come to my house for the feast tonight," he invited each and all.

Iskifa's house stood on the outskirts of the main part of Chunuli, in a grove of hardwood trees on the banks of *Hayi Bok.* Tension gathered in his shoulders as it came into sight, surprising him. "Precious Nanitana," he whispered, inaudible amid the tumult of childish chatter. He heard Chola's territorial yipping, alerted by their approaching noise. "Only a flight away now," he said to himself, "and here I am, as nervous as a young man on his wedding day."

He stopped a half-flight from his house, reached into his pouch, pulled out his bird-bone whistle, and blew it to a certain pitch. He saw dust fly when Chola hit the road and began to count. Before he reached *pokoli,* ten, Chola sprang upon him, almost knocking him down with a leap straight into his arms. Fortunately, he was only a medium-size dog. Iskifa let him bark and lick and wriggle with excitement a little while before easing him down. Chola tried to jump into his arms again, but summoned all the dog-will he could muster on Iskifa's gentle command: "*Biniili,* sit."

Iskifa felt dismayed to see Nanitana did not come out to greet him, but, this is her way, he thought. He told the children to stay outside.

Nanitana stood with her back to the door, before a table laden with pottery, wrapped *banaha,* and other food waiting to be served. He could smell *tanfula* aging in a pot by a low cook fire outside. Her silver-streaked raven hair hung past her waist, delicately disguising the tawny grace of her hips. The sight of her, nevertheless, caused him to relax, exhaling a sigh of relief. He paused in the doorway, awaiting her word.

"You could have sent a messenger," she said coolly, without turning. "I know you. You have invited everyone within fifty flight to our fire tonight. I have so little time to prepare."

His heart fluttered to the sound of her voice. He was doubtful of the tactic because of her stern tone, but walked softly up to her, pulled her shining hair back with the gentlest touch he could manage and kissed her ear.

"*Sinti Yopi*, Swims Like a Snake," he whispered, "*hullo okchanya*, love of my life."

Her shoulders drooped, hearing his pet name for her and his expression of eternal affection. She dusted the flour from her hands and turned to embrace him with the energy of a woman half her age. She kissed him as passionately as she had when they were young lovers. "Oh, Iskifa," she said, clasping her hands around his face, "I missed you madly, as always."

He saw kind tears of joy in her eyes, telling him the story of their lives together. At once they said, "I'm so happy you're safe, and I hate every breath you are away from me."

She released him and turned again to her cooking, wiping her eyes. "You turn me into a young girl, you owl. You make me embarrassed."

Iskifa, too, wiped tears away and reached to pull her firm, muscular backside up against him, feeling the same warm surge of passion and intense love he had known almost from the first day he met her.

He gently pulled her hair aside again, exposing and kissing her neck. "Nanitana, my wise and beautiful dream. My heart ached for you. Not even the exotic ocean, the coastal forests, nor the fire flowers of *Alaka* can match a single gleam of your eye. I am well now, whole again. I am home."

CHAPTER SEVENTEEN

TOCHINA

COLORFUL TENTS, CAMPSITES, AND PEOPLE OF EVERY DESCRIP-
tion and costume—hundreds, as far as Taloa could tell—over-
spread the landscape around the travelers. They were still at
least a half-day's walk from Tochina, and the spectacle of the
Yamohmi already passed her grandest expectations.

Naturally, the sight of Robert Williams and Lizbeth created an
immediate sensation when they arrived at the immense campground
near a substantial Allahashi town along the way. Such excitement in-
vigorated Taloa. She reveled in the grand mass of humanity, the cultural exchange, and anticipations of unimagined marvels to come. She
even felt proud of her association with perhaps the most interesting
local event—the white man and his hitherto unknown beast.

Anli Basha's son, daughter-in-law, and grandsons set up their tents,
which looked drab compared to some ornate dwellings around them.
Exhilarating as the spectacle was, it could also drain one's energy, so
Taloa felt anxious to resort to a tent and gain a respite from the crowds,
along with Robert.

They left Lizbeth tied to a pole amid a milling clutch of curious
children and some adults who likewise could not withhold their curiosity. One of Anli's elder grandsons stood watch over the goat.

"This is good," Robert said, his words garbled among chews on a piece of jerked meat. "I'm starved." They had forced their walk that day, hoping to arrive at such a place as this. They had not eaten since mid-morning, and the sun at the time stood but a sixth above the horizon.

Taloa felt happy. She studied Robert, whose attention stayed with his meal. The white man had grown an amazing cover of dark brown hair on his face during the half-moon since they met. She felt glad to help this strange man she had grown accustomed to, and for whom she felt a compelling, if sometimes confusing, sense of responsibility.

The meal and the rest restored them from the fatigue of a long and somewhat eventful journey. A violent thunderstorm overtook them near where the big river called the Tanasi meets with the bigger river called Ohiyo, the Good River, and exacted a lot of energy from them. It only lasted a night, and three canoes awaited them the next morning on the Good to carry them to its confluence with the *Misha Sipokni*. Anli hired the canoes from the brother of the man who ferried them down the Tanasi.

Anli glanced at Taloa while he retrieved his pipe after the meal, and she politely excused herself. He and Robert would smoke, a pleasure only taken by men in civilized company. As for Robert, though he still would confess a lot of ignorance about the ways of his new friends, he yet learned to appreciate the pleasures and importance of some basic ceremonies.

With her first step outside the tent, the "new civilization" that had sprung up around this once small town again thrilled her. Her eyes could not be full. Everywhere she looked she saw men—and even some women—smoking strange pipes, people wearing fabulous ornaments, and an incredible assortment of trade goods.

She walked around, hearing a number of languages unheard before, and mishmash mixtures of tongues she knew to differing extents—her mother was Chikasha and her father one of the Chahta, and she grew up in Chunuli speaking a dialect of both languages, each widely known in this part of the world. She noticed what seemed to be religious rituals in some quarters of the camp. Exotic plants dangled trembling in the wind in pots hung about the bizarre assemblage of temporary structures. Merchants sold goods she had never seen or imagined. If this was only a sample, she wondered, what splendid discoveries awaited them in the grand city of Tochina?

She could barely sleep that night, but she and her fellow voyagers woke before dawn, packed, and took back to the road by first light, expecting to see Tochina before mid-day. When the mounded city appeared on the skyline, her wildest imaginations were surpassed. The enormous log stockade surrounding Tochina stretched for tens of flights, and the great temple and palace loomed over the wall, visible even from far way.

Many merchants' buildings for a great distance outside Tochina looked permanent. Anything she could imagine, and much she could not, was offered for trade—food, drink, clothing, pottery, rugs, blankets, shiny metal art and ornaments, and even prostitution, judging from the way some women dressed. She felt shocked, but in the thrall of such sophistication, she accepted these things as the high and low marks of a highly developed civilization, one to be admired and learned from.

Again, Robert and Lizbeth attracted an immense following. Although there were jugglers, storytellers, players, and sporting and gambling games going on all around, many residents and travelers abandoned them to surround the white man and his goat. People offered Robert small gifts, and many felt compelled to touch him or his animal, making both a little nervous.

Taloa noticed watchers in the background, marked by their lack of excitement or participation in any distractions around them. None of this, however, seemed frightening or disturbing to her. This was her time of discovery—certainly, she thought, her coming of age.

She studied the enormous logs in the wall, with their sharp parapets, and remembered Iskifa's words of warning: all that seems glamorous is not virtuous. She thought briefly about his historical analogies between the *Yamohmi* and all its cultural mix and the debacles the Yukpans' ancestors suffered. Still, she could not imagine how such ancient history might fit into such a modern, more enlightened world.

Robert seemed to enjoy his celebrity. Someone had given him a beautiful beaded shoulder bag, and he filled it with food and local crafts from canny merchants who intuited it might be good for trade if the one who promised to be the constant center of attention possessed, and hopefully displayed, their goods. "*Yakookay! Yakookay!*" she heard him say often, using the common expression of gratitude.

At length they approached the main gates of the stockade, flung wide on that day. Taloa saw tough-looking Allahashi warriors approach in a group, marching around a very official-looking elder wearing an ornate costume, perhaps of a high priest. The crowd parted while the warriors and the elder came forward to greet Anli Basha's entourage. Anli's son and grandsons stepped aside to allow the personage to meet Anli, who walked in the center of his group.

The warriors also divided in close order to open the way for the elder, who introduced himself, extending a hand toward Anli, "I am Holabi, high priest of the Allahashi." Holabi thus greeted him in the Chahta language, displaying his education.

Anli extended his hand to grasp Holabi's forearm. "Thank you, my wise and spiritual friend," he replied in the Allahashi tongue. "I am Anli Basha, wordmaster of Anoli."

"Welcome to Tochina," Holabi continued, "the great city of the three rivers."

"In the ancient times this city was known as Boktochina," Taloa whispered excitedly to Robert, "which means 'three rivers,' but Yo-shoba's father shortened the name to Tochina, which means simply 'three.'"

Anli presented an Anolian calumet to Holabi, and Holabi offered a similar Allahashi gift to Anli. "We are honored to be greeted by such a distinguished person," Anli said. "You humble us with your presence."

"It is I who suffer indignity in your presence," Holabi answered ceremoniously. He spoke to Anli, but Taloa saw his dark eyes flit past him, distracted by Robert. He continued, in an exaggerated tone, so all around them could hear, "The Great Sun, ruler of the Allahashi, has instructed me to escort you to the Honor House, to receive our humble hospitality as his special guests."

Taloa could barely contain her excitement. "Isn't this wonderful!" she whispered again to Robert, who hardly reacted, seeming transfixed and overwhelmed, staring at the armaments Holabi's warriors bore. She elbowed him gently. "That's not polite," she murmured. "Take your eyes away."

He did, at once.

"Again, great priest, your kindness surpasses our best dreams," Anli continued in oratorical voice.

"Follow me, great man of knowledge," Holabi said, sweeping his hand dramatically toward the center of Tochina. He stole another glance at Robert before turning to begin the deliberate procession customary for a man of importance and achievement. The warriors gathered around him again, in formation.

The grandeur of the city all but mesmerized Taloa. She marveled at countless platform mounds with elaborate buildings atop them, recalling how many told her the largest earthworks in the northern world stood in Tochina. In the distance, even eclipsing the mounds in the foreground, rose what she thought must be Yoshoba's palace, built atop a massive earthwork the size of a small mountain, taking her breath away. The warriors led them to a cluster of lower, flat-topped mounds in the center of an enormous plaza, passing the wide walkways between them.

Her usual shyness around people had left her, and she felt proud to be included among such a noble, triumphal procession. She became conscious of the crowds along their path, full of curious people who could not help but see her among the royal and important, and who of course would gape at the bizarre white man with his strange costume and the confusing collection of ornaments he wore and the strange little animal he led along. She told herself to walk straight and dignified.

She leaned toward Robert. "This may be the playing field we have heard so much about," she said. "It is said that Yoshoba worked on it for ten winters." Inside the compound spread the largest and most immaculate stickball field she had ever seen. She almost gasped. "This field must be ten or twelve flight long and half as wide! How wondrous!"

Robert only blinked at it. Irish hurling fields could look vast, but never like this.

"This is more magnificent than we have heard, great priest," Anli exclaimed. "It must be the utmost in the world."

"Thank you, wordmaster," Holabi answered pompously, "we are very proud of our accomplishments."

Taloa wanted to pull off her sandals to feel the lush, thick grass against her feet, but did not wish to seem undignified in this procession. She wished she had dressed better. She had not anticipated such glamour or imagined she would be part of it.

"You must be hot, tired, and hungry," Holabi observed hospitably. "Let me show you to your quarters, where you may bathe and eat."

Taloa noticed unusual openings underneath the mounds—entrances with heavily beamed frames and large, double wooden doors. She imagined they must have to do with the unusual burial customs of the Allahashi. She had heard of bizarre Allahashian ceremonies and customs, but thought it all only gossip generated by skeptics like Iskifa to discredit this clearly advanced civilization.

The Honor House was a name given to a collection of buildings a long walk from the stickball arena. The accommodations in the unmarried women's quarters were clean and comfortable, and many women had already settled in. A comfortable chatter enlivened its atmosphere, apart from two women who quarreled over a bedding spot.

Taloa felt some anxiety at separating from Anli, Robert, and the other members of their group. Her feelings toward Robert were particularly confusing, even if she considered his predicament pitiable—a man separated from all he knows and everyone he loves in a strange, unknown land. She strained to dismiss her misgivings and confusion in favor of the excitement and elation of this place and this day.

Isunlash, wordmaster of Tochina, had greeted them earlier after they climbed up the beautifully landscaped stairway to the Honor House. "Welcome to my council," he had told Anli and repeated to Taloa. Taloa felt flattered to find this great man aware of her position as an heir to the wordmaster traditions.

"We will hold our meeting at the wordmaster house, the second mound inside the gates, after the *Yamohmi*," he told her and Anli. "In the meantime, we have seen that everything you need for comfort and rest is provided here."

"Do you know if the Yukpan Confederacy team has arrived yet, Isunlash?" Anli asked him. "They left Anoli before we did, but we were delayed by a bad storm."

"They arrived here two days past, Honorable Master," Isunlash replied. "They started their workouts yesterday in their own practice area. They are a fit group of athletes and have assured my independent referees they will be more than ready tomorrow."

"Tomorrow?" Taloa gasped. "I thought there were several days yet before the contest."

"The Great Sun, Yoshoba, declared we will start a few days ahead of schedule," Isunlash continued in an official tone. "The weather is tricky during this season and the teams are ready. There is no profit in delay."

Taloa felt shocked and annoyed, but knew better than to challenge or criticize matters beyond her control. She suspected that cutting the Yukpans' practice time was a trick by Yoshoba to gain an advantage. She had little time to speculate, however, having to find a spot to unpack her belongings near the center of the large house, which already was almost full.

Her thoughts turned back to Robert. How tremendously mysterious this must all seem to him, she thought, recalling how he protested briefly when the appointed hosts led Lizbeth away to a pen at the foot of the Honor House mound. She felt some of his pain, knowing Lizbeth was his only connection to his previous life. His pale skin barely surprised her now. In certain lights, especially when he smiled naturally, she found him, his dark hair and icy blue eyes, almost handsome. She stood taller than most of the men and boys she knew, which made for a few awkward situations among men, and it pleased her that Robert stood taller than she. Her thoughts ended with an impulse to find him and see how he was doing.

She found him nearby outdoors, sitting under an arbor, staring through a small gap between two huts into the bustle of the city around the mound. Taloa sat beside him and waited for him to speak. He kept silent, as if unaware of her.

It seemed, she observed, he had lost the enthusiasm he showed earlier in the day and again felt overcome by his problems. After three weeks with Robert Williams, she had begun to understand his moods. She had watched his physical wounds heal and saw him gain strength along their long journey from Anoli to Tochina. She had come to admire how athletic he was and how quick, willing, and efficiently he acted anytime there were loads to bear or work to do. They had plenty of time around campfires for Robert to tell her the stories of his life—his country, his ship, his parents, and Celia—although his wistful, lighthearted stories about the latter troubled her, if oddly.

"Did you see the people with almost black skins?" she asked. Still nothing from him. "And the group of tall men with pointed beards?" she queried, trying to distract him from his worries. Again he did not respond. "It is said that the dark ones and the tall ones are people who live many days' walk to the west, but who originally came from across the great eastern ocean, like you did."

He seemed to awaken to that and turned to her. "Do they have boats?" he asked.

"I do not know. It is said they have been with the western people for many generations, and that they like it there and never want to return home."

"And why not?" he asked incredulously.

"Look around you, Robert. This is a fine, rich land. They say they came from a land that was corrupt, crowded, and without hope. They have intermarried with the western people who welcomed them, and they now feel rich."

"I cannot believe that," Robert said, apparently straining against tears of frustration. He looked pitiful. His bushy hair flopped forward when he let his head drop, perhaps to hide his face. His dark, unruly beard made him look wild. She kept talking, turning to a sympathetic tone. "I have heard a number of stories during my life of people coming from across the ocean. The great Kahuweya of the Onoyota tribe in the far northeast sailed across the ocean many winters ago and lived on some big islands with light-skinned people for a season. Kahuweya even married and brought home a bride from the white tribe." Taloa reasoned these old stories might cajole Robert into accepting a different fate from the one he strived for. "Many believe the civilizations across the ocean have died. Except for a few scattered communities that kept their old ways, the people of which you have seen, these wayfarers from your world have intermarried and been adopted and absorbed into our world."

Robert only looked away.

A jolt of embarrassment struck Taloa. She hoped he would not interpret what she said as a desire for him to "intermarry" with her. She felt herself blushing and changed the subject. "Have you heard that the *Yamohmi* is tomorrow?" she asked, with abrupt quickness. "I had thought we had many days before it came."

He turned back to his view of the city. "Yes, I heard."

"I can hardly wait for the Yukpans to demonstrate our superiority on the field of honor," she chirped with a smile, hoping to cheer Robert up. He did not seem moved.

She tried to think of something else to say, but felt at a loss. He seems so sad, she thought. She saw Anli approach from the direction of the men's Honor House quarters, a somewhat familiar-looking young man—an Allahashi, judging by his dress—beside him. The young man bore a wordmaster's campfire symbol in a tattoo on his left shoulder.

"Oh, here you are," Anli called to Taloa, sounding relieved. "I've been looking all around." He turned to Robert. "Robert Williams," he addressed him, directly.

Robert turned quickly, surprised.

"Your presence is required in the palace of Yoshoba," Anli continued in his language while Taloa translated.

Robert's surprise withered into anxiety.

"Nothing to fear, Master Williams. Quite the contrary," Taloa translated. "The Great Sun wishes for you to sit near him at the *Yamohmi*, as a guest of honor. He asks that you come now to discuss the details," Taloa said, excitement rising in her voice.

Robert shook his head and crossed his arms. "No. No, I won't," he refused, firmly.

Anli looked confused. Taloa understood Robert's fear, but did not translate his refusal. Instead, somewhat against her nature, she challenged Anli. "This poor man has suffered greatly, Master, and we are under Apesa's strict orders to keep him in our custody until after the *Yamohmi*," she said in Anli's tongue.

"I worked all that out with Yoshoba," Anli countered cheerfully. "He has assured me that he respects Apesa's judgment, and I will also be seated with Robert to satisfy the order. Is it not wonderful that we will enjoy such high placement in this event?"

Taloa felt a flush of excitement at Anli's explanation, but felt compelled to stand her ground for Robert's sake. "I'm afraid he will rebel and be hurt by Yoshoba's guards," she answered. "There will be no one to translate for him. Master Iskifa will never forgive us if anything happens to his white man."

"Don't be such stickler for the rules, Taloa," Anli scolded. "I, of course, considered the language problem. Isunlash eagerly offered his best wordmaster apprentice, my young friend here, to assist Robert." Taloa realized she now recognized the young man as one who came to Anoli two winters ago to observe and learn what he could of Master Bannet's English. "He will interpret for Robert and see that he is treated royally." Anli paused and waited, his hands folded before him. The Allahashian apprentice smiled and nodded. "Robert will be all right, and Iskifa will never know of any intrigue. Persuade him now," Anli concluded, adding, "I'm losing my patience."

Taloa knew she could not win. "Robert, you must," she pleaded reluctantly in English. "It would be the most grievous of insults if you refuse. I hate to think what might happen to you—and us, if you continue to be so stubborn."

Robert glanced at her, a tear of weariness and anxiousness forming in the corner of his eye. He looked awful—scared and tired. "Robert, you must," she repeated. She saw resignation on his face.

Two temple warriors came up behind Anli. Taloa recognized them from Holabi's escort. Robert saw them, too, and hung his head. He seemed to be thinking. Taloa felt afraid. He could not be so foolish as to refuse this request, she thought.

He sat for what seemed an eternity to her. At last he stood, slung his shoulder bag around his neck, and faced the warriors. "I am ready," he said softly.

"*Chiibaaya'achi*, he will go with you," Taloa said to the guards.

Taloa and Anli watched from the arbor while Robert, the Allahashi warriors, and the interpreter walked past the corner of the last men's quarters, toward the north stairway of the Honor House mound. She focused on Yoshoba's palace in the distance atop the enormous earthworks near Tochina's north wall. A disquieting uneasiness came over her. Robert vanished from the foreground in her line of sight.

CHAPTER EIGHTEEN

THE FASHIONABLE EVENT

TALOA WAS LOST. SHE TRIED TO CROSS THE NARROW CREEK, but had to stop, immobilized at her knees by quicksand. "It's only packsand," she whimpered, trying to allay her growing fear. The trees, white blossoms of the flowering thistle, seemed warmly familiar—"*Ii*, yes, these are the banks of the *Hayi Bok*. I'm in Chunuli. *Yakookay! Yakookay!*" she cried out, halting at the yip of a fox nearby. She listened for another to answer, but heard no reply. Every effort to free her feet took her deeper. She turned every way she could, desperate for help. A faint sound like a child's cry came to her ears, and she squinted into the dim light to see a baby raccoon cowering near the water, calling for its mother. Her heart filled with sympathy. Movement rustled in the creek-bank underbrush, and the fox, a young one, came sniffing upstream from her. The fox saw the baby raccoon and fixed on it, kneeling into a crouch. Taloa summoned her angriest voice. "*Malili! Malili!*" she tried to shout, but only a strained breath came out. She tried again, and still only a whisking breath issued from her tightened chest. The fox quivered in his hindquarters, setting for a pounce. Before Taloa could cry again, he sprang, snapped his jaws around the tiny raccoon's neck, and disappeared into the brush. Taloa's panic returned to the mounting horror of her predicament. The air felt almost chilly, but sweat began to sting her eyes. As abruptly as the fox, the high priest Holabi stepped out from a curtain of tall reeds along the bank. His familiar face gave her a surge of hope. He was dressed in the same raiment as when he greeted their party at the gate of Tochina. "Oh, help me, please. Pull me from this quicksand, kind priest," she entreated him. He did not speak, and she noticed his eyes—odd, pale yellow, and reticent, their pupils enlarged. Short feathers sprouted from his face. "*Kitiini*," she shuddered. In the span of a few thundering heartbeats, Holabi shrank to the size and form of a horned owl. With a few flaps of great, wafting wings, he lifted out of his robes, which fell onto the moist sand of the bank. She watched with horror while the owl vanished into the wet pre-dawn air, flying away upstream. She could not breathe, but tried again to scream, and as her voice leaped out of her at last, she awoke in a cold sweat. She found her legs bound in her blanket and women around her sitting up and rising from their pallets to see to her, rubbing their eyes, blinking at her. She felt confused and embarrassed, even if relieved, to realize she only suffered a nightmare.

The women nearest her whispered comforting words. "Thank you," she whispered back. "It was just a bad dream. I'm all right." They returned to their beds.

The sun was not yet up. The vague, gray light of early dawn glimmered through the door. Taloa sat soaked with sweat, and her heart still pounded. She swept hair from her eyes and shook her head to clear it, but bits and parts of her dream remained in her thoughts with a curious persistence.

She got up, feeling the same chill she felt in the nightmare, wrapped her cover around her shoulders, and tiptoed to the door overlooking the practice field to lean against the post and watch a few people move about below. The sight of a sleepy city soothed her. She let her eyes wander until they stopped, arrested by a sight at the top of a tall pole in the center of the field. Upon it, facing her as if watching, sat a large horned owl, the same as the one from her dream. He spread his wings and sprang off to fly toward her, closing with disturbing speed to about half the distance between them before wheeling away toward the center of the city. Taloa watched until he vanished from sight. The appearance of the owl on both sides of sleep troubled her deeply. "I must speak to Master Anli about this," she muttered. She washed quickly and slipped on the dress she would wear for the *Yamohmi*.

She skipped down the stairway from the quarters on the Honor House mound to the walkway at its base. Tall privacy fences adorned with flowering vines separated the guest quarters atop the lengthy, medium-height mound and required one to descend one stairway and ascend another to visit other quarters. She took short strides like a *shokhata*, a possum, and tried not to look up at the players' quarters, although she would have liked to have seen Iyapi or Shakba. Speaking with Anli came first.

She noticed torches lit in the athletes' house, but managed to avert her eyes. It was very bad manners to distract athletes before an important contest. When she reached the steps to the building where Anli and his family stayed, a serious-looking, young and dark-skinned Allahashi man, not as fearsome as the temple warriors, blocked her path.

"I wish to see Master Anli Basha of Anoli," she announced firmly.

"No single women are allowed here," the stern young man answered, in a broken mixture of Allahashi and what she believed to be a Siouan tongue.

"My message is of the utmost importance and cannot wait," she told him in as clear an approximation of his language as she thought he could understand.

"No!" he replied, forcefully.

His stubbornness angered her. She tried to step around him, and he blocked her again with his spear, point up and throwing end wedged into the ground. His knuckles dug into her chest.

"No! Woman, no!" he declared.

The rudeness of his manners angered her. "*Yalhkapa*," she blurted, and stalked away. She instantly regretted saying that, hoping he would not understand the insult meaning "feces for breakfast," which Taloa heard her Chikasha mother hurl at her Chahta father on heated occasions. Each time, she made Taloa swear never to repeat the word.

Still, the last thing she expected at the *Yamohmi*, especially considering their reception, was a spear point in her face and a strange man so rude as to touch her. And she had never been in a city where she could not move about freely. She hurried back toward the single women's quarters, feeling more confused by such rudeness than by her dream.

The glamour of the *Yamohmi* began to lose its luster already, and she had only been in Tochina one night. A wave of enormous disappointment tried to swallow her. She had looked forward to the event ever since she heard the first rumor and later the official announcement. "It's the dream, it's the dream," she muttered, straining to hold back a surge of angry tears. She prided herself in not easily crying, like many other girls she knew who would never advance in knowledge like her. "I'm sick of being scared by stories. They're not true. They just tell them to children to keep them in line," she whispered. "I'm not going to have my great event spoiled by childish fear." She composed herself and entered the women's house.

The early sun sent streams through the doorway, adding light to the laughter and chatter of excited women dressing and preparing for the *Yamohmi*. Taloa's anxiety eased at the sight of their colorful clothing— some familiar, some exotic. She diverted herself by trying to identify the tribes represented within their speech, drawing on her already immense knowledge. One could not be a wordmaster or a wordmaster's apprentice without understanding that identity in all its forms is carried by language.

"At one sixth this morning," she told herself quietly, taking a deep breath, "the greatest *toli* event ever played by humankind will begin." Again, the great good fortune of being present for the *Yamohmi* began to mollify her anxieties, and she began to discount them as momentary.

I hope Robert is all right, she thought. "At least he has some decent things to wear," she said aloud to herself. She felt sorry she could not be with him during the event. She had grown accustomed to the attention he attracted, which gave her status also, yet felt sympathy for him even if she could only guess how lost and alone he must feel. She thought she perhaps helped ease the pain of his loneliness when she translated and explained things to him.

Low vibrations arose as if from the earth, causing the house walls to tremble. She knew they came from the large drums used to announce the make-ready phase of events like the *Yamohmi*. She felt her heart answer like a drum in her chest. It has begun, she thought exultantly, what we've been waiting for. The women hurried to finish preparing, and some began to walk outside to await their escort to the game.

Four Allahashi temple warriors marched in formation up the stairway to the top of the mound, two stopping at the top step and the others circling around behind the women. The drumming in Taloa's chest gained tempo while they began their march down the stairs toward the center of the city. They wound through throngs of merchants and tourists buzzing amid Tochina's byways. When they entered the stadium, she thrilled to the sight of thousands of people standing and sitting on the array of mounds on either side. She thought she would burst at the sight of the Yukpan team, arrayed in their game regalia with long, plumed tail feathers, working out in disciplined drills at one end of the field. She felt proud and certain they would win the day.

At the other end, the Allahashi team drilled, clad in black breechcloths and studded ankle bracelets. Their shaved heads reflected the midmorning sun. She recognized their traditional single braid topknot with an eagle tail feather hanging from it. Their faces were painted yellow and black—the colors of sickness and tragedy, meant to intimidate their opponents.

She felt flush with pride for her Yukpans and strained to see Iyapi and Shakba, but her group of honored women passed through the entrance near the center of the immense playing field, and she could not see well enough to tell one player from another. The warriors guided them to the center observation mound on the west side and up the steps to its top. She looked straight across to the east and saw Yoshoba's observation mound, its array of chairs and canopies visible even from so far away. Thick ranks of temple warriors stood in lines up and down its slopes, flanking the seated dignitaries. She assumed Master Anli and Robert sat somewhere in there, near Yoshoba.

Dozens of huge, thundering drums set on small mounds at the four corners of the field continued their awesome rumble, increasing in volume and speed, so loudly she could hardly hear the Shoshoni girl who befriended her on the way there. The girl seemed nervous because she came alone, and Taloa was glad to have a comrade, even if she could barely understand her. Some words sounded like Nahuatl, but the Shoshonis were a distant people to the north and west and had little historical contact with the scattered nations of the *Misha Sipokni* bottomlands and tributaries.

A new exhilaration overtook her. How wonderful, she thought, that the *Yamohmi* could bring together Yukpans, Shoshonis, and so many others who had never before met! The drums fueled her enthusiasm— they were always loudest and fastest as the start of the game came closer. When they stopped, the game would begin.

The number of spectators made for more than the leaves on all the trees, she thought. What a variety! Colorful clothes, pelts, mats and awnings, and merchants trading everything imaginable! Surely this was her finest hour, her day of triumph!

The drums stopped. The chattering crowd fell silent, by custom, in tribute to the great athletes of all the nations. After a moment a great cheer arose from them. Taloa felt the hair stand up on her neck, and her skin bristled with bumps. She thought she might burst with joy. Her heart jumped again while she watched each opposing team form three ranks of athletes and march toward the center of the field to face one another, the Yukpan Confederacy team facing north and the Allahashi team opposite.

Taloa could see Iyapi and Shakba standing in the center of the front line of Yukpans. She felt thrilled to see such a valorous array of the Yukpans' finest, with their colorful tail plumes and faces painted red and white—red on the left if they were from war towns and white on the left if they were from peace towns.

An official stood at the center of the field, holding a *towa*, the small ball made with a rock at its core, wrapped in deer hair and laced with tightly wound leather cord. Twenty-four other officials, also respected men, stood distributed to each side of each half of the field, twelve from the confederacy and twelve from the Allahashi, in alternating positions of six officials apiece, according to their nation, about a flight apart. To be selected as an official for *toli*, stickball games, was among the greatest honors. Cheating or even accusations of cheating by *toli* officials were all but unknown.

The center official raised the *towa* overhead, bidding ten players from each team to step forward. The remainder scattered to offensive and defensive positions up and down the field while the center official offered up a loudly voiced prayer in the Allahashi tongue.

Taloa's heart again pounded in her eardrums, wild with anticipation of Yukpan glory. Iyapi, one of the taller Yukpans, waited at the center for the jump ball. She watched Shakba maneuver to an offensive position about halfway to the Allahashi goal. The crowd grew silent again, also by custom, and for an instant the aroma of cook fires, the beauty and scent of the hair-adorning flowers of the women around her, and the smell of green grass and exotic beverages flowed like a river into Taloa's senses.

She gasped as the official threw the *towa* in the air. Every player had a *kapocha*, a ball stick, in each hand, and a clackety battle rang forth, a feverish conflict that seemed to go on forever as the tangle of players, like a writhing knot of snakes, struggled for the *towa*. A small, tough-looking Yukpan finally scooped it with the pocket of his stick and tossed it up again, toward the edge of the packed group.

Iyapi shouldered his way between two Allahashi and leaped into the air like an escaping deer, so high Taloa could barely believe he was a man. He caught the *towa* between his sticks, sprinted into the open field toward the Allahashi goal, a swarm of opposing players only a few steps behind.

A very quick, muscular Allahashi player intercepted Iyapi, dropping his sticks one stride before he reached him and grabbing him around the waist. The Allahashi lifted him into the air and just when he began a violent spin move to throw him to the ground, Iyapi launched an amazing throw almost a flight downfield.

Another Yukpan player, all alone, caught the pass on the run and launched it again before the Allahashi defenders could close on him. Two more expert throws guided the ball toward Shakba, who dodged two Allahashi defenders assigned to stay on him. The throw fell short, and he ran upfield for an amazing diving catch with his sticks, letting his momentum carry him through a roll back to his feet.

He pitched the ball to a small, stout Yukpan player standing alone at the middle of that end of the field. Tens of Allahashi players sprinted toward Shakba and the small player. The small player did not move. Taloa screamed, "*Malili!* Run! *Malili!*" but the Yukpan stood his ground with insolent self-assurance, as if to taunt the Allahashi.

The Allahashi streamed in large groups to and fro, like swarms of flies. Just as one stampeding group reached the small player, he jumped to make a throw to Iyapi, who caught it between that group and another that hung back to cover Shakba. Looking confused, half that group and the entire number of men chasing the small Yukpan player quickly closed on Iyapi. The scouting reports apparently were quite emphatic about him. The primarily Yukpan spectators on the western mounds yelled frantically. It was a sweet sound to Taloa, but deafening.

Iyapi leaped so high into the air Taloa thought of nighthawks. He launched the ball to a Yukpan left alone toward and down the east side of the playing field. The Allahashi players were now spread all over the field. Communally sensing the strategy for an attempt on goal, most sprinted toward the north goal and the east quarter. Iyapi also raced that way, passing many slower Allahashi players. Two more diversionary tosses on the east goal quarter drew a large number of Allahashi close. Three deft throws straight across the field to the west, untouched by defenders, put the ball in the hands of Kochcha, a young friend of Taloa's from Anoli. He ran an entire flight untouched to within a flight of the goal.

He cleverly faked a throw back east, causing most Allahashi defenders to freeze or go with the feint. He paused, turned, and threw the ball into the northwest corner to Shakba, who had slipped away from his baffled defenders. After catching the *towa* with his sticks, he sprinted to the north end line. He was so fast, most Allahashi instinctively ran toward the goal to amass and prevent a score.

Shakba, in one of the most athletic runs Taloa had ever seen, head and body-faked to elude six defenders. Before the Allahashis heading to defend the goal could turn, he jumped into the air at a full run and threw the ball the remaining half-flight over their heads, scoring a dead-center hit at the top of the goal post.

Taloa and the people crowding the western mounds erupted with exultation. Confederacy spectators jumped, whistled, shouted, and hugged. The Allahashi players, walking dejectedly back to midfield, had been completely outplayed, outmaneuvered, and outrun. Taloa knew one or two goals in an all-day game between top players often were enough to win. She felt ecstatic. Yukpan players congratulated each other and sprinted past the winded and bewildered Allahashi to make ready for the next jump ball.

The game had only begun, but there would be no rest period until the teams had competed for an entire sixth. The Allahashi managed to reorganize their defenses and even muster some advances toward the south goal, but the battle surged back and forth without another score. A number of players fell injured, but play did not stop even for them to be carried from the field.

Taloa's ceremonial deerskins began to feel uncomfortably warm. She looked forward to the half-game intermission so she could freshen up. Others crowded under the large, intermittent shade arbors scattered about the mounds. Conversations among the women wandered from the game.

Just before intermission would begin, Taloa saw Allahashi temple warriors appear, marching about as if to spread around the field. She felt a little puzzled by such a show of might, yet assumed they intended to protect players from contact with spectators during the break, and that they would escort them to training areas to rest, drink, and take a light meal. It was common practice before big games for athletes to fast from food and women for an entire day and night before and not partake of food until the break. Still, to Taloa, the oddity of the warriors' behavior grew. A large number, armed with spears, girdled the field and a second rank, all archers, filed through the entrances to line up behind the spear-carriers. Such a display, if it was merely to protect players, seemed excessive to her. In fact, polite custom, even for warriors or watchers, required them to leave their weapons in their lodges during events like the *Yamohmi.*

While she calculated these irregularities, she noticed the entrances on the east side of the arena fill with men who, even from this distance, looked like warriors. She thought a moment, remembered Iskifa, and felt a puzzling nudge of panic. Could it be a trap?

Others in the crowd seemed to notice, too, muttering with confusion. She turned to stride to the top of her mound and saw Allahashi bowmen amassed all around its base, moving up the sides. She sprinted toward the entrance end, Iskifa preaching in garbled fragments in her mind. The full terror of the moment grasped her.

Armed Allahashi warriors sealed the entrance. She felt the sting of regret for her stupidity and the jangling clamor of fear, but knew not to panic. She dashed back among the confederacy crowd on the mound. "Run! Murderers! Run! Fight! They're trying to murder us! Flee and fight!" she screamed in one language after another.

The people began to scatter, although hesitantly, as the Allahashi archers reached the crest of the mound and turned to launch a volley of well-aimed arrows at the Yukpan players on the field.

On the field, Iyapi stopped running, looking puzzled at seeing the large doors in the base of the mounds swing open and warriors come pouring out. He looked toward Taloa and she toward him, just as an arrow pierced through his neck. He fell where he stood.

Her whole body jerked at the horror of the sight, but she did not cry out. Yukpan players fell everywhere. Bowmen moved through the spear warriors to cut down players on the field. Taloa saw Yukpan players speared to death while they tried to escape.

The archers turned against spectators on Taloa's side. Assassins hidden among the Yukpans pulled knives from hiding to attack, and hand-to-hand fighting raged around Taloa. Two paces below her, an assassin raised a dagger over an old woman. Taloa jumped by reflex, landing on one foot and kicking him through the hinge of his knee. He buckled and dropped his knife, which the old woman quickly grabbed to thrust into his neck, her hand so quick Taloa barely saw it. The woman stabbed him again and he fell still. Then the old woman, a Mvskoke, lifted her head and pealed forth a high-pitched war cry that drove all fear out of Taloa. Though the Yukpan Confederacy was known for trade and not war, some people like the Chikashas and Mvskokes were renowned as the best warriors in their world. Taloa's people were reserved and devoted to peace, but it was a very bad idea to anger them.

Taloa leaped to help another Yukpan woman, bleeding from a wound in her chest while she valiantly wrestled another assassin with a knife. Again, Taloa kicked the Allahashi's knee joint, but he didn't fall, and instead turned on her. The wounded woman sprang upon his back, clamped her arms around his throat and throttled him. He stabbed her in the arm and she fell away. Taloa jumped forward and kicked him in the groin. He doubled over, and the other woman lunged into his legs, toppling him. His head hit the ground, and he let go of the knife, which Taloa snatched up, drove deep into his chest, and let go. He tried to rise, grasping at the knife, staggered and fell backward, both hands on the blade, and moved no more.

Still, the battle seemed lost. Arrows flew all about, the gnawing whisk of broken air everywhere. Taloa scanned the people around her, all bleeding, moaning, screaming, or dead. Yukpans and other non-Allahashi people surrendered to be rounded up. She looked for a way to escape.

From the north a group of spear-bearing warriors headed her way. She bolted south, only to see more, and whirled, realizing she was surrounded. She stood still while the warriors tightened their circle around her. The frightened part of her wanted to scream and cry out, yet she would not pay them such satisfaction, she decided. She would die honorably. Three warriors emerged from the circle, one of them the ugly young man who kept her out of Anli's quarters that morning. He nodded to the others with him, seeming to communicate, "She's the one."

Strangely, she felt no fear. She kept her eyes fixed on his spear, which he raised while he shouted something she did not understand. The other two grabbed her arms. She struggled while they tied her hands behind her and directed her at spearpoint toward loose ranks of other prisoners also moving, also bound.

The chaos of fierce battle was over, replaced by the ugly shouting of orders by the Allahashi brutes and the whimpering and moaning of the dying and injured. While she marched down the mound toward the field, Taloa began to feel the stings of several bloody cuts.

Her beautiful dress hung torn, bloodstained, and dirty from battle.

She realized most of the Yukpans were dead or headed for slavery. New terrors for the lives of Robert, Anli, and Anli's family rushed into her thoughts. The sight of hundreds of dead men and women numbed her, yet her numbness fled in the face of her anger to see Allahashi women in their vulgar skirts, kneeling over the dead to strip them of their valuables. She bolted toward one about to spoil a Yukpan's corpse and kicked her in the side of the head to send her tumbling. The woman yelped like a dog.

She aimed for another kick, but a blow to her head with a spear shaft sent her to the ground. Her head swam while prods and the painful tugs of hard fingers brought her back to her feet, and she fell in, resuming the dreary march. The Allahashi herded her and other prisoners toward the gated caverns under the mounds.

She recognized a temple guard speaking with the ugly young warrior from that morning. The guard came to take her by the arm, guiding her eastward across the field, away from the rest. They passed Kochcha, who lay grotesquely contorted in death, so many arrows in him she could not count them.

Pain engulfed her mind and body. She prayed silently to *Aba Binnili* to receive the players, the honorable men, whose bodies they passed until the guard shoved her into the chamber under the royal mound, already filled with people. Guards barked at them to remain silent and knocked a few to the ground for trying to speak and reason with them. The warriors closed the heavy wooden doors behind her.

The darkness inside was complete. She heard men and women cry, but mostly stillness—the mute misery of a defeated people. She could not summon a thought. The pain from her wounds grew intense. She managed to move to the earthen wall of the vile cave, illuminated only by a tiny shaft of light peeping through a crack in the door. Taloa pressed her back against the wall and slid down to sit on the cool, moist dirt. She fought past the throbbing in her head and remembered the story of creation told to her by her Chahta father—of wet clay people emerging from the earth of *Nanih Waiya* cave into the light. "*Yaaknaat ittihoobataa*—is this the same earth?" she puzzled, bewildered.

CHAPTER NINETEEN

GLORY

YOSHOBA FELT PANTHER-CLAW TENSION BIND HIS SHOULDER muscles while he pretended not to watch his warriors encircle the playing field. He could hear the Yukpan nobles and masters begin to murmur nearby on the royal spectators' mound. Still, he felt confident it was all happening too fast for the dull-witted Yukpans to realize his masterful trap was about to close. His only anxiety was that they might try to run before his warriors were ideally in place.

He felt pleased by the presence of the strange white man, whom he seated among the most important Yukpan headmen, like Anli Basha. Like most others, Yoshoba was fascinated by how odd the man looked, and he understood immediately how he could take political advantage of the attraction he brought with him.

At the precise moment he rehearsed a hundred times in his mind, he raised his stone scepter in his left hand, signaling Shatanni behind him to send his warriors down among the honored guests. At the same time, elite guards on the field opened the mound crypt gates to let out four hundred heavily armed men who had waited inside.

The white man and the Yukpan dignitaries sat guarded by two elite warriors apiece, each carefully instructed in Yoshoba's step-by-step scheme. The Yukpan luminaries sat transfixed, as Yoshoba predicted, when they saw the vault gates open. Only the Mvskoke chief, Monahwee, seemed to figure out what would happen.

Apparently Monahwee was a suspicious sort—he hid a knife in his clothing. He sat lower on the mound and after turning to spy Shatanni's warriors closing in, he bolted, knife drawn, shouting and dashing down to the field. An Allahashi archer from high above dropped him dead with an arrow in the back, between his shoulders.

Despite Monahwee's alarm, Yoshoba's timing paid off. The Yukpan leaders reacted uncertainly to the Mvskoke chief's death and before they could realize their own perils, each found two spear points at his neck. As planned, the elite warriors quickly bound and blindfolded the high-ranking Yukpans and hustled them away over the top of the mound while Yoshoba's delegates watched, muttering with mild, detached confusion. As soon as the nobles left, Yoshoba raised his scepter in his right hand, and the archers began the slaughter of confederacy players on the field, and assassins pounced among the spectators on the west side.

Elite temple guards closed around Yoshoba and Ilaponla to escort them as they swiftly departed the arena toward the palace mound, while the other warriors marched the Yukpan dignitaries to a disguised underground prison and posted a heavy guard.

Exhilarated, Yoshoba took a perch at the palace's highest point to witness the carnage that followed. A sense of accomplishment overwhelmed him while he watched the one-sided battle rage in the near distance. The dead littered the field—the best young men of the troublesome confederacy, his last formidable enemies, cut down in one brilliant action. All over Tochina, he could see Yukpans dying like vermin.

The city gates closed according to his schedule. In less than an hour the entire Yukpan contingency in Tochina lay dead or captured. His glory and pre-eminent place in history was perfected before his eyes.

Ilaponla did not speak during their brisk march back to the palace. She emerged, her clothing changed, when the battle was nearly over.

"Your finest achievement, my Sun," she said with mere flatness in her voice, walking to stand beside the emperor. "Your trap worked. What now?" She did not sound exultant.

"You will see, squash blossom. You will see." He refused himself the temptation to look at her, knowing whatever opposition she might have planned no longer held promise for her. Along with the rest of the world, she was now firmly under his thumb. "Go to your rooms and wait for my command," he said tersely, catching her stubborn glower in the corner of his eye. Her resistant attitude evaporated after two guards stepped toward her. They escorted her to her quarters.

For the next few hours Yoshoba sat on his terrace, under heavy guard, while his warrior captains arrived one by one to report the statistics of battle and the disposition of the prisoners. He felt himself as golden as the sun that set in the west, illuminating his meetings. The palace seemed to reflect his magnificence even more than in the past.

A few resourceful Yukpans managed to escape, which did not disturb him. A handful of frightened survivors to carry the message of his might and terror worked well into his plan for northern world domination. He had instructed Holabi and his priests to set a council in what once was the judges' mound shortly after the battle to receive and appease city officials' complaints about the massacre and Yoshoba's failure to warn them. He felt confident the sudden chaos of war, not to mention fear for their own lives, would consolidate his local political adversaries into supporters, at least for the short run. He had strategies available to extinguish durable dissent to his imperial ambitions. He went to sleep that night under heavy guard and enjoying a full measure of contentment with his victory.

The next morning he sent orders to Ilaponla to dress in her most royal garments and to appear with him at two-sixths for the first public ceremony to celebrate their victory. At dawn several hundred workmen began work on a vast wooden ceremonial platform in the center of the playing field, with a raised podium in its midst for his and Ilaponla's seats of honor. Before two-sixths, criers ran through Tochina declaring all present, including guests from the north and west, were to assemble on the arena mounds for the ceremony.

Yoshoba ordered the Yukpan nobles and masters brought out of their prison, bound and gagged, to be arrayed for public view upon the royal visitors' mound. Robert and Taloa were taken from among them, strung up by ropes binding their hands, and left dangling from a crossbar at the south end of the platform. He intended for them to serve as symbols of his new dominance over the Yukpans.

Once everyone assembled, he ordered Holabi to lead the ceremony with a speech, authored by Yoshoba, which began with a condemnation of the Yukpans for their treachery and unholiness. He pointed out Robert as "the pale-skinned *hattak okpolo*, evil one" whom the Yukpans brought into the innocent Allahashis' midst to bring a curse upon them. He condemned Taloa as a whore to the unclean white man, as well as a symbol of the wickedness of Yukpan women and their societies. Translators at strategic points in the arena converted the message to other tongues represented in the crowd.

Holabi further proclaimed the unlimited prosperity and strength Yoshoba's courageous victory made possible for the Allahashi and their noble allies. "The Yukpan Confederacy will now dissolve," he declared, "and we will no longer need to worry about them allying with our enemies to the south against our northern tribes."

The high priest made for a persuasive orator. He enticed the sympathetic audience with visions of wealth, power, and new hunting and trading territories, all now taken from the jealous control of the weak and evil Yukpans. Still, following Yoshoba's orders, Holabi did not disclose details of the Great Sun's master plan, particularly the part that included executions of a few Yukpan nobles to instill fear of Yoshoba and trading others back to their peoples in exchange for the political and territorial concessions necessary to consolidate the empire.

His speech drew to an end, and Yoshoba gave a signal to light the wood stacked and prepared in a vast clay-lined fire pit cut in the middle of the platform. Another signal brought forth Lizbeth, the white man's goat. She bleated and resisted, nervous and confused. Two of Holabi's priests tried to bind her hind legs so they could hang her up between Robert and Taloa. Lizbeth began to struggle violently, kicking, bleating, and snapping at her captors. She made contact with a priests' arm, drawing blood, so they held her down while another bound her legs and her mouth. Made desperate by her bonds, she still fought even after they hung her between Robert and Taloa. Holabi declared to the crowd that the unearthly animal proved a further example of Yukpan witchcraft—their fellowship with the underworld—that ultimately held no power over the Great Sun of the Allahashi.

Three priests, on a signal from Holabi, bore forth a great copper dish to hold under Lizbeth, who dangled and writhed, her bleats muffled. On Yoshoba's signal, Holabi took a long, shining black stone knife from a ceremonial table and cut her throat with a swipe. The crowd cheered wildly while Lizbeth's blood splashed onto the dish, but soon their cheers subsided to discomfited murmurs, turning from grim entertainment to unsettled suspicion while she struggled and jerked for several minutes. At last she hung still.

Yoshoba did not lose his subtle smile, even while the white man bellowed what sounded like curses in his strange tongue during the instant of unexpected quiet after Holabi slit the underworld animal's throat. The white man, cut and bruised all over from a fight against the warriors who bound him, kicked and flung about, screaming straight at Yoshoba, who nodded to one of the guards. The guard struck the white man hard in the belly with the handle of his spear, and he gasped and fell quiet. Yoshoba could also hear Taloa Kinta, shouting deliriously and struggling against the ropes tight about her wrists, "*Chi imimatobbi-acho!* You will pay for this!"

A priest severed Lizbeth's head and impaled it on a long pole, which he set upright near the south end of the platform. The three dish bearers poured her blood into the fire, which guttered and spat. The crowd rebuilt its enthusiasm, cheering while Yoshoba rose to stand, scepter raised, to receive their praise.

The priests gutted and skinned Lizbeth with quick efficiency, threw her hide and offal into the fire, and slid a long, heavy pole through her carcass, like a spit. They carried it to a pivoted rack to swing it over the fire. The crowd, plied by the merchants with drinks fermented from wild musk grapes, cheered even louder. Yoshoba felt amused to see many wore souvenir ornaments, clothing, and other manner of items all scavenged from the corpses of Yukpans, whose bodies now lay buried in mass grave ditches concealed in dense woods east of the city.

The din of shouts, dancing, beats of small drums, and cheers reached its apex when Yoshoba rose with Ilaponla and gave a signal. The priests swung the goat, partly roasted by then, off the fire. Holabi handed Yoshoba and Ilaponla copper platters, larger than the plates his novices gave to other dignitaries—chiefs and headmen of some of the major northern tribes and their wives—standing with them on the platform.

After all the dignitaries were served sizzling slices of goat, Holabi carved and handed Yoshoba and Ilaponla large pieces, and together they ate, the men sharing triumphant smiles, as if at a secret joke. The crowd cheered again while Yoshoba raised his cup of wine toward the throng, a signal for guards to prod the Yukpan nobles back into their prison and for the drunken celebration to spread throughout the city and beyond. The guards let down the white man and his Yukpan woman and dragged them back to their heavily guarded stockade. Yoshoba had not fully thought out every detail, but he intended to save the two for public execution soon after. The festivities in Tochina continued long into the humid night under a full summer moon climbing into the blue-black sky.

Yoshoba and Ilaponla returned to the palace mound, where he immediately dispatched his queen to her quarters, still under guard. The goat still had longer to roast. Priests handed out small slices to Allahashi subjects curious for a taste of the exotic animal.

Yoshoba reclined on the west terrace of his palace and called for a group of fetching young slave women captured during earlier skirmishes with other remote tribes, selected and groomed by overseers to dance for him and his elite guards. He chose some warriors for the honor of going off duty to indulge their pleasures with the women. As the moon declined toward the western horizon, he admired its reflection shimmering upon the broad waters of the *Misha Sipokni*.

He limited his drinking, not wanting to lose track of his agenda during the chaotic revelry, yet felt his voice relax in the warm poultice of the ferment while he spoke, his eyes fixing on moonbeams reflecting from the great river, "All that you have seen beneath you this night, Moon Woman, is mine."

CHAPTER TWENTY

THE CURSE OF YIMINTA

ISKIFA AWOKE, EYES WIDE IN THE DARKNESS, DRENCHED WITH sweat. He spread his hands about himself, comforted slightly to feel his home bed and the touch of Nanitana's warm skin. Still, for the second night in a row, a dramatic and disturbing dream had dumped him out of the cradle of sleep.

The night before, the woodpecker his Chahta father and kin called the *biskinik*, the news bird, appeared to him, perched in a strange tree with smooth, skin-like bark the same pale green color as the biting grasshopper. The *biskinik's* head was larger than normal and had four faces, one toward each of the four directions. In his dream, Iskifa saw the bird and the tree while he fished on the banks of the *Hayi Bok*.

The *biskinik* was one of his favorite climbing birds, of medium size, with a simple song and a tap-tap-tapping. Many people claimed the *biskinik's* tapping was its way of speaking. Its sharp, black beak looked fearsome fourfold in its strange, outlandish head. And it spoke.

"I speak for *Aba Binnili*, the Creator of All," the bird said to him. "Hear and give ear, for *Aba Binnili* has spoken. I have nourished and raised children who have rebelled against me. The dog knows his master and the turkey his master's grain, but the Yukpans do not think or consider. Ah, foolish nation, a people loaded with stupidity, a seed of evildoers, corrupt children. You have forsaken your Creator, people who are walking backward into anger. Your heads are sick and your hearts faint. From the sole of the foot clear up to the head, there is no soundness in the body, but wounds and bruises and rotting sores; they have not been closed up, nor bound up, nor soothed with poultices. Your towns are burned and desolate and overrun by strangers."

The *biskinik's* oration burned Iskifa's ears like hot pepper juice. He could feel his throat swell shut. His head spun because the *biskinik* changed languages, one after another, speaking the same tongues Iskifa heard along his journey to the sea and back. Each time the *biskinik* changed to another language, its face would turn to its left and another more dazzling and frightening beak and face would appear, its pearl-black eyes the only constant feature he saw. Iskifa spoke to the bird, almost choking on his words. "But our land is rich, corn fills our granaries, our water is sweet, and our songs fill the river valleys."

"Iskifa speaks the words of a naïve child," the *biskinik* replied scornfully in his native language, turning another face to him, one that held a shimmering likeness within its frightening radiance—Iskifa's mother. "Yukpan daughters are left as a hut in a cornfield, as a watchman's hut in a burned garden of squash, as an inundated city."

The *biskinik's* head spun once more to speak in the Allahashi tongue. "Hear the words of *Aba Binnili*. To what purpose is your repetition of many prayers and offerings to me? I am full of grain and the fat smoke of your hunting fires. I do not delight in your drums or songs. Bring no more vain ceremonies. Your burning cedar is an offense to my nostrils; your new moons and your appointed feasts are silliness; they trouble me; I am weary of them. Put away your evil doings, your dim-sighted foolishness; cease to do evil."

The bird squawked angrily and flew away. Iskifa pulled on his tight fishing line, but it broke easily. He fell with a *thud* on the creek bank and awoke in his bed, gasping for breath, sweating. He rose to walk outside and spent the rest of the night studying the moon and puzzling over his dream. He was unable to work or eat the next day and spent much of his time alone and confused, wandering the banks of the *Hayi Bok*.

Now this new dream, on this night. In it, he saw people dying, defenseless, arrows and spears rending their flesh, blood spilling from their bodies, and he heard their screams of anguish. He gasped at the sight, as if through flames, of Robert and Taloa strung up by their hands. Others stood near them, but their faces were the only ones he recognized. He read Taloa's lips saying, "Master, save us." He wanted to awake and go to help them, but could not. The images repeated, over and over, until the landscape of his dream changed to the smooth, flowing waters of a great, wide river. Again, he sat on the bank, fishing, but a rope slipped down from a tree to slide around his ankles like a snake, whip him upside down, and dangle him with his face only a short interval above the flowing waters. Fish of all kinds came to the surface, first turning glimmering eyes toward him, then standing on their tails atop the water, laughing at him, raucous and taunting, like elder women. In the water he saw the reflection of a flock of crows drawing near from the western riverbank, first shimmering black specks, soon swooping, swelling images, and they landed on him, gripping his clothes and shoes and hair with sharp claws. One by one, they began to tear small pieces of his clothing, then his flesh, as if he was carrion. Their raw voices grew louder until his head throbbed. Just as he thought he could stand no more, the four-faced *biskinik* appeared in the water's reflection, growing from a speck to full form, and landed on the bottom of his feet.

"Be gone, *chalhha*, black birds," the *biskinik* spoke, and the crows vanished. "Listen, wordmaster," he said, "and let us reason together. If your people become wise, as they once were, you will eat of the good of the land." The *biskinik* began to sing the familiar song Iskifa loved, and his terror grew less.

The *biskinik* again spoke. "The nobles and masters are rebellious, the companions of thieves," it said. "They each love gifts, art, shiny metal, and personal gain. They have forgotten their communities, their crops, the widows and motherless children, the ancients, the weak ones, the sick. They care more for trade than for honor and truth. If they continue they shall be as the dry leaves of oak and as the deadfall in the forest, and the spark of their own foolishness will kindle a fire that consumes them and none will be able to quench the flames. You must lead them away from the enemies, back to wisdom, or they will perish."

The *biskinik* squawked and pushed away from Iskifa's feet. He watched its head gently turn while its reflected form in the water diminished and at last vanished. For a moment, all was quiet before he felt his heaviness increase, and the rope wound tighter around his ankles. It broke, and he fell face-first into the river, feeling the instant tug of its heavy current. The cold shock awakened him.

As he did the night before, he arose quietly, so not to awaken Nanitana and need to explain his odd behavior to her. He walked out into the midsummer moonlight, piecing together the scenes from the two nightmares and the warnings of *Aba Binnili*, and realized a new and disturbing message—that Robert and Taloa might be in danger, and many of his friends, neighbors, and allies might be the same or worse. Anguish flooded his soul. He admonished himself for not warning his people more forcefully about the treacherous Allahashi, for his failure to assert himself as their elder, and for not insisting they come to their senses and disdain the *Yamohmi*.

He admitted, however, that human foolishness knew no bounds. Such truth was no more evident to him than in his remembrance of the follies of his youth. He prayed and thought and wept, walking the familiar *Hayi Bok* path. He knew he must go to Tochina, alone. No one would believe him or his dreams, he could not risk any more of his friends' lives, and he could not afford to be slowed by their doubts.

He felt the most grief over his failure to protect his young apprentice, Taloa. Why had he not insisted she return with him to Chunuli, instead of letting her walk into the *Yamohmi* trap? And *Aba Binnili* sent him on a special mission to save Robert on the great water's shore. He prided himself on his faithfulness to *Aba Binnili*, yet felt compelled to confess his failure to follow through with this strange, pale-skinned man.

By first light he had gathered what he needed for the journey and what might, perhaps, help him to free some of his people. He stood in the doorway of his log house, staff in hand, bags over his shoulder, aching with love and pity for his partner of uncountable winters.

Nanitana awoke. The yellow light of dawn dimly illuminated her shapely beauty as she sat up, squinting toward his shadowy figure in the doorway.

"Why are you dressed so?" she asked sleepily.

"I had another dream, sweet one," he replied with all the concern and affection he could project in a few words. "I must go to Tochina."

Nanitana shaded her eyes with her hand. Her brow furrowed. At first she looked angry while she collected the meaning of his words and his tone.

"Our people need me," he told her, sadly. "I must go."

Her expression relaxed into one that seemed both a frown and a smile. She walked to him and raised her hands to squeeze the sides of his face, looking into his eyes. Her dark eyes always seemed to him like windows into a better world and never so much as at this moment. Still, he felt frightened and boyish in her gaze. She kissed him and let her hands slip down.

He turned to walk into the road, feeling the ache of parting in his belly, even with the assurance of her blessing. The leaves of his beloved trees shimmered and rustled in the morning breeze while he followed the *Hayi Bok* westward. He estimated that if he kept at it briskly, he might reach Tochina in seven or eight days.

Along the way he ate strength-giving roots and nuts and gathered herbs and plants he needed. He slept only adequately, walking until well after dark and beginning again before dawn. He gathered forbidden mushrooms, ones his *alikchi*, medicine, friends warned should be used only under the most extreme necessity. Few knew their exact powers, and many considered them instantly deadly, even to the touch.

He followed the well-traveled creek-bottom roads mostly through Yukpan lands, avoiding towns, friendly or otherwise, to avoid delay. As he drew nearer to Tochina, he skirted the bluffs and bottoms of the *Misha Sipokni* to stay clear of Allahashi settlements. On the morning of the eighth day he caught his first glimpse of Tochina. He had not seen the city since he was a teenager traveling with his father in a buffalo hunting party, only a winter before Yoshoba's grandfather slaughtered, drove off, or converted the last practitioners of the Creator religion in the north. Few Yukpans without important purposes had hunted beyond the south border of Allahashi-held territory in many winters, even if their treachery of that time was all but forgotten. Since invitations to the *Yamohmi* went out two winters before, the more interior confederacy tribes persuaded themselves they should no longer think of the Allahashi as threats. Even so, others living on the edges of the confederacy's territory still regarded them with distrust and suspicion.

While Iskifa walked, he hatched a plan. He remembered lessons from the early part of his apprenticeship, ones in which his mentor Atanapoa vehemently criticized the sun worship of the Allahashi. Among his stories, one character, Yiminta, captured Iskifa's imagination. Yiminta was a pre-Allahashi prophet of great renown in the days when the Allahashi, now the "Children of the Sun," still called themselves the Good River People.

Yiminta's significance lay mostly in the fact that he predicted an ungodly heathen people would defeat the Good River tribe, many winters before that prophecy came true. One of the first deeds of Okpulo, Yoshoba's great-grandfather, in his purging of the Creator religion in the north was to send assassins to kill Yiminta. Yiminta predicted on his deathbed that he would return from the dead in the future, and a horrible and deadly disease would consume anyone who tried to kill him after his return.

Iskifa managed to steal some old-fashioned Allahashi ceremonial garb from an unattended farmhouse. He decided, well knowing the risks that followed, that posing as Yiminta gave him the best chance of getting close enough to the palace to rally confederacy prisoners for an escape. He knew Yiminta's resurrection prophecy would be forgotten by everyone but the priests and hoped they might be called to investigate his claim to be the resurrected prophet. That could give him enough time to do some good, and he had to admit it was a long shot, but it was the best he could come up with, given so little time. Besides, he reasoned, if the destruction of the Yukpans was as complete as his dream portrayed, no one should expect an enemy to walk straight into Tochina in plain sight.

The imposing city loomed ahead for a great distance while fear and calculation jostled each other in his mind. The hot air of river-bottom summer cooled overnight and braced his courage somewhat as he started before dawn to approach Tochina. The trees looked old and ominous along the stretch of the *Misha Sipokni* where he slept before he prayed for a long time, his whispered petitions flowing atop the *swoosh* of the great river's current.

As the sun broke over the horizon, he stopped at a creek, bending to work its thick, dark mud into his hair, which he twisted into spikes to stick up from his scalp. He rubbed the darkest mud on his face, let it dry, and daubed white pigment from his pouch around his eyes to give himself the most risen-from-the-dead appearance he could conjure. He checked the potions he thought he might need, mixed at stops along his journey.

He moved hidden among rows of green *tanchi* in fields extending tens of flights west of Tochina, skirting farm villages, arousing only an occasional dog's bark. As he came closer to the city, the fields gave way to smaller gardens and clusters of houses. It surprised and disconcerted to him to see such a large population spread around the city.

Within a few flight of the city, the houses and merchants' buildings became so dense he knew he must show himself. He hoped he would encounter a priest before he caught the attention of a watcher.

He walked into the center of the town closest to Tochina. Women took one look at him, grabbed their children, and slipped into their houses until an old man accosted him.

"Who are you, strange creature?" asked the elder, first coming up to walk beside him, stretching hesitantly to examine Iskifa's face.

"I am Yiminta of old," Iskifa replied in a gravelly, ghostly Allahashi tongue. "Be forewarned not to touch me, lest you die."

The old man jumped a surprising distance away. Perhaps he recognized the name.

"Fetch your priest, young man," Iskifa told him, not breaking his slow and stately stride.

The old man left straightaway and returned with what must have been his best estimation of a holy man, another skinny old man bedecked with odd piercing ornaments, tattoos, and charms. The medicine man held a strange grass doll with a rabbit's-foot head in his hand. Iskifa recognized it as a traditional good luck charm and a rather cheap one, at that. Even so, the skinny Allahashi must have hoped or believed it might also ward off evil, because he kept it raised toward Iskifa, with comic insistence.

"Is that your best medicine, young man?" Iskifa asked blankly.

The skinny man stared, keeping his distance, seeming unable to speak. He whispered nervously to the other old man, waving the cheap little doll up and down. Now and then Iskifa heard "Yiminta" among his tremulous whispers.

"Take me to Holabi," Iskifa interjected, expressionless, as if that were the obvious thing to do. Anli Basha had mentioned the high priest's name while they talked about the *Yamohmi* in Anoli.

The medicine man motioned in broad circles with the shivering doll for Iskifa to follow him, keeping a fair distance. A troupe of amused and curious children fell in behind them.

"I must walk in the center of the *Hina Aalhpisa*, the forward path," Iskifa chanted to himself as the last march to Tochina began. In line with that sentiment he let himself, without smiling, enjoy the sight of children, especially the daring ones who ran ahead, some playing hoops and arrows.

It would not be Iskifa's first time to face danger. At sixty-five, there was little he had not seen—births, murders, war and peace, betrayal, and fierce loyalties. He allowed himself to notice the attractive young Allahashi women eyeing him along the way. He had just passed his fortieth winter with Nanitana and was always careful not to yield to the temptations of fertile young women. On the other side of his mind, the sights of the young women also summoned shards of the unhappiness he felt when his first wife quit him for his unfaithfulness and wandering eye. Still, the lighthearted, if devious, nature of the attraction eased his inner preparation for the hazards ahead inside a city full of people who proved themselves worthy of scorn.

The words of his father, Itti Toshtuli, rose in his memory, as if to prompt him. When he was a teenager, they received word a marauding band of Allahashi warriors were headed to Chunuli. "Defend your family, your people, but do not hate your enemy," his father had said, because he regarded how hungry the Allahashi must have been to range so far south. "Hate can only kill the one who does the hating."

His father taught him all he knew about wood, weaponry and fighting, and agriculture, but Atanapoa trained Iskifa in holy things, as a judge of language, in comparing religions, and in the medicines of the forests. Taken together, these two men provided him with the knowledge that gave him a comfortable and useful life. "All will come to bear before another moon rises," he thought.

On his deathbed, Atanapoa's last remark to Iskifa was a question. "What have you learned, apprentice?"

"This is the essence of what you have taught me, Master," Iskifa replied, choking back grief at the sight of his beloved teacher about to leave his body. "I really believe in the design. I believe the Creator has a design for every living thing, and that we should study the design with the curiosity of a child and with the cheerful anticipation of a child and expect that something good is going to happen."

The memory both cheered and saddened Iskifa. His answer showed how naïve he was at that age. He remembered how Atanapoa condemned religious "show knowledge" and openly rejected misplaced zeal and prejudice. The teacher died before he could respond to his student's declaration.

The gates of the city rose in sight. The huge, high, weathered oak fortifications were the largest by far that Iskifa had seen. The open, unguarded gates suggested the Allahashi believed all immediate threats were past. Guards stood in every parapet around the perimeter, however, proving they still felt cautious. The city, on both sides of the gate, teemed with colorful trade, athletic games, and merchants of all descriptions.

Inside the gates, Iskifa spotted the watcher before the medicine man did. The watcher came forward, and the skinny medicine man spoke with him, alternately pointing the doll charm toward the center of the city and back in the direction they came from.

The watcher approached Iskifa for a closer look—a grim-looking young man, tall, muscular, and well armed, with incredibly dark skin and an ugly pink scar across the side of his face. Iskifa saw aggression mix with bewilderment on his face. He seemed to wish not to get too close. The watcher motioned for Iskifa to follow, his gesture grave and authoritarian. The medicine man started to follow also, but the watcher backhanded him to the chest soundly, and the old man reeled away like a child's hoop, vanishing into the bustle around them.

Surrounded by so much noise and activity, Iskifa attracted far less attention. They walked several flight before stopping at the bottom of a precipitous stairway up the manicured sides of one of the multitude of platform mounds. The watcher made a sign to two guards near the top, who came down to talk with him. Iskifa understood their tongue well enough to hear a crude rendition of the Yiminta myth, their perception of a necessity for interpretation by Holabi or one close to him, and a clear warning not to touch this creature.

Iskifa felt the cold fingers of fear trying to grip his heart while he watched the guards, marking them by their bearing and demeanor as heartless men, trained to kill. "I am content, like the wild flower," he sung inside himself, recalling a song his mother loved to sing anytime he was afraid as a boy.

The guards took places on either side of the stairway, glowering at Iskifa and pointing upward with their spears. They gave him a wide berth, but no choice as to what his next move would be.

At the top, one of the guards prodded him tacitly with the shaft of his spear to move to one side. The other went inside the building and returned with three young men in priestly clothing, all bald except for topknots at the backs of their heads. Each wore a glaring red tattoo of the sun on his jowl, a sign of his class.

The young priests motioned for Iskifa to enter. "Sit there, old man," one said, pointing to a chair alone in the middle of the airy room.

Iskifa stepped toward it, but lowered to sit on the ground instead. The young priests frowned, but made no comment about that while they took seats on benches around him.

"So, you are Yiminta, whose story we've heard?" one asked, hardly sounding persuaded.

"You are correct, pup," Iskifa replied in a hoarse monotone.

"Will we die if we touch you?" another asked, casting a skeptical smile to his associates.

"If you do not believe, touch me and see for yourself," Iskifa replied, pausing between each barely audible phrase, hoping to make the prospect of touching him seem even more foreboding.

The young priest's smile turned down. He looked at each of the other priests, who only raised their eyebrows, as if to suggest, "Go ahead." He jumped up, jerking his head toward the door, and they followed to huddle just inside the entrance, not out of Iskifa's earshot. "This old fool is a fake and a fraud," the young priest who asked about dying said. "We should throw him down the hill."

"Maybe so, hothead," another novice priest said. "But even if he is a cracked pot, the story he tells is powerful to the citizens among us who still secretly practice the old ways. Master Holabi will want us to be careful with him. We don't want to give them another martyr." Their whispers grew quieter, but he could tell they decided, to his relief, to wait for their master to examine the one who claimed to be Yiminta.

After a few minutes, one of the cutthroat-looking guards came to stand squarely in the doorway, to guard against escape. Iskifa saw the three novices descend and calculated at least part of his plan worked. They would shift responsibility up rank for a decision about how to deal with this odd man. He prayed his next meeting would be with Holabi and tried to think over details of what he would do next, but so much lay beyond anticipation. He decided his time was better spent preparing himself spiritually. He believed the Creator influenced human events, including the rise and fall of civilizations, and his focus was better placed on the *Hina Aalhpisa*. "Remain in the center of the path," he chanted to himself. He let himself relax from the self-control of his masquerade and mellowed into his own senses, noting the smell of this city and the hums of insects floating in and out of the priest house. He could see the impressive architecture of the palace atop its great platform mound through the door opening. He had heard it was the greatest earthwork in the northern world. His eyes confirmed that claim. He also noticed an absence—the songs of birds.

He knew about great towns, even palisaded ones, but no cities this large in the southeast where he lived. Nevertheless it seemed even in his region of Chunuli, near no major waterways, that the population had increased a great deal in his lifetime. Generations including his father's were content with being farmers, woodworkers, and fishermen, but since the new corn came in, about the time of Iskifa's birth, narrower specializations had developed. Whole cities sprung up solely on trade, fostering specialties in commerce and paring away the more generalized skills and wisdoms he learned to value among men and women. Humans were not created, he reasoned, to be partial beings, but creatures of knowledge and balance, understanding earth, sky, animals, people, medicine, and the arts and crafts necessary for complete health and accountability. Even with these values, Iskifa acknowledged the irony that the rise of the importance of the *anompolichi* came from increased preference for wider trade routes and the diversity of language expertise they required.

As he processed the city's offerings into his senses, a hummingbird flew in through the doorway, hovered a moment, and edged closer to him—attracted, he supposed, by the embroidered images of red lilies on his stolen ceremonial Allahashi vest. He remembered the breastplate fashioned from hummingbird feathers his mother kept in a special covered basket. She inherited it from her grandmother, who said hummingbird feather ornaments pleased the Creator, so they were used only in the most sacred ceremonies. Iskifa regarded the appearance of the hummingbird as a very good sign—a sign *Aba Binnili* was pleased with his mission here.

With less than a sixth of daylight left, a troupe of well armed and more elite-looking warriors arrived at the priest house to take him into custody and march him to the main priest mound nearer the palace. They prodded him with their spear points up the long stairway, and he soon found himself in the presence of Holabi.

Holabi's countenance was intense. His deep-set eyes were shiny black, like the glinting rock from western volcanoes prized by knife traders on the river. His incredibly long hair looped in braids under his arms, pinned to the shoulders of his immaculately crafted and colorful high priest's mantle. Woven into the braids were small fans of hummingbird feathers, a detail Iskifa found disconcerting.

"Yiminta of old, welcome," Holabi spoke in a tone affecting high oratory, contradicted by his crooked, nonchalant smile. "For decades we have awaited your return."

Iskifa tensed at his arrogance—even if he wasn't Yiminta, this priest seemed only to worship himself, he could tell. "Give ear, foul priest," he retorted, in perfect dialectical Allahashi. "Your reign of terror has come to an end."

The warriors raised their weapons.

Holabi scowled, but raised his hand. Furrows crossed his brow. "You speak boldly, mud-face ghost."

"I speak the truth, false prophet."

"Your intestines will soon foul my floor, and your tongue will please a dog's palate, fool's crow."

"You know the curse," Iskifa replied in a ghostly voice, again pausing significantly between sentences. "Go ahead."

Holabi turned to walk to a table where he dipped a gourd full of water from a clay vessel and returned to extend it toward him. "You must be thirsty from your journey." His expression, a mix of smile and sneer, gave away his experiment—human or spirit?

Iskifa knocked the dipper from his hand to the floor. "You face your reckoning, evil one," he said blankly.

"Guards! Bind this putrid-smelling wretch and take him to the stockade that holds the white man and the girl," Holabi ordered.

The guards hesitated to touch him. Holabi repeated his order, louder, and their superstitious fear of Yiminta proved to be less than their practical dread of Holabi. They tied Iskifa's hands behind him, cinching the rope painfully around his wrists, but only poked him with their spears to move him out the door and down the mound steps.

Iskifa showed no discomfort, buoyed within by relief—and great amazement—that his plan worked so well. The manipulative priest knew the legend of Yiminta thoroughly and tested it, with no risk to himself, by making the guards touch him and by throwing him in with prisoners who also would die or survive, either way.

The walls of the stockade stood the height of three men, built of round, green timbers sharpened to spikes. The brutish guards shoved Iskifa into a chamber by himself and wedged the door shut. On the way inside he counted only four guards posted around the compound that sat in a clearing about two flight inside the main gate. The guards took his bags to check for hidden weapons, but missed the small bladder of liquid he kept tucked under his breechcloth, perhaps because they didn't wish to touch him again. Iskifa listened to the guards chuckle—in one of the bags they found an Allahashi woman's dress. They hooted, joking about an old man who liked to dress as a woman.

Iskifa pulled out the little bladder and dug a small hole to hide it before he crawled to peer through a thin space between the timbers into the next cell. He could make out the forms of four men, all badly beaten. Judging from their tattered clothing, they were Mvskokes, and two were elder men of rank. Three lay still, and one elder sat awake.

Outside the guards fell into boredom. Iskifa heard stories they told, although no conversation about their prisoners aside from unenthusiastic details about the crazy old man they just brought in.

He crawled to the other wall to find another split and looked through to see Robert and Taloa lying in the shredded, stained remains of their clothes, either unconscious or asleep. He saw welts from whipping, but no other wounds, and felt encouraged to see they were breathing. With so little daylight left, he decided the rest of his plan, however risky and dependent on whether his young friends could walk, could not wait for later.

Because he loved the cadence of the language, he began to sing in the Chikasha tongue a song of the great historic battle of Chunuli, a ballad most Yukpan children knew. It told of victory during the last great war with the remnants of the Hokays and their cohorts who fought many winters against Yukpan tribes east of Chilantak's town, trying to retake territory the Yukpans held for centuries after the great Anoli liberated them. The Hokay alliance laid waste to many tribes in between, but met ruinous defeat in the decisive battle on the prairies south of Chunuli. He wanted to sing loud enough to awaken Taloa, but without the guards hearing.

He saw Taloa sit up and look about for a moment before she crawled to the wall between them, to look through the crack. He moved away a little so she could see him.

She began to sob. "Master? ... Master?"

Iskifa nodded and shushed her, tapping his lips. Still singing, he gave her the sign to watch. He dug up the bladder, pulled its plug, and slouched against the opposite wall, changing his tune to a popular Allahashi drinking song, slurring the words and blaring loudly.

"What's going on in there?" one of the guards demanded. Others joined him to listen a moment before they hustled around to the gate. "Hey, duck-brain," one cajoled the main jailer, "your crazy old man's got some *shonti*!" The jailer unlocked Iskifa's cell with an irritated frown, stepped inside to regard the prisoner warily, and reached to lift the small bladder from Iskifa's hands. He gave one last look at the old man who lay quiet as if passed out.

A younger jailer snatched the bladder away for a quick swig. "Hey, don't be greedy!" the older jailer chided him, sounding glad for a break in the boredom. "There's enough for everyone—and this *shonti* must be strong stuff. We don't want Shatanni to catch us at it."

The older warrior closed Iskifa's cage door, but forgot to replace the wedge in his eagerness to get the small bladder back for a sip. The guards' conversation turned giddy. The *shonti* was indeed strong—Iskifa seasoned it with a pure extract of forbidden mushrooms he prepared during his walk to Tochina. When he was young he used to experiment with the mushrooms and found that in small doses they held the power to make men see visions. In a larger dose like he used that night, he expected unconsciousness, perhaps even death, might result. Either way, their minds and senses would cease.

Soon the guards staggered back to their posts, slid down the stockade walls to sit, and after a few minutes all slumped, out cold. Iskifa pushed his door open and stole over to the next cell, where Taloa had awakened Robert. They waited, cowering near the front wall. Iskifa dragged one of the limp guards inside, moved to pity by the sorry sight of his friends—weak, almost naked, starved, and defenseless.

"There's no time to waste," he urged them. "Robart, strip this dog of his clothes, put them on, and put your clothes on him. Make him appear to be sleeping."

Taloa translated, but Robert hesitated, looking groggy and not sure he believed the strange-looking man could be Iskifa.

"Your eyes do not lie to you, my friend," Iskifa assured him in the most soothing tone he could muster in such a rush. "Do as I say. Now."

Robert grinned with recognition, although wearily, and set to work. Iskifa retrieved most of the things dumped from his bags. He tossed the dress that caused such amusement among the guards to Taloa, who put it on and buried her Yukpan garb.

Iskifa unfolded a small, beeswax-enclosed package. "Tell Robart this is oak tannin mixed with my finest rendered bear oil. Have him rub it onto his face and skin. He needs to change into an Allahashi."

Robert seemed bewildered by the Allahashi costume, so Taloa helped him get into it and helped to rub the tannin into his skin.

Iskifa and Taloa heard the Mvskokes plead through the wall, "Don't forget us."

Iskifa opened their cell, instructing the young Mvskokes to exchange clothes with the insensate guards, and to be sure to tuck away their knives and weapons. The elders turned their Yukpan garments inside out and put on some of the guards' ornaments to appear Allahashi, at least at a casual glance. They carried a stockade guard outside the back wall, taking care and stealth to set him up to appear as if he was alert and on duty.

"It will be dark soon," Iskifa told them in Mvskokean. "We must escape. Don't try to free your women or children," he warned, pointedly. "It is useless to try. They are too well guarded."

They protested, but Iskifa carefully described the Allahashi military presence and after compassionate but firm argument, persuaded them the best they could do was to escape themselves. That would be a daunting task, but it offered the only prospect for liberation of their people and others enslaved by the Allahashi. Taloa translated to Robert, who seemed to collect his wits enough to call up reserves of strength and focus.

Iskifa washed the mud and pigment off and turned his ceremonial garb inside out to look nondescript, choosing not to change clothes with a guard—a relatively short old man with silver-streaked hair would never pass for an Allahashi warrior.

Iskifa whispered to the Mvskokes, "After dark we must leave this compound in two groups—my friends and I at first. You follow a five-hundred count later. If we are caught, we will make noise and attract a lot of attention, which may serve as a diversion for your escape. As you know, the *Misha Sipokni* lies due west and only about twenty flight away. It will be a dark night, and there are two towns close together between here and the river. After we pass through the first town, we can walk through the cornfields in the bottoms and be well downstream before dawn. We should hide in the woods the first day, because the area is well settled. Tomorrow night's walk will put us in less settled places, where we can travel in daylight if we are careful. Do any of you know their language?"

"I speak fairly well," one of the younger men replied in a dialect of Allahashi. "My father is a shell trader."

"Good. You must handle any encounters you cannot avoid," Iskifa instructed.

The Mvskokes asked many questions about the river route and conferred about the best ways to find food, the necessity of minimizing fires, and even ways to kill or incapacitate enemies without making a sound. While darkness fell and they made ready to leave, the guard leaning against the outside wall began to groan. They froze and listened. He groaned again, louder.

"Wait!" Iskifa whispered.

CHAPTER TWENTY·ONE

SICKNESS

I AM DYING!" YOSHOBA SCREAMED, REELING IN HIS BED. A DOCTOR whisked to his side and began to mop his brow with a cool, wet cloth. Yoshoba slapped him away. Another chanted in the corner before an altar set with a fat burning lamp, idols and fetishes all about. Scattered oil lamps infused the room with a dim yellow glow.

"Stop your jabbering, you fool!" Yoshoba snarled, words gurgling in his raw, swollen throat. He gasped and coughed miserably and suffered every time he looked at or touched the oozing sores on his chest and arms. "You idiots could not cure a scratch, much less this evil that has befallen me!" he moaned, exhausted, hanging his head and rolling it slowly, without strength to lift his chin off his chest. "I've burned without relief for three days. My head has an arrow point in it. I cannot eat. I soil myself and throw up bile. Have you no spell for me, you witches?"

"We're doing all we know, Great Sun," the nearest doctor answered timorously. "Even I feel ill."

"It's not enough, you rat! How fares Ilaponla?"

Silence.

"Ilaponla! Does she live? I demand to know!" he rasped.

"She ... she died last night, Great Sun."

"Good," he muttered. "I don't have to kill her now."

"What?"

"Never mind."

"Six others who were with you on the platform and ate the white man's beast are also dead," the doctor fretted. "All who were on the platform are badly sick, save one."

"And who is that, you wretch?"

"The High Priest Holabi, Great Sun. He served, but did not eat."

"He probably knew," Yoshoba groaned, weakly. "He and the woman were bedding together, and the skunk let her be poisoned, anyway. His death will be as certain as hers. Call him to me! And not a word of warning, or you die, too!"

The doctor sent a guard, and Holabi soon appeared.

"You called for me, my Sun?" Holabi asked.

"What is your judgment about this Yiminta lunatic?" Yoshoba asked as if to conduct business as usual, despite his struggles to speak.

"None of the guards who handled him have died," the priest reported with a confident smirk. "I checked just a little while ago. I assume he is a crazy old fake and should be simply put to death." Holabi cocked his head. "Would you like to see him yourself, Great Sun?"

"No! No! I need no more curses than the one I suffer now, you fool. Kill him and be done with it."

Holabi nodded toward two temple warriors. They left.

"Done, Great Sun."

"So. Who will succeed me when I die, priest?"

Holabi cleared his throat, looking uncomfortable. "You shall not die, Great Sun. I have prayed to the—"

"Do not try to deceive me, priest! Who, I ask for the last time, since Ilaponla is dead, will succeed me?"

Holabi stammered, "Either—either I, who holds the highest office besides yourself, or—or Shatanni, who is very popular with the people, Great Sun."

Yoshoba burst into a coughing fit, finishing minutes later with a trickle of blood at the corner of his mouth. He fought to breathe. "The end of my time draws near. Come closer, high priest," he gasped, "that I may whisper my will to you."

Holabi swallowed with hesitation and approached to incline his ear to Yoshoba's mouth.

Yoshoba put a hand behind his neck to pull him closer. "It won't be you, priest," he whispered. He drew a slender stone dagger from under his cover and shoved it into Holabi's abdomen under the rib cage, twisting it.

Holabi exhaled a blood-spattered rasp and fell upon Yoshoba, collapsing him onto his back.

The doctors stood about as if frozen, gawking.

"Get this dog's carcass off me!" the dying monarch gurgled. "Bury him at once without drawing attention, or you will be next."

CHAPTER TWENTY-TWO

ISKIFA'S STRATEGY

"WE FORGOT TO LIGHT THE TORCHES," ISKIFA WHISPERED while they listened to the guard groan outside the stockade. "Light them at once," he told one of the young Mvskokes, who found a jar of coals and swiftly finished the evening ritual around the outer compound of the jail. The amber flames cast an eerie glow on the guard propped against the timber wall, who began to loll his head about, as if to awaken soon.

"You must quiet the guard," Iskifa told the other young Mvskoke. "Make his sleep certain, but leave no marks or blood." Iskifa, Robert, and Taloa kept watch while the young man stole catlike through the outer door. They heard a quick gasp from the guard, and silence. The young man crept back to them.

"Now we are ready," Iskifa said. He turned to the elder Mvskokes. "One of you count five hundred, the others pray for guidance and protection. *Aba Binnili* will deliver you." He put his arms around Taloa and Robert, who still looked beaten and drained despite their eagerness to flee. "We will survive and continue, my young friends. Follow me."

He nudged the gate open just enough to peer about and saw only the bustling nightlife of Tochina to the south, but from the north, two armed warriors strode toward the compound. Jolting fear jabbed his heart, and the hair stood on his neck. They did not see him, but he needed to act quickly. The Mvskokes, known for their skill as archers, carried bows and slings of arrows they took from the jailers. Iskifa, gesturing for quiet, directed them to positions at the front corners of the walls.

"You must stop them without a possibility of their crying out," he whispered, pressing his forefingers to his neck to indicate their targets. "Don't shoot for their hearts," he added. "Their breastplates are seasoned oak and can stop or turn an arrow." They nodded with grim understanding, drew their arrows, and notched them on their bowstrings.

Iskifa guided Taloa and Robert as close to the gate as possible, and Robert drew his Allahashi knife with a trembling hand. Iskifa took a spot opposite the gate so he would be the first one the warriors saw. When he heard the gate open, he pulled up his breechcloth and squatted down in profile to appear to relieve himself.

"Hah!" the first warrior blurted with disgust at the old man's undignified pose. The second warrior followed, but the first turned far enough to catch sight of the bowmen in the corner of his eye and raised his spear, but too late. Four arrows flew to their marks, two in each warrior's neck. The second warrior collapsed at once. The first staggered toward the Mvskokes, wounds spurting. An elder Mvskoke drew another arrow, notched it, and confounded Iskifa's estimation, shooting it through the Allahashi's breastplate and his heart. He fell backward to lie still.

Taloa and Robert wasted no time dragging the other warrior clear of the gate and saw he blinked and gasped, not yet dead. Iskifa saw a wild, angry look in Robert's eyes as he raised his knife to finish the man and sprang to catch his forearm. Robert looked up, squinting against the stinging sweat trickling down his forehead. Iskifa registered the depth of agony on the young white man's face and took his hand to guide it over the Allahashi's mouth. Robert pressed on it, and the warrior, with blood pooling around his neck, died quickly, eyes open.

Iskifa then watched Robert take from around the temple warrior's neck the rose-colored beads that belonged to his dead friend on the beach. Robert wiped off the Allahashi's blood that had spilled onto the string of beads with their little crossed stake, and put them around his neck.

"Hide the bodies," Iskifa whispered to the Mvskokes. After taking more weapons from the temple warriors, they opened the small underground pit on the afternoon sun side of the compound—a pit they were all too familiar with—and dumped the bodies inside.

"Now we must go," Iskifa said, shouldering his bags again. *"Aba Binnili aapichi, Aba Binnili's* favor," he blessed them, grasping the forearms of each of his Mvskoke allies. He led Robert and Taloa out.

Apprehension and caution gripped Iskifa. Frightening eyes fixed upon them in the Tochina night, but all looked away. Traders and others from the northern and western nations plied their wares during the day and reveled in Tochina nightlife. He hoped strangers like themselves would not attract much attention in that stewpot of humanity.

He felt hungry and knew Robert and Taloa must be starved. The sorry casts of their countenances faded into the dark of the moonless night. Even so, torches and bear-oil lamps spread too much light about for his comfort. He tried to keep to the shadows.

Getting food without stealing it was better accomplished inside the city, so Iskifa sat his weary companions at a table obscured by shadows outside a merchant's hut. He traded a black pearl pilfered from one of the guards for some jerked venison, fresh vegetables, dried fish, and as a bonus, some fruit, and the friendly merchant filled his water skin. Taloa and Robert lunged for the food, hungrily. "Only small bites of the dried meats and squash," Iskifa cautioned, "so your stomachs can take time to adjust."

On their way again, they stopped at another hut so Iskifa could trade for three light pelt blankets bearing Allahashi designs. He wrapped them around their shoulders. As soon as they cleared the ominous gates of Tochina, Taloa and Iskifa glanced at each other, smiled, and embraced with warmth and relief.

They looked at Robert, who tried to smile, but an uncertainty remained in his eyes. Taloa slipped her arms gently around him and hugged, and his eyes closed tightly in her embrace, sudden tears gushing from them. He made no sound, Iskifa noticed, communicating firmly his awareness of the need to survive. Still, he looked pathetic, weeping like a frightened child in her arms, the blanket hanging from his drooping shoulders.

Iskifa led them away from the town where he encountered the skinny medicine man with the rabbit's-foot doll earlier that afternoon. The few people they passed hailed them and spoke politely. Taloa and Iskifa responded in their simplest and best Allahashi dialect. After they made it to the expansive corn plantations, out of sight of houses and people, they sat to eat again.

"We must walk most of tonight to make it to the *Misha Sipokni*," Iskifa told his friends. Taloa translated to Robert, who looked drained. "Then we will find a good hiding place and stay there after the sun rises."

The trails through the massive crop fields seemed relatively safe to Iskifa. The only person they encountered was an old man camped in a watchman's hut in the middle of a large cornfield. The man told them he lived there and kept the raccoons out of the corn. He seemed apprehensive to Iskifa and unused to human visitors. Robert and Taloa waited outside while Iskifa explained, in the Allahashi tongue, that they were on their way to the river to fish and needed to keep going. He gave the man a couple of plums. The watchman seemed relieved to understand they meant no harm and quite pleased with the plums.

They walked for long hours along a game trail through the river-bottom thickets to a hidden and rocky ravine where Iskifa had slept on his way to Tochina, an all but eternal day and night before. A creek flowed from the bluffs toward the *Misha Sipokni* and formed the ravine under a canopy of trees amid a thicket of briars and woods.

"This is a good place," Iskifa said, knowing Robert and Taloa had to be exhausted and weary of being clawed by thorns along their way. "We will be safe here." They rolled up in their blankets with no further words and withdrew deep into the womb of sleep.

The sun rose to a sixth before the drumming of a large woodpecker awakened Iskifa. He lay still at first, scanning the almost solid overhang of branches and vegetation. He sat up to take stock of his companions who slept like stones. Taloa looked beautiful and peaceful. He felt a deep sense of relief at being able to bring her at least this far from the jaws of death. Her crow-wing black hair caught a glisten from a shaft of sunlight. Some leaves lay tangled in it, recalling to him a story his mother liked to tell of the forest spirit queen, a sister of Mother *Yakni* herself, who gave birth to the entire race of little people. The little people's stewardship and knowledge of the herbs of the forest had certainly delivered him and his friends.

Robert lay face up, snoring with long, tormented spasms of breath. His tears had streaked the tannin, leaving little white semi-circles under his eyes. They would need touching up before they continued through hostile territory. Iskifa lifted his shoulder to turn him onto his side and quiet his snoring. The dense creek bottom thicket was not safe enough for them to push their luck.

Iskifa's worst fear was in knowing their escape would be discovered that morning, and the Allahashi drum system would soon pass warnings and alerts about them and the Mvskokes into the outlying provinces. Of the many languages he knew, none seemed more valuable at the moment than the codes of the *teponaztli*, as they called them in the southwest—the slit drums. Because of them, messages traveled up and down the river much faster than the swiftest runners or boatmen could carry them.

Besides that, their present territory was still too risky to allow them to travel in daylight. He let Taloa and Robert sleep, hoping they could regain enough strength to continue later. In the meantime he fashioned a blowgun from cane growing in the ravine. With one of the very sharp knapped-stone Allahashi knives they captured, he whittled darts two hands long from three straight hardwood limbs, taking care to give them needle-sharp, barbed points. He fletched them with rabbit fur from his pouch.

So far, *Aba Binnili* had blessed his strategy, with results turning out very much like his best hopes. According to the plan he thought out during his long journey to Tochina, considered in every possible detail, their first day of hiding and resting after escape would be devoted to just what they did now—refreshing themselves, and preparing weapons for the rest of their journey.

He finished the blowgun and built a small, hot, and almost smokeless fire to harden the darts. Done with that, he relaxed to play softly on his flute until his friends awoke.

Iskifa explained to Taloa, who in turn explained to Robert how to use the blowgun. He took a small, innocuous-looking ball of beeswax from his pouch and explained it was hollow in the center and held an extremely deadly, jellylike mixture refined from the venoms of the rattlesnake and the *sinti basoowa*, a small, fatally poisonous snake with red, yellow, and black stripes. "If I need to use it," Iskifa explained, "I cut open the beeswax ball and dip the dart point into the poison. One dip can kill ten men."

Taloa handed the darts to Robert, who inspected them with wide-eyed interest, turning them over in his hands. Iskifa had not wanted to draw any kind of attention while they fled Tochina and so elected not to carry a bow and arrows in order to look as much like Allahashi commoners as possible. The bows and arrows he left to the Mvskokes. He made sure Robert and Taloa each had a sharp knapped-stone knife taken from the Allahashi guards and took time to show Robert how best to carry and use one.

They ate the jerked venison, fruit, and squash from the Tochina market, and Iskifa watched his friends regain strength—a benefit of their youth—although not completely, which he expected after the horrible abuse and torment he knew they must have suffered.

Another large Allahashi town lay a short walk to the south. At a sixth before nightfall they started. Iskifa planned to leave the thickets before dark and head for the smoother floodplain of the *Misha Sipokni*, which formed wide bottoms on both sides that held the immense cornfields surrounding the next town. Almost all the population lived inside the town.

Iskifa led his friends through a perimeter cornfield to its edge, and they climbed a shallow ravine grown up with timber to a bluff overlooking the town. He felt sure no one lived on the bluff, but he noticed a defensive watchtower on his earlier walk toward Tochina. The woods stood dense for at least a hundred flight east, so he felt certain the tower was built to keep watch for threats along the river.

As soon as they topped the bluff they heard drums from the direction of Tochina. Iskifa crouched to listen, filling with dread, certain their escape was found out.

CHAPTER TWENTY·THREE

DRUMS ACROSS THE BOTTOMLANDS

SKIFA COUNTED THE DRUM BEATS ON HIS HANDS, BUT THEY stopped before he could decode the whole message. "I could only get part of it," he whispered to Taloa. "All I could make out was something about death and calling a council."

"That's what I heard," Taloa agreed, adding, "and I think I heard something about Yoshoba."

After a few minutes the message repeated, and they got it for sure: "Yoshoba, the Great Sun, and Holabi, the high priest, are dead. Clan chiefs and town leaders must come to Tochina for high council."

Iskifa relaxed, relieved beyond measure—not a word about their escape, which might have been overlooked during the confusion and turmoil over the headmen's deaths. He looked at Taloa. "I heard the same," she confirmed, looking as amazed as he felt.

She translated for Robert, who almost smiled. "That's very good news," he whispered, with a glance of gratitude toward Iskifa.

For the first time since the terrible dream that sent him to Tochina, Iskifa felt a sense of joy and success, if only for a moment. An obvious question thrust forward in his mind. "Who killed them—Yoshoba and Holabi?"

"Maybe Anli and some of the others broke out," Taloa suggested, betraying some excitement at the idea. "Or maybe Yukpan warriors counterattacked. It's been almost two weeks since the massacre." She translated their speculations for Robert. In such situations Iskifa most appreciated his choice of Taloa as his apprentice. She could seamlessly translate a conversation for a third listener in the most natural way.

Robert spoke to her, and she translated to Iskifa, "Robert thinks it may have been a coup, an internal takeover, perhaps by the warrior chief Shatanni. He says that while he was imprisoned with the nobles before the feast, he thought he heard Yoshoba and Shatanni arguing with each other."

They soon exhausted their fund of possibilities about the mystery of the two Allahashi leaders' deaths and settled in a thicket on the edge of the bluff. In time Iskifa spied a man carrying a slit drum on a strap over his shoulder, climbing up the watchtower ladder. The villager reached the platform and played the same message on his drum, reverberating through the bottomlands. He waited a few minutes and repeated the same message. Iskifa again heard the message from the direction of Tochina. After the villager sent the message a third time, Iskifa heard another drum repeat it farther downriver. This might continue all night, he thought. He decided they should take a deeper detour through the woods.

"*Minti*, come with me," he beckoned, leading his friends inland. The going was difficult and painful, but undetected. The drum messages, always the same, stopped about midnight, and the three managed to get well beyond the Allahashi town before dawn. Iskifa realized he was somewhat lost, so they walked well into the new daylight along a ridgeline above a wide *Misha Sipokni* floodplain, having left the last cornfield many flight behind.

They had not seen another human being since the man in the watchtower. A number of towns and villages strung along downriver from Tochina, but each sat close to the *Misha Sipokni* on mounds or bluffs. Iskifa asked Taloa and Robert to wait in a deep and lushly wooded ravine watered by a small freshwater spring while he ventured farther south about five flight and turned east for a similar distance before making his way back. He declared their campsite safe for their day's rest.

He got out a line and his white bone hook, the same he used to feed himself and Robert during their journey inland from the great water, musing how it seemed like many seasons had passed since then, rather than only a moon. He frowned because the Allahashi guards lost his favorite small knife when they dumped his bag at the stockade. Still, they left his fishing gear, so he followed the spring rivulet about two hundred paces through the thicket at the bottom of the ravine, to where it flowed into a creek. He soon caught some small fish and carried them back to their day camp, where Robert had gathered some wood, and Taloa built a small, hot fire. They roasted the fish on sharpened green limbs from a nut tree and began to feel a bit more relaxed and safe, or so Iskifa thought, when Taloa burst into tears.

"I cannot believe they are dead," she lamented at last. "Iyapi, Shakba, all the others. The Allahashi are evil and they deserve their deaths for this, each and every one," she snarled through tears. Resentment and anguish mixed among her words. Robert slipped closer to lay a gentle hand on her shoulder while she continued, "And who knows what has happened to Master Anli and his family and all the others they captured? I think they jailed the Yukpan guests of honor in those horrible vaults they put us in after they ambushed us like cowards." She buried her face in her hands and wept fiercely.

"Your sadness is justified, my young friend," Iskifa told her. "It is a terrible thing to see your friends cut down like grass, especially so many so young and vital." He also laid a hand on her shoulder. "But you must be strong, Taloa. We may be Anli's and our other friends' best hope for liberation and life. I think Robart may be right—Shatanni or someone has taken over, but probably nothing has changed. The Allahashi will not kill the nobles. They will use them for ransom or bargaining in their ambition to get Yukpan tribes to join their alliance. We must warn our allies of their tricks and make plans to resist them." He patted her shoulder, and her sobs began to subside.

After a short silence, Robert spoke. "I know you are hurting for your friends and relatives who were murdered," he said. "Believe me when I say I know how you feel. I hurt every day when I think of my friends at the bottom of the cruel ocean. It is the same ocean I must cross if I am ever to see my home and family again."

Taloa turned to embrace him, her head laid on his shoulder. Another rush of weeping overtook her before she sat back to rub her eyes. "I want to see my mother and father and my sisters and brother so very much," she said in English, fighting not to sob. "I haven't seen them for three winters. I am so thankful they did not go to the *Yamohmi*."

She translated what Robert said for Iskifa, who nodded gently. "You will see your loved ones again," Iskifa assured her. "And you, Robart, have been sent here for a purpose, which may include you carrying news of us back to your people. You may get your big boat, but your first task is to stay alive until we can get ourselves back to friendly land."

Taloa translated to Robert and his response, "You are a great man, Master Iskifa. Even if I never get home, I am eternally thankful for your courage to rescue us and for all you have done for me."

"*Chokmashki*, my interesting friend," Iskifa replied. "We do what *Aba Binnili* makes us do. Listen carefully, now. I am going to explain the hazards between us and our freedom." Robert and Taloa drew closer. "We will be safe if we can make it to the Hatchie River. We can follow it south and be safely into Yukpan territory in two or three more nights' travel, especially if we can steal a canoe without getting caught."

"That sounds risky," Taloa remarked, dubiously.

"Hear me out," Iskifa contended. "The only serious concentration of enemies is at Sawanoki Town at the mouth of the Ohiyo River, where it pours into the *Misha Sipokni*. If we can get a canoe or raft of some kind, we might be able to sneak past it in the middle of the night. We will have to watch out for night fishermen. It's still our best chance, because there are Sawanoki farmers living all over the lands above the mouth on both sides."

"I think we will surely be killed," Taloa disagreed, matter-of-factly.

"Why? We know their language. We are wearing Allahashi clothes and carrying Allahashi weapons. We must be convincing and not flinch, no matter what happens. I'm depending on you to thoroughly prepare Robart for these encounters," Iskifa said, raising his attention toward a movement catching his eye, up the wooded slope from them.

An old woman appeared from the northeast, a direction Iskifa had assumed to be safe. She walked along the top of the ridge overlooking the ravine where they hid. Robert saw her, too, and started to take out his knife, but Iskifa held him still with a wave of his hand.

"Hello, grandmother," Iskifa called out in perfect Allahashi. "Would you like some fish?" The old woman laughed while she made her way down the wooded slope. "Welcome. Join us and have some fish," Iskifa repeated in his most hospitable voice.

The old woman sat down with a bagful of oyster mushrooms gathered from the woods. "No, thank you, grandfather. I'm not hungry," she answered at last in a singsong voice. "I smelled your smoke. Would you like some mushrooms with your meal?" she asked. "I can roast a few for you."

"No, but thank you," Iskifa replied cordially. "We have finished our breakfast."

"Do you have anything to trade for corn?" she asked, demonstrating her main interest was commerce.

Iskifa ignored the question. "Do you live near here, grandmother?"

"Yes, I do, young man," she said, laughing loudly, revealing she had lost a number of teeth. She was dressed like a farm woman, her clothing simple but clean. "My two grandsons, both fine warriors, live with me. Their mother and father died during a raid by the Washashe when they were little. I have raised them ever since. We are fishers and raise some corn. We are Chepoussa, but we do not like towns. We live by ourselves on the river just west of here."

Her words struck fear in Iskifa, and he saw alarm pass through Taloa's eyes. Robert sat dumbly, staring into the fire. "Do they cultivate corn this day?" Iskifa asked.

"No, they left two days ago to do some trading in the town just upriver," she replied, stirring the campfire coals with a stick. "We have a lot of corn and some furs," she mentioned, still angling for a deal, and returned casually to the subject of her grandsons. "They said they wouldn't stay there too long and may be home now, if they have not found any mischief to get into."

Iskifa quickly devised a plan, although a risky one. "We would like to trade for some corn." He opened his pouch and showed her their few trade goods—some good tobacco, several black pearls, and a hair ornament—taken from the Allahashi guards.

"Let's go," she said, eager to make a deal, grabbing her bag of mushrooms and rising to lead the way.

Iskifa had discussed such instances with Robert and Taloa, so they knew what to do if they encountered local people. "You will be believed," he whispered reassuringly to Taloa while they put out the fire and gathered their things, "because you speak their language."

Taloa explained on the way that Robert was her elder brother, and she looked after him because he was mute and had mental problems. She said Iskifa was her grandfather, and that they had been to the *Yamohmi.*

"Oh, yes, I heard they had a terrible fight up there," the old woman remarked, sounding scandalized. She cast a critical, if perhaps not obviously skeptical, glance at Robert. "You should give your brother a shave. He has too much hair on his face."

"We are Miami," Taloa went on in the sisterly tone heard often when women converse, "from north of Tochina. We are fishing the creeks and rivers on our way down to Sawanoki Town where the Ohi-yo meets the *Misha Sipokni.* My aunt married a Sawanoki trader, and I have cousins there I have never met. We want to see them before we go back home."

Iskifa never felt more relieved that wordmasters and their apprentices typically elected not to wear facial tattoos. Their masquerade as Allahashi would be impossible with such marks, although they were common among tribes. The reasons were quite practical—so they would exhibit no apparent bias during sensitive negotiations between different tribes.

They approached the woman's house built on high ground near a point where the bluff came close to the big river. She pointed out her nice stand of ripening corn below. Iskifa noticed a canoe lying on the bank by the river.

In the house, the old woman served *shonti*—no doubt, Iskifa thought, to loosen him up for trading. Taloa asked her not to pour much for Robert while they sat in the small, two-room house. The woman brought out some furs and a large bag of dried corn.

Iskifa kept his eye on Taloa, who acted as interested and natural as possible, chatting and reaching to pick up and examine a particularly beautiful, almost pure white fur. When she did, Iskifa saw the old woman look down, her eyes narrowing to focus on the tiny tattooed symbol representing a raccoon above and inside Taloa's left ankle. Iskifa realized he should have warned her to cover it. The Chepoussa woman would recognize it as a mark of the dominant, widely known Raccoon Clan of Taloa's inland tribe. The Allahashi were superstitious about the raccoon and would not wear such a mark. He knew he and his friends were found out.

The old woman tried to resume a natural pose, but was not a very good actor. "I think I'll get some more corn," she declared abruptly, turning to leave. Iskifa sprang to stop her, and she screamed. Robert leaped to cover her mouth, and she bit his hand, causing him to release her, and screamed again. Iskifa punched her, and she fell to the floor, silent at last.

"She will not be out long," Iskifa said. "Find rope. We must bind and gag her." Taloa found a rope to secure the woman to the house's center pole. "We must break for it by river," Iskifa told his friends, "before the grandsons return." On the way out, he grabbed a Sawanoki calumet set on display.

They ran down the well-worn path to the *Misha Sipokni*, loaded into the canoe, and pushed off into the river's slow, but powerful current. Robert, the seaman, took the bow paddle, Taloa the stern. To Iskifa's disappointment, he spotted the grandsons' canoe gliding toward them from upriver.

One of the men stood and yelled, recognizing the fleeing canoe.

The young Chepoussa warriors were at most a flight behind upriver when they pulled away to land below their house. One jumped out and dashed up the bluff, to check on his grandmother, Iskifa surmised.

"Paddle for your lives!" he shouted. Robert and Taloa rowed more like fresh athletes than fatigued prisoners. Iskifa regretted they had only two paddles and kept watch on the old woman's house. Too soon her warrior grandson burst out to rejoin his brother, and the chase was on.

Even with a three-flight lead, Iskifa knew the young men would overtake them. The river made a sharp turn, forking into two channels around an island. The narrower and swifter channel was closer, to their left, so they turned that way, but after they passed the first eddy, Iskifa ordered them to beach the canoe. Taloa and Robert protested, but he insisted, pointing toward a flat, sandy clearing with a gentle upward slope. "We must make our stand there," he said while they landed. "They are much faster," he explained while surveying the surroundings, "and will catch us, anyway." His eyes lit on a large sycamore lying partly uprooted, much of its trunk leaning over the channel, hovering about the height of two men above the water.

"Can you climb that tree, Robart?" he asked, pointing to the tree. Robert didn't need translation; he nodded. "Go," Iskifa said, waving to let him know he wanted him to climb out as far as he could. Taloa relayed his further instructions for Robert, who scaled the sycamore like it was the main mast of the *Manannan*, to hide among the branches on the farthest end of its trunk. The Chepoussas still paddled behind, giving Iskifa time to tell Taloa to jump back into the canoe with him. They paddled furiously about another half-flight downriver, to the next open landing.

"Taloa," he said while they got out, "one or both of these warriors will come ashore. You must lure them into range of my blowgun. It's our only chance. Do you understand?"

"Yes, master, I understand."

"*Aba Binnili aapichi*," he said tenderly. He unpacked his bag, took out the blowgun and darts, and tucked the beeswax ball in his mouth, while he scaled, light-footed as a boy, the first large tree with good cover up the riverbank. Taloa slipped into a tangle of bushes below him.

The young warriors' canoe came around the bend, steering close to the bank after passing the eddy. Robert carefully timed their approach and at the right moment, arose with knife in hand, ran down the sycamore's trunk, and jumped onto the canoe. He went right through the bottom, close enough to the warrior in its stern to seize and drag him underwater. They plunged and surfaced in desperate contest, again and again, until Robert got the best of the Chepoussa and stabbed him. The young warrior grew weaker, and Robert pulled him to the shallows to finish him off, holding his head under until a ribbon of blood flowed out of him into the rushing water and he became still.

The canoe swamped and sank as soon as Robert tore through it. The other young warrior lost his knife when he fell out of the bow, and he dived twice to find it. The current carried him and the remnants of the canoe downstream toward Taloa and Iskifa. He swam cross-current to the riverbank a short distance upriver from them. Taloa stepped out to draw his attention.

"You fight like women, Allahashi skunks," she yelled in his language.

With fury in his eyes, he charged toward her, knife drawn, past the tree limb where Iskifa crouched, too fast for the wordmaster to take a shot. Iskifa knew Taloa could fight—she grew up playing *toli* with a rough brother and rougher cousins. When he drew close, she turned and rolled into a backward tumble, sprang off her arms, and kicked him squarely in the chin.

The young man sailed backward to sprawl for a moment on the sand, but jumped to stand just as fast. He shook off the blow and began circling her on the wide beach, slowly, smiling in spite of the blood filling his mouth. "You have killed my brother, you whore," the Chepoussa snarled, spitting blood. "It is your turn to die."

Iskifa could not shoot with Taloa turning step for step between him and the warrior. The young man stalked closer until they were almost face-to-face. She stopped and stood her ground. "Go ahead," she said in a submissive tone. He raised his knife, and she kicked him in the groin so hard she lifted off the ground.

Groaning, he buckled to his knees. Taloa sensed Iskifa's position and swept away to her left. The young warrior staggered to his feet, growling and tracking her with his eyes. Iskifa blew the dart into the side of his neck, into a large, pulsing vein.

The warrior slapped at the sting, but the barb kept it lodged. He turned to see Iskifa squatting on the limb, already loading the second dart, its point dripping with terrible poison. Their eyes met. The young warrior stared almost cross-eyed, his face contorted. He pulled the hardwood dart from his neck, and Iskifa blew again, striking him in the center of his left eye.

The warrior let out a blood-curdling scream and stumbled toward Iskifa before falling face down into a bush at the root of the tree. Taloa sprang to take his knife and turned him over, raising the knife, about to strike.

"Wait!" Iskifa called.

She let the knife down. The warrior lay still, his remaining eye wide. His arms and legs grew stiff. He trembled, gasping for air, and then stopped.

"He is dead," Iskifa proclaimed flatly. "He is dead."

Robert sprinted downriver, reaching them just after the young warrior died. "Thank God," he uttered numbly.

They bound the dead warriors to heavy rocks and committed their bodies to the *Misha Sipokni*. Robert took clothes from one of them, and Taloa helped him reapply more oak tannin mixture to his skin. The three loaded into the canoe and paddled downriver a fair distance to a promising hiding place.

"When the old woman realizes her grandsons are not coming back, she will try to stop someone on the river and sound the alarm," Iskifa told Taloa and Robert. "We have to put as much distance as possible between us and her."

They waited until dusk, uncovered the canoe, and continued down the powerful river all night, keeping as close to the bank as they dared. Iskifa estimated they had traveled at least fifty flight before they found a good hiding place to stay while it was daylight. They made camp, found blackberries and goosefoot, and caught some fish, which they ate raw, cut into small pieces, not risking a cook fire. They slept in shifts, taking turns standing guard. The drums started up again at dawn and repeated once again at midday and at sunset, still communicating only the deaths of Yoshoba and Holabi and the call to council.

They got back into the canoe at dusk and paddled all night again, taking occasional rests, and floated watchfully into the first sunlight the following morning through a sparsely populated stretch of river. They repeated their daytime hideout, this time risking a small, hot fire to cook a rabbit that Taloa snared and skinned.

Iskifa saw familiar landmarks along the river and calculated they were within a half-night's float to Sawanoki Town. "If my reckonings are correct," he told them, "our journey by river this evening should take us past Sawanoki Town after midnight." At dusk they set out again.

When they began to see houses and cornfields near the river, Iskifa knew they came close to the large town of the Sawanokis, an enemy tribe and a strong ally of the Allahashi. They switched over toward the west bank, opposite the town, but spied a village on that side, too. As they drew near it they came upon a relatively treeless beach at the mouth of a large creek. Much to their chagrin, a small group of Sawanokis camped there, their two long river canoes pulled up ashore.

The Sawanokis saw the travelers before they could slip past and called out to them, taking them for night fishers. "We must stop here and treat with them, or they will be offended," Iskifa explained. Taloa complained and Robert uttered a doubtful murmur, but they landed. Iskifa told the Sawanoki men—all warriors, he noticed—the same story Taloa told the old woman, changing only the name and place of the town where their fictional relatives lived to that of another one farther downriver. He also explained they didn't like crowds, so they did not attend the *Yamohmi*.

"I have cousins there I have never even met," Taloa chimed in, speaking in a dialect the Sawanokis would recognize as Miami. Iskifa made sure to show them the Sawanoki calumet he took from the Chepoussa grandmother's house—a powerful token, and one that Sawanokis would give only to trusted friends.

The Sawanokis explained they were on their way in answer to the disturbing message passed by the drums. Theirs was an advance party, headed to Tochina to make arrangements for the arrival of their chiefs, who would follow in a few days to attend the high council. The Sawanokis summarized accounts of the *Yamohmi* they heard from their people who attended and returned. They admitted they did not know how Yoshoba and Holabi died, although all were eager to learn. Iskifa and Taloa told them they didn't know, either; the first they heard of it was in the drum codes. Taloa made sure to keep her left ankle and its raccoon tattoo away from firelight.

CHAPTER TWENTY·FOUR

OKLAFALAMMI TOWN

FTER CONVERSATION WITH THE SAWANOKIS IN THEIR CAMP settled down, Taloa returned to the canoe to get the old woman's white fur to offer it as tribute for allowing them to pass through their territory and fish their waters. "I wish you safe travels and a successful council in Tochina," Taloa said with kind ceremony as she offered the gift. The Sawanokis received it warmly and in return expressed wishes for their Miami friends' safe travel.

The three set out again, feeling nervous after such a near encounter, but relieved to be alive, and floated through the rest of the night without meeting anyone else. The next morning they decided to keep paddling, emboldened by the success of their ruse with the Sawanoki warriors. When they encountered other watercraft on the river, Iskifa or Taloa would show the Sawanoki calumet. Each time, people accepted their story without question, smiling and waving while they paddled away. Robert passed as the mute and mentally disadvantaged brother of Taloa. Iskifa caught more fish, and when they stopped to rest, Taloa gathered roots and wild fruits and vegetables.

They left the *Misha Sipokni* at the wide mouth of its tributary, the Hatchie, which would take them safely into Yukpan territory.

From its source in the hills they would be within a few days' walk of Chunuli. With each flight they traveled up the slow, meandering Hatchie, Iskifa felt more certain of their escape. He was pleased to watch Robert gradually recover from the terrible harm he endured and observed how he and Taloa conversed comfortably in Robert's language, occasionally laughing and scuffling, much like a brother and sister might.

Two weeks of difficult travel and struggle had all but exhausted Iskifa. His shoulders ached from sleeping so many nights on the ground and from the turns he took paddling the canoe so Taloa or Robert could rest. Taking the lives of other human beings, although a terrible necessity, had left him feeling more disturbed than he imagined it might.

They progressed a half-day up the Hatchie, and at last Iskifa told his companions to cast off the Allahashi ornaments. The first people they met after that were Chikashas who lived in the upriver town of Oklafalammi, out that day to hunt squirrels. The three camped that night with the Chikashas, free to tell their remarkable and engrossing stories of war, imprisonment, and escape. Iskifa ingratiated the hunters with humorous personal stories about their wordmaster, Hishitohbi, who had grown up in Chunuli and moved with his young wife forty winters before to Oklafalammi, her family's hometown. Hishitohbi had apprenticed with Notintowa, the twelfth wordmaster of Oklafalammi.

Iskifa's group reached Oklafalammi the next night. Hishitohbi and a group of townspeople came out to greet them and brought all to a pleasant, shaded campground between the river landing and the town proper. They had heard the bad news about the *Yamohmi* and spoke in angry voices of their wishes for swift blood revenge. They wept to hear Taloa's grim story of the massacre in the stickball stadium in Tochina.

She translated as much of the conversation for Robert as she could keep up with, but one comment left her dumbstruck for a moment. The people in Oklafalammi had heard from eastern traders about the white man and his animal whom Iskifa found on the eastern coast but,

"What's more," the elder woman speaking to Taloa continued, "there are rumors that another white man washed up on the beach barely alive, and he is cared for by a small tribe further south of the Onnahas along the same coast." Taloa hesitated, thinking of Robert's tender emotions, before translating the surprising report.

Iskifa overheard the elder woman and studied Robert, who at first looked stunned and blinked backed tears before his brow furrowed deeply and a wave of emotion overtook him. He buried his face in his hands and sobbed, mumbling things Iskifa couldn't understand. Taloa told him Robert suspected the survivor might be his strong young friend, whose name was Denny. Iskifa comforted and calmed Robert by going over with him, through Taloa, the various ways the woman's report offered hope for his future. Robert soon seemed to embrace the hope.

The townspeople wearied of war talk and adjourned from the campground. After sitting so long in a canoe, Iskifa enjoyed the leg-stretching walk to Hishitohbi's house on the edge of Oklafalammi, on a bluff over the river. Hishitohbi's wife and her kinfolk had prepared a large meal. He enjoyed the warm reception and the feast, but most appreciated the clean, soft bed they laid for him that night.

Sometime before dawn, Iskifa dreamed he awoke lying flat on his back and felt an uncomfortable weight on his feet. He lifted his head to see the four-faced *biskinik* perched on his feet, gripping his toes.

"When I speak, you should listen," the *biskinik* said clearly in Iskifa's first language. "Let there be no compromise in your resolve." As before, with each new sentence the *biskinik* spun his head and presented a completely new face, each different, at once terrifying and sublimely colorful and beautiful. "All of you that are thirsty come to the water, and you that have no trade goods, come, buy, and eat. Why do you spend your wealth on that which is not cornbread and dried fish? And your labor on that which does not satisfy? Listen carefully. Turn your ear and heart to *Aba Binnili*. Eat that which is good, speak that which is right, and your souls will delight in fatness."

After the *biskinik* spoke his last word, he turned toward the doorway of Hishitohbi's guest house and propelled himself outside with a graceful flap of his wings, ascending out of sight with his four-faced head gently spinning. Iskifa did not awake until shortly after dawn.

He felt perplexed, but not upset by his dream. Taloa and Hishitohbi joined him to kindle a morning fire in a small outdoor pit between the wordmaster and guest houses.

Iskifa told them about his latest *biskinik* dream and asked them to help interpret what it might mean, especially among the other amazing and prophetic dreams and events of the two moons past. They talked at length about different ways to free their friends and relatives from Tochina, acknowledging how hazardous each idea sounded. Taloa and Iskifa agreed they should rest in Oklafalammi for two days before taking the last leg of their journey.

Iskifa observed in the meantime how the promising news that one of his shipboard friends might still be alive seemed to invigorate Robert and greatly improve his demeanor. The people of Oklafalammi were naturally intrigued by him—the children liked to touch him and show him things, and he laughed with older people while teaching them a few words of his language. The town organized a stomp dance on the second night of their stay as a tribute to the memory of the fallen Yukpans and to honor their guests. During more private conversations inside the wordmaster house, Robert seemed to enjoy his celebrity while Taloa translated his stories of Europe, which enraptured Hishitohbi and Iskifa.

After two days' rest in a clean bed, Iskifa awoke early, refreshed and ready to leave. At the river's edge, he thanked Hishitohbi for the bundle of food and provisions for their travel. The package included a gift for Hishitohbi's sister, who lived in Chunuli. Iskifa turned to face him and other people of Oklafalammi who gathered to see them off and promised to send word as soon as a consensus emerged among the tribes to the east and south about how to respond to the Allahashi treachery. He, Taloa, and Robert launched their canoe once more, waving reluctant farewells to friends old and new, to finish their journey to the headwaters of the Hatchie and then overland to home, to Chunuli.

The accounts of the life-and-death struggles of Iskifa, Taloa, and Robert, and of their escape from Tochina through enemy land, inspired pride and hope wherever told, as the stories spread throughout the confederacy of the Yukpans, the blessed, the laughing people.

OOTAALHLHI
◦ THE END ◦